Book One
of the *Lucy's Crypt* series

The Invitation

The Invitation

Published by Wendy and Wetherall in Australia, 2024

ISBN 978-1-7638350-0-9

A catalogue record for this book is available from the National Library of Australia

Typesetting and Cover Design by:
Charlotte Mouncey, www.bookstyle.co.uk

Map illustrated by Maria Priestly and Kerrie Turner

Printing and Distribution Channel: IngramSpark

Book One
of the *Lucy's Crypt* series

The Invitation

Katie Webster

With special thanks to Tim and Sarah,
for your help with and faith in this book.

A note about destiny

*D*estiny is a universally misunderstood concept. It is regularly refuted as whimsical nonsense but it is foolish to refute something that is not understood. While it is nearly impossible to curtail the complex concept into a box, let us make some corrections. Destiny is not the plan of some ethereal being. It is not a script by which way our lives are outlined - line by line; scene by scene. Destiny is also not unavoidable - or inevitable - despite how often those terms are incorrectly intertwined as two threads of the same string. Destiny is a much more abstract and indefinable concept - but it moves and operates from the moment we are conceived. Destiny is a force, the drive of which is inextricably linked with who you are at your core. The force will continue, until the moment you die, to drive you toward it; toward certain choices, paths, and opportunities. It might reveal itself from time to time, as a series of mystifying moments - the coincidences in life that are marvelled at momentarily and then shelved and forgotten about. But it is not immune from the puncture of intervening choices. It cannot save you from the choices of others that may steer you away from it, and nor can it prevent your own choices that defy it. But it remains there - the force - controlled by no one - characterised not as living or dead - nor spirit nor ghost- and it will try to guide you toward it, until the day you die.

Signed: *X. Bear, Spiritual Adviser to His Majestic Eminence and His Imperial Lord, Wooden Floor Borders, Archmond*

Our hero must be noble
Our hero must be brave
Our hero must be selfless for our lives he has to save
Our hero must be honest
Our hero must be bold
Our hero must be compassionate
Our hero must be determined
Our hero must be well spoken
Our hero must be clever
Our hero must be agile and quick
Our hero must hurry

N
W E
S
Yerkey
Subplateau
Que
Gemini
Rumustica
Pyramid Bay
Archmond
Alexandria Plateau
Coby
Lake Okinawa
Arlequine Ocean
RH
Josso Jungle
Trimany
Mervent Currents
WFB
Meta Emery
Chupners Forest
Timid Sea
Long-hell Sea
Winnapea
Jaratua Sea
Sanguine Seas
Mazouri

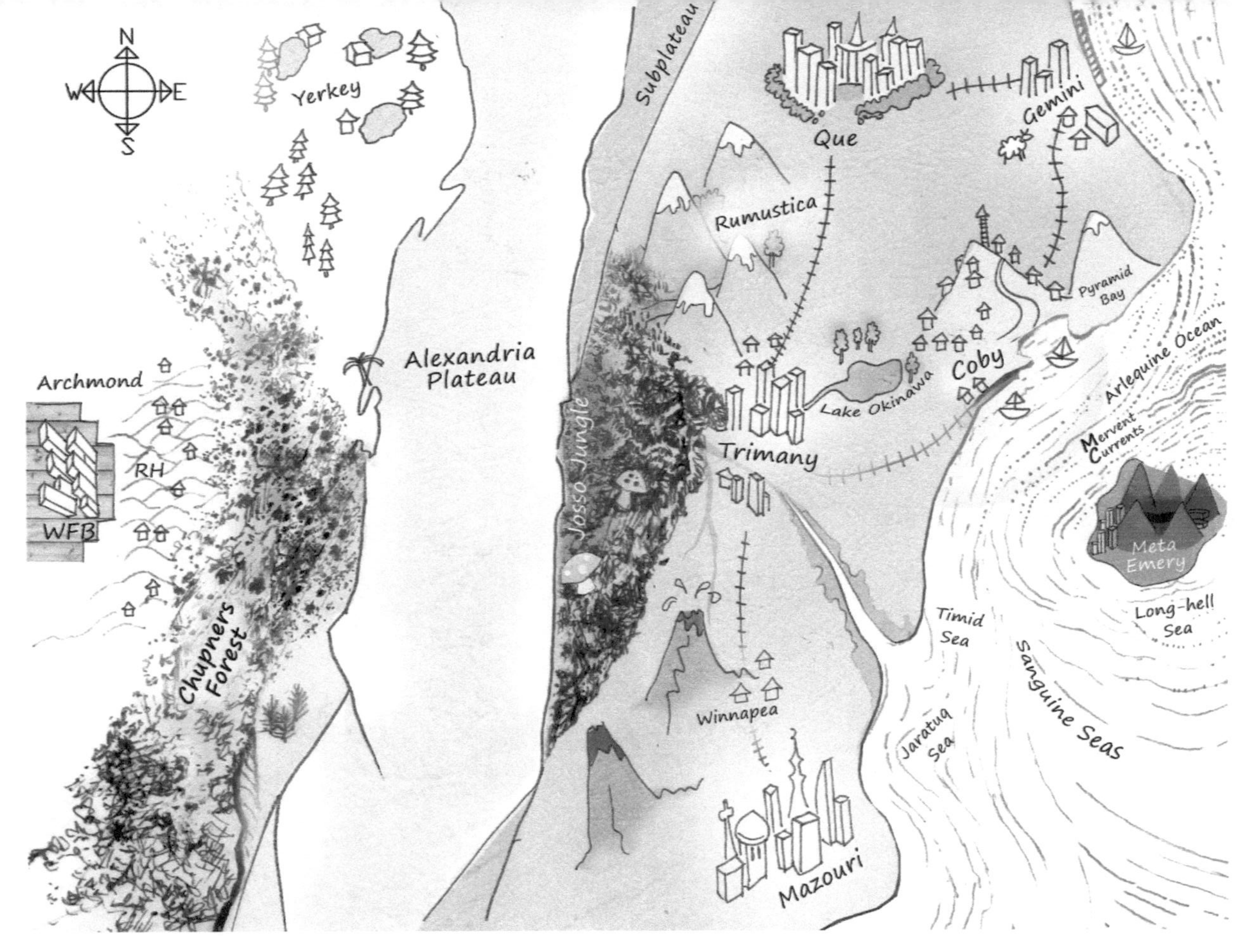

6

Chapter 1

The only star in the sky

It was about six-thirty in the evening, but the sun, though concealed by vaporous clouds, was still happily nestled in the final quarter of the horizon, not wanting to set. The sky was not yet giving way to darkness, but it was already colourless, empty, and vague. The sunset tonight would be unremarkable.

Lucy was dragging her feet along Locket's Lane, the breeze was licking at her neck, causing her fringe to shift irritatingly in front of her face. Her dog, a little rugged fluffball named Crumbs, was nose to the pavement, taking the opportunity in his master's slow stride to take in all the odours of the ground and examine the street for canine enemy markings.

Lucy was not trying to avoid going home, at least that was what she told herself, not that she often let her mind turn to such reflection. She was just walking, vaguely, as empty in purpose as the sky was of colour.

She was seventeen. Her aunt on her mother's side swore she had their family's pale complexion, but this was only because of a lifetime in the sun-starved climate of Scotland. Whenever the summers were warmer or longer, which was not often, her skin took toward the olive hue of her father's Italian heritage. But for the most part with her blackish hair, light skin, and blue eyes, she was exquisitely contrasted. Not that it seemed to help her popularity at all. Teenage social circles are complex.

School had wound up some hours before, and after taking off alone, her pup trailing behind, she had filled these last few hours with empty wandering. The day had been upsetting, frustrating.

Mary, a charismatic classmate of Lucy's, who always appeared to be perfectly feminine, perfectly pretty, perfectly dressed, and perfectly equipped, had made very public her mockery of Lucy's shabby shoes and faded second-hand uniform. Even some of the boys thought it was funny. Lucy had given no response. It was true, the cleaner did have better shoes, what could she say? She only shrugged, pretending not to care, and looked away. But the initial remark snowballed into a series of nasty attacks, with everyone wanting to have a go. So the hours of walking were helping to exhaust the images out of her memory. In particular, she wanted to dissolve the vision of Mary's pretty face, laughing, throwing her head back with delight at every new insult. It caused her stomach to churn. 'Come on, cheer up Lucy,' she'd said at the end, as though it was all a friendly dig. It wasn't.

Lucy was poor, but she never understood why. She was an only child, both her parents worked, though her mother less and less, and they owned their home outright. But they never had any money. Lucy didn't question it. She didn't really question anything at home. It just was what it was.

But it wasn't just the school torments causing her to do laps around the town parklands; these last few days had been strange. Lucy stopped to allow a van attempt to turn itself around in the middle of the lane. The van belonged to the chicken shop in the main street. She knew the owners, but she couldn't tell who was driving it now; the windows were tinted. It passed her with no acknowledgement.

She hadn't walked the entire time since everyone drifted their separate ways at the end of class. She had spent one of the hours of the afternoon sitting at a bus stop, watching the trees shift in the wind across the road. An unruly row of cypress trees bordered the entrance to the nature reserve. Before them, several oak trees dotted the grassy picnic area. Beyond them, dense undergrowth was almost impenetrable. Only a maintained path carved its way through. The cypresses were bending in the wind, periodically allowing a view to the lush plant life beyond them. There was a shadow that blurred itself, in the dense bushes behind the cypresses. She had thought it was a face watching her. But the leaves and branches shifted again, and whatever she thought she saw was gone. She was just imagining things, she thought, but it prompted her to keep moving in any case.

Now, Locket's Lane was leading her home, to High Street which would eventually lead her to Parker's Way, and then all the way home to Ursula Avenue.

As Lucy came on to High Street, a strong breeze picked up and she grabbed at her coat pulling it tighter around her. She screwed up her face in agitation; the cold air was not welcome in the middle of spring. It steadily rolled a cluster of rubbish and leaf litter down the main street, which was as empty as the sky above.

Lucy saw someone cross the street behind her, only in the corner of her eye. She turned to see if it was someone she knew, but whoever it was had disappeared already. Above her came a gentle electrical hum as the streetlights flickered on. Slowly but surely, the moody shadows of evening were creeping in. Lucy stopped for a moment, examining the deserted street. Most of the shops were closed. The green-grocer, the bakery, the butcher, the drab clothing store for old people. The fish-and-chip-shop was open, but it didn't seem like anyone was there. Lockerby was lifeless at night. The people here are so boring, Lucy often thought. Although, they were the only people she'd ever known. She'd never left Lockerby, not even for a holiday.

Lucy had decided, a quarter of an hour ago, that she should proba-bly be getting home. It was late and not long until her mother served dinner. Still, she could not foster any urge to hurry. She stopped by the old post office to pull a note from her pocket. It was the third one of the kind she'd found over these last few days. Days where she couldn't shake the feeling of being watched, even when she was on the move.

The first note had blown towards her three days ago, mixed up in a cluster of litter just outside the school grounds. It tumbled along

the footpath in the breeze, before it collided with her shoe, and then
it rose, sticking across her ankle in the force of the wind. It was just
a white square about the size of a 'post-it' note. It had rough edges,
as though it had been torn out of a larger piece of paper. But the
markings on it were not something she imagined anyone in the school
would draw, or anyone in the town for that matter. The ink was black
and fluid, while the etchings thin, as if drawn with a quill. It was a
circle, thick like a reef, with intricate 'criss-cross' patterns filling it.
Alternating thick and thin lines gave the appearance of depth and
shadow in the patterns. Across the circle through the empty space at
the centre, the letters E.W, were barely legible in a font she'd never
seen before.

But the strange part was not the first note, it was the second one. It
was pinned into the picket fence outside her house the very next day.
As she neared it, noticing instantly it was the same size as the odd note
that stuck to her leg the day before, she thought she heard her name.
The whisper sounded distant and faint, yet close and personal all at
once. Maybe it was her mother inside? Or in the backyard, calling
out to her? When she went to unhinge the note the pin pricked her,
blood spurted from her fingertip across the fine metal pin and down
her finger. Disconcertingly, the wound, and the amount of blood it
caused, seemed grossly out of proportion to the size of this pin and her
incidental contact with it. In shock she had dropped it, but when she
bent down to pick up the note the pin was gone, carried off somewhere
by the wind she assumed, even though the evening was still. As she
opened the note, she heard her name again, subtle, almost inaudible.
'Lucy'…was it just the wind? Or her slow descent into insanity?

'Lucy,' the word had ushered past her again, 'you're a liar Lucy.'

The markings were of the same Celtic style, but the picture was
different than the first one. In this one, three swirls, each with a cross
through the centre, were all woven together. The same strange letters
were this time at the bottom, 'E.W.'

This last one, which she now looked over by the side of the post office, she had found only hours ago, when she was sitting at the bus stop, trying to determine whether the shadow in the bushes really was someone watching her. Deep down she knew it wasn't. There was only a dense growth of bushes with straggly limbs and overgrown grasses. Who would hide in there to watch people? Then as the branches shifted and the face like shadow disappeared, the folded white note came rolling down the road in the wind, sticking to the side of the bus stop. Maybe she was losing grip on reality by trying to find meaning in these symbols, but when she opened the note, this one only said, LIAR.

She had considered that someone was playing a trick on her, someone from school. It was for that reason she only chose to look at the notes when she was alone. That and, everyone already thought she was odd, it wouldn't do her any favours to tell people she was being haunted by notes with strange drawings. There was a sudden crash and clanging. Crumbs was barking furiously at a car with a trailer that clanked off down the street carelessly, ignoring the speed bumps and sending its load crashing noisily down. The jolting noises snapped her from her daydream though, so she was glad. She shoved the note back in her pocket.

'Sorry Crumbs,' she said with her hands in her pockets smiling down at her fearless protector. He stopped barking at once to gaze up at her adoringly, 'I'll stop messing about, we'll go home now.'

As she neared her street, she thought to herself, as she noticed that the sky had quickly become lost under a swishy new canvas of grey clouds, that it would rain tonight for sure. She glided vacantly through the home stretch; Ursula Avenue, a thick and winding street that rolled over contours in the country land. Lockerby was a somewhat forgotten town. Wide open spaces and predominantly historic housing, aligned the run-down roads. An absence of modern facilities, malls, centres and whatnot, and the otherwise cold climate, greyed the non-working hours of the conservative community.

There was little employment in the town if you weren't somehow engaged in the rural activities. It was a simple life. The town seldom fostered ambition in its youth. Work in a store, do a trade, work on the land, or for girls, marry and raise children; they were the presented options. But it was a pretty little town, mind you, engulfed by grasses and greenery every summer, which turned golden and red in the autumn, before the white frost and snow of winter. Of course the town's old-fashioned ways weren't so strange to a girl who knew of nothing else.

As she neared home, the air swam with the rich aroma of flowering gardens. Lucy stared at the roses as she strode dreamily past. The way those roses grew without ever a bad batch would forever fascinate Lucy. Her mother had struggled for years to grow just one fine bush. Lucy stopped to stare at the purple flowers reaching from their pots and clambering over the iron tips of the fence. They were irises, not that Lucy knew that. She only knew that the petals were very velvety and fresh. It was a pity no one could say the same for the hag that grew them. Of course the pitiful old bag hadn't always been so reclusive and hateful. It began when her husband passed away, a few years back.

'Your dog's made a mess of my garden,' Mrs Hurlock said.

In typical fashion she seemed to appear from nowhere, hobbling out from the side of the house, pointing over at Crumbs, who was nowhere near the garden.

'What?' was all Lucy could think to say, confused.

'You won't be going anywhere until it's cleaned up,' whispered Mrs Hurlock, leaning down so close to Lucy that their noses were almost touching. Lucy became nauseous. Mrs Hurlock wasn't just a bitter old bitch, she was sickeningly hideous. Her skin was weathered and old, almost entirely comprised of wrinkles and dirty crevices where two wrinkles had folded together to form a valley in her face. Her eyes were pale and grey, and her teeth had eroded into yellow-brown posts that stood boldly in her blood red gums. Lucy coughed at the foul stench coming from Mrs Hurlock's mouth; the presence of something rotting inside was mildly masked by brandy. She looked back to the garden, it was pristine, there was no mess in sight. The woman was just mad. Lucy made a noise of concern, then scooped Crumbs up into her arms and turned away.

Finally, Lucy and Crumbs paced up the stony path that dissected the maze of potted disasters before her house. It wove its way boastfully about the lattice of dying plant life. Once they were the prize-winning arrangement of tulips, daffodils, and pieris of the late owner. A fuzzy circle whizzed past her, missing her face by an inch. She stood dazed momentarily. A group of youngsters stood cringing in the distance of the neighbour's yard. A yard much more contemporary than her own. The Breemer children played forever energetically.

'Sorry Lucy!' called out the eldest, a lad who was a few years younger than herself. She smiled half-heartedly, and fetched the ball from where it had lodged in a hanging basket. She launched it back toward them over the fence.

'Thanks,' he said and laughed, leaping to mark it mid-air. She had never really found friendship with those children, a bunch so alive and exuberant. They knew not to waste their efforts with their mysteriously withdrawn neighbour. Though there was a time when they had tried. Once. But Lucy had responded with the same indifference she gave to everything at that the time.

Chapter 2

The last supper

*I*t began as rightly as another ordinary night at dinner. Seven o'clock, the understood time. Her mother and father sat at opposite ends of the elongated timber table. The usual silence, though absent of courtesy dialogue, as Lucy slyly slipped pieces of cheese to Crumbs by her feet while she ate. Her father, Mario, hadn't changed since he staggered home from work. His fingers and arms were still covered in the grime of a hard day's pay. His large muscular physique was the only thing he had to show for nearly twenty years of intense labour. That and a deep tan, which was probably in large part, a legacy of his Italian heritage. Perhaps Lucy's temperament came from her maternal side.

Lucy's mother, Alice, was a quiet and graceful lady, small and petite like her daughter. Her hands were soft and pale, like the rest of her skin, and beautifully decorated by her long pearl nails, and solitary diamond ring. The dining room air was dusty, with the scent of wood, the same that wafted through the house. Nothing these three were cognisant of though, after years within the ageing walls. Their fantastically ancient family home was heritage listed.

It was one of the first built in the early days of Lockerby. It was a large manor, for the governor at the time. It had been built for him when Lockerby had been envisaged as a thriving centre for surrounding rural and mining lands. But the population died off over the years, through various forces of time and change, forgoing the need for someone of his title. The manor had been auctioned off to a wealthy man, who had passed it down to his son. The son later gifted it to his daughter as a wedding present, she passed it on to her son, a loner, who died soon after, leaving it to his cousin, Alice.

The first of the owners had maintained its baronial style, with simple and occasional maintenance. But it had grown weak over the recent decades and creaked with age and fragility. The manor was dreary and cold to visitors, and the neighbourhood children rumoured it haunted, daring each other to front the cob-webbed angel chimes that wailed warnings on windy nights.

Through the course of the meal Lucy began to pick up on something. She could feel the air fermenting; although not unusual, something was wrong. As they finished eating her mother cleared the table. An instant familiarity came from the way she moved so gently and timidly, hands fumbling with the petite condiment saucers. The silence was expected. Mealtime had always been such. But the flashes of eyes upward, the clenching of sweaty hands into lace napkins. Awkwardness was clotted with the constant clearing of croaky throats. The animosity was obvious, especially to their daughter. Agitated and restless, Mario jostled his way out of the room. Now safely alone, Lucy encouraged Crumbs to jump into her lap, and she sat there stroking him, very quietly. Crumbs looked up into her crystal blue eyes, then looked down and licked dinner's residue from her fingers. She raised him to her face. He licked at her pink cheeks, but she pulled him back as his eager paws clambered across her school sweater. He was a pleasant distraction, she even giggled…

'This is bull, Alice!' His large and powerful voice echoed from somewhere in the house, above. Concerning heavy thumps began cascading down the staircase, vibrating the delicate chandelier. Closer, closer, closer…Instinctively Lucy ducked under the table. The door swung open. Lucy watched the ends of Mario's tattered work pants and the steel cap boots they strayed over, temper into the room. He couldn't stand still, pacing and turning, back and forth.

'ALICE!' he screamed with frustration. The aqua heels strayed slowly into the room.

'What?' Alice asked. She hushed her voice as though it might hush him back down to earth.

'You stupid bitch!' his deep voice murmured, a voice so deep that even a whisper bellowed, 'you think I won't find out hey? You're so stupid. That's what you are. Stupid -' he paused as if to re-assess his insult, 'a stupid whore.'

'What are you talking about?' She was both wary and exhausted. But she was not wholly surprised at the line of questioning; it was not new.

'You screwing him? Hmmmm? That why you were at Ollie's? He take you to lunch after a good one?'

'Are you talking about today at the café? Did one of your friends tell you that? Marz you're being ridiculous - I work with David - that's all.' There was a cheery tone in her voice as if it would expose the absurdity of the accusation, but in truth she was desperate to convince him.

'LIAR!' Insinuating clamours nauseated Lucy, as she stressed about whether or not to be a witness to what was being done to her mother, above the table's finish.

'You think I'm an idiot? You think you can just go and have lunch with some lad? What's he getting for that lunch aye?'

'We chatted…I'm sorry. Marz, please, don't do this…believe me it was *nothing!*'

Alice began to choke desperately through the drizzle of tears and a nose running with blood.

'SCREW YOU!' Mario shouted so loudly there was no doubt the neighbours heard. Then with another scream, Lucy saw her mother hit the floor. The sobbing of the sweet voice became like the bawling of an abused child, substituted occasionally with deliriously incoherent begging. Lucy's heart sank, and she tried to hush her frantic breaths by twisting her sweaty fingers in the ends of her dress. Crumbs was stealthily still, pressed into the carpet like a commando.

'Shut up! Stop crying!' the loud voice ordered but the crying continued.

It was always such a gory noise. Both the sobbing and the violence. It was often impossible, when she overhead them, to match the sounds with the actions. There was just rants and screams, gasps and collisions, moans and squeals. There was often thud after thud. Tonight, although the draping tablecloth meant she could not see, she could imagine, which may or may not have been worse. A deafening crackle and the golden light feature had exploded. Perhaps he shot it? Perhaps it combusted with the room's anxiety?

Shadows hung upon the walls as light hummed from under a shut door. Trying desperately to hold herself together Lucy shivered gently in the cold. A coldness, mind you, that was brought on by something other than weather. She tried to shut her ears, but his ranting and raving wouldn't mute. New movement. Lucy squinted at the shadows, was her mother being dragged up onto her feet? Yes, because then, with a yelp and a thunderous growl he shoved her into the precious fine china cabinet. Lucy spun around in desperation to keep track. The weakly structure toppled, and the glass and china shattered everywhere. Hundreds of little pieces joined Lucy as they flew under the table. Lucy's mind raced rampantly - the importunate question - was this it? Lucy shuddered and pulled Crumbs tighter to her body, unaware she was almost choking him. The spring night had so suddenly become icy, and frightened cold tears ran down Lucy's face. Though she knew for her life she must stay silent. As sad as this moment was in Lucy's life, the love she had for her mother seemed to selfishly subside. In that moment all she knew was fear, and all she felt was her need to survive. Her young smooth hands were trembling uncontrollably, as was her soft breath.

Bloodied head to the floor, Alice gagged at the sight of her daughter's figure through the tassels of the stained white tablecloth. Mario faltered; a short-lived shame that was more surprise than regret. Shame manifested into a heightened state of madness. Furiously he made for the table. Alice screamed. In the first inkling of courage she'd exhibited all evening, she hurtled a lit candle toward the tablecloth. The flames happily devoured the field of wine-soaked cotton and crystal glass splinters; clouding the room with black smoke as they whipped toward the ceiling. Lucy scurried from underneath the blazing framework, over to where her mother lay; weak and unresponsive. In shallow disbelief Lucy gripped the straps of her mother's dress, deeming them handles to shake her with, and felt herself dry-retching at the sight of the blood down her mother's face and neck. What had he done to her? Her mind froze with the unwillingness to comprehend.

Alice coughed, wheezed. Further panic, Alice was asthmatic. The Ventolin - where was the Ventolin? She had started the fire to save her daughter, but now the smoke may kill her. But the time had come for Lucy to leave. Mario grabbed at Lucy's ankles, dragging her from Alice.

'She needs her inhaler! Please! Please!' Lucy shrieked.

'I deserve respect, Lucy. RESPECT!' he shouted hoarsely, shaking, and with vein bulging eyes that were welling with water. He couldn't hear her. He couldn't hear any words but his own. Lucy was being choked in suspension, feet dangling, neck consumed by her father's enormous hand. Then, without any perceptible cause or instigation, her father suddenly toppled over in a mysterious agony. Lucy crashed into the clutter of the once cabinet, as her father snatched up a part of it, construing it as a weapon, an enflamed bat. It swung toward her, but Lucy had dived back, her sobriety a slender advantage. And it was then, at this juncture, that it really was time to leave. She ran. Without remembering Crumbs, or her mother, or the Ventolin, and with her father's rage now in her direction, she ran. Tunnelling through the corridors, and finally bursting into the pouring spring rain.

Somewhere far, far, away…

'Well? Have you nothing to say?' Soleman asked almost boastfully, looking up proudly from the telescope, his gaze turning through his cracked spectacles, to his partner on the other side of the stone chamber room. Between them a table was cluttered with faded papers and glass trinkets.

Ronald, his partner, leaned back into the armchair, and shrugged, apathetically.

'What does it matter? It's done now. Blood has sealed the spell,' he replied.

'You don't think that says anything? About character, about purpose? Instinct?' Soleman exclaimed, almost exhausted, as though he was growing tired of stating his case.

Ron sighed, and rolled his eyes, looking away in a short burst of passive aggression. His long grey hair fell in a ponytail down his back and curled at the base of the ruby armchair. 'This is a *severe governing risk*, you can't just be sure about it in your own mind - on some personal hunch. The effort we go through to get this right… Our resources are finite. The candidate must be tried-and-tested, the preponderance of proof must be ascertained!' he cried. Soleman waved his hand dismissively, his white robe swishing about as he did.

'You have no sense for these things, Ron. As sure as sure can be I am, we have it right.'

There was a silence, Ron rapped his fingers along the armrest rhythmically, - *one - two - three -four -five*…a moments pause, then again, *one - two - three - four - five.*

'Eh-em,' he slapped his hand across the armrest with a sudden idea, 'our hero must be noble, our hero must be brave, our hero - '

'Yes, yes, Ron, we all know the creed. That's precisely why I know we've made the right decision.'

'*You've* made the decision,' his partner corrected, blatantly.

Soleman smiled, amused at his partner's irritation and patted down his white hair with water from the emerald basin beside him. He walked out onto the balcony. Spying down from so high, he saw hundreds of others all going about their daily nothings, despite the heat, beneath the patchy sky. When they saw the figure presenting himself, looking down on them, they began to swarm into masses and waited attentively. He rose his arms and he cried loudly, 'let the glorious word be spread, our hero's name can now be said!'

Cheering and screams of excitement filled the toxically perfumed air, and tiny hundreds began jumping, bopping, twirling around, drunk on new hope. Those who had been inside rushed out to seek the cause of such commotion, to bask with the others in the joyous news. Canisters of confetti, long ago prepared for this very moment, exploded into the air from the curtain walls of the castle. Ron joined Soleman on the balcony. He looked down at the hundreds upon thousands below them, all awash with this newfound hope. He sighed and shook his head. He looked to Soleman as if to speak, but he was silenced with the raise of a hand.

'There's a reason I over-rule you. And, like you say - it's done.'

Back in Lockerby...

Chirpy morning birds chorus loudly, calling, trumpeting, ordering the world to wake. In Lockerby common species of sparrow and robin, fulfilled their duty on the branches of lacklustre town trees. The crisp frost of the morning stuck to the windows, and a freezing sensation slowly wafted in through the cracks of the timber and closed in on Lucy, spontaneously waking her. Offsetting the dark dawn in the attic, was a soft white morning light, starting to flood the room. Her school dress was dirty, torn and damp; she had managed to climb up and into the attic, and had lay there in the dusty mess. Crumbs too, did not look his best; his pedigree fur was tangled with dirt and thick with icy vapour. He gently nuzzled his way beneath her arm and her dust covered face smiled down at him.

'It's morning,' she said and coughed, looking around curiously. In fact, it didn't seem quite like morning. Not the morning she knew as waking time. It looked far earlier than that. Without a clock, she had only the gloomy purple tinges beyond the window frames, and the clammy air to go by, which suggested it was just before dawn. But it wasn't, it was just before seven a.m.

Lucy crept quietly down into the house, tiptoeing, not wanting to wake anyone. The house seemed oddly peaceful. The mess from the broken china cabinet had been swept into a pile. A bright square of red colouring in the faded carpet, boarded by dusty edges, was all that marked its prior place. Another table lay in replica of the former, this one much smaller, and made of plywood, or so it seemed as she bumped it. None the less, it filled the space identically, covered by another of the white patchouli patterned cloths. There were some black smoke marks on the ceiling, not many though, almost as if nothing had happened. *Almost.* But it had happened. And the presence still singing in that room choked her. It choked her enough to know that now was not a time to be here. It wasn't safe to be here. She had to leave.

She showered under quiet low-pressure in the downstairs bathroom, before rushing upstairs, emotionally disjointed. In her haste she clunked the floorboards carelessly. She flung open the door to her white room. It was a classically mirrored antique room, from the four-poster bed, polished by the decades, to the cream-coated copper stencilling, where ivy fingers wandered down from the ceiling. A room of absorbed history and worldly trinkets. She hauled open drawers, tearing out garments of this and that, shoving them into her school backpack. She wriggled on a clean school pinafore - but had no intention of attending. Trying to collect her thoughts, to plan to her next move, she stood to just breathe.

What was the time? Lucy glanced at the rickety clock her mother had crafted. Just after seven. The clock was odd. Upon the surface of a painting was a white rabbit in formal attire, who was himself concerned with time. Her mother had a strong fondness for white rabbits, it seemed. If you could call it a fondness. Or perhaps a suppressed obsession. It seemed a common theme in all the things her mother cherished. Vibrations from the western wing.

'Who's there? Lucy?' he bellowed from the other side of the upper floor.

She felt the ground shudder slightly, as he must have blundered angrily out of bed. Whatever she had would suffice, she thought, snatching the backpack. No time to zip it up. She hurtled down the central staircase. There was a cry for Crumbs, and then they were out the doors, clearing the garden fence, and away, free.

Racing down Ursula Avenue in the freezing dawn-lit fog, Lucy could almost laugh. It was the high she got from having escaped him, endorphins charging to her brain. But that was short lived. The avenue turned into another street some time on, and before long she was tracing the main highway that carved through the town. She watched morning traffic bypass her. Impatient drivers of semi-trailers honked angrily at the slower moving family-vans and hatchbacks, swimming casually in the silver blue light that filtered through this unusual cold fog. But the fog meant she was masked, blurred by the mist. That served good purpose. She didn't want to be seen. To keep hidden, she was headed for seclusion; she was determined to go back to the nature reserve that had given her haunting feelings only yesterday. She couldn't understand her own reasoning for this, given it had spooked her so much. Crumbs *was* with her though. He was the only stable constant in her dysfunctional life. So Lucy elevated him to a greater role in her life than a mere pet. He was her only true friend. And he was here. Besides what else would she do today? Face school? To have to justify herself to that gossiping bundle of pretentious, cupcake, house-whores that composed the school clergy…oh god… not today…she couldn't face it.

A siren blaring ambulance cut wildly through the traffic, curving off in little more than blue flashes. Lucy speculated timidly for a moment, chewing the frayed tips of her fingernails neurotically, but then thought it best not to entertain morbid ideas. The nature reserve was in view, so it was now time to be cutting across ovals and through the gardens of (at this hour) unoccupied primary schools. The progression of the hour meant the lifting of the fog and the emergence of Lockerby suburbia into the scents and sounds of daylight. Porridge and raisin toast. Breakfast radio and church bells.

'Lucy! Is that you?' an excitedly feminine voice made itself heard. A mousey blonde girl hung the top half of her body over the red brick wall.

'Ha! It is you! Geeze Louise what are you doin' out so early?' Asha - the closest thing Lucy had to a *human* friend, hauled the rest of herself up, and tumbled over onto the footpath.

'Could ask you the same? And whose garden's that you climbed out of?'

'Plum?' Asha offered from the handful she had gathered into the knitted blue school jumper.

'Are they…Mrs Johnson's?' Lucy recognised their prize-winning texture, 'is that what you're doing out at this hour? Stealing plums?' Lucy chuckled at the absurdity.

'Well I'm not ganna do it while she's awake and crocheting budgies on her pillowcases am I?' smirked Asha cunningly, finishing off the one she'd started with a firm and final bite. Lucy helped herself to one.

'Well? You didn't answer my question. It's not even eight yet…don't tell me you joined the bloody choir?' Asha vacantly asked, while she fixed her hands beneath her curly bob, pushing more volume into it.

'Don't be stupid you know I can't sing.' Lucy shrugged trying to be as lively as Asha, but finding it difficult.

'Brilliant. Let's take off now then. I think the music teacher is there early with the choir and I needed someone to help me keep the coast clear while I fetch my make-up back from the staff room,' she paused to pose and imitate upset, *'What? You lost my cosmetic bag - but…but…*

it was a, a gift from Aunt Valerie, before she…she…passed away! Oh, my father's only sister!' Asha practiced before bursting out with laughter and battering her mauve eyelids. Clearly, she had plenty of make-up at home.

'Oh. Sorry. I'm not going to school today Ash, and…yeah…don't mention to anyone that you saw me.'

'Oh, Lucy don't you pay bother to little Miss Mary. She's got a mouth fit for swinging a baseball bat into. Both her and Rhiana'll have fallen into their own mirrors or drowned into their own narcissism before much longer.'

Lucy smiled happy to have someone on her side, but then calmed again with a hushing sigh, 'no, it's not Mary, or Rhiana.'

It grew awkward for a moment while Lucy fidgeted, trying to keep her emotions below the surface. They were crossing the road at this point towards a park, though neither of them had initiated the walk. Asha stopped at the curb, a foot or so taller than Lucy, and looked down at her, almost maternally.

'What's wrong Lucy?' Asha's temperament suggested she needn't have asked. She had begun to collect the clues together over the years as they splintered off their rushed yet momentous encounters. Lucy gave an empty smile and Asha needn't ask anymore.

'Well…you want my jumper then? It's bloody freezing this morn'n, and I can grab another.'

'No, you keep it. I'm really not that cold.'

Crumbs stood by the side of the road splashing his feet in the puddles. As it started to present itself, coming out from its misty blanket, it was safe to guess another wet spring day had arrived. Once again the sky was a vacant white. The distant nature park, which had been a lively arrangement of coloured plants and animals only yesterday, was now a wet, spongy canvas of dark green smudges. The neighbouring gardens looked messy; there had been a storm last night, but the morning although wet and cold, seemed to promise a calm day.

Lucy sat at a picnic table in the grassy patches before the reserve. It was wet, but she swept off the puddles with her backpack. Across the road was the bus stop she'd sat at only yesterday, and wondered, watching the trees, if there were eyes watching back at her. Crumbs leapt atop the table and began sniffing over it for leftover morsels of food. Lucy sighed with hopelessness. It would not be long before someone would notice her, someone would see the school uniform and take it upon themselves to call the school, report her truancy. Report some troublemaker was making trouble in the park. But she had nowhere to go.

She looked into the reserve; perhaps its dark shadowy enclave could be her shelter today? An archway, metal framed and thin, stood at the beginning of the path. It was all but covered in wisteria, the purple flowers only just starting to bloom. By the base of the arch, wooden posts described the various walking tracks along with their distance, difficulty, and time. The wind whistled down the pathway like a tunnel. Lucy shuddered. The dense acres of forest gave off a foreboding feeling at the best of times, but this morning it would also be marshy, murky and wet. Lucy retrieved the white notes from her tunic pocket, and laid them out across the wooden table. Crumbs began to sniff them excitedly; there was a scent on them that alarmed him. His lips drew back, and his fangs came keenly forward as he growled at the paper.

'Shush,' snapped Lucy, pushing him away, 'I'm trying to read, Crumbs.' But she wasn't. There was nothing more she could take in from the Celtic shapes and strange lettering, and the accusation of 'liar' meant nothing to her. The wind picked up, and as it did it picked up the notes from the table, snatching them and carrying them off down the shadowy path into the reserve. Lucy stood almost instinctively as if to curse at the wind and order the notes back. But instantly she felt foolish for her defiant stance and sat back down. Then the thought came back to her. Perhaps the reserve *was* where she should go.

With her gaze unfailingly on the path, she stood again and picked up her backpack. She was not just considering the idea, now she was transfixed by it. She made her way to the archway, her backpack hanging limply in her right hand, her eyes still not darting away for a moment. Crumbs followed behind by several feet, reluctant. He barked relentlessly, at the shadows in their way and at Lucy's impending decision. He was begging her to stop. But the air of foreboding had morphed into a morbid curiosity. And from somewhere else inside her…defiance. Maybe someone had been watching her. Maybe she would confront them and tell them she wasn't afraid. Not anymore, not of anything. Eventually Crumbs broke his stance at the archway and followed after her down the path. The forest around them was devoid of animal life. The birds perhaps had found a drier place to spend their day. The ground was soggy, and Lucy's boots quickly became mucky with thick black slodges of earth. But as they went on the shadows, grim as they were, did not pose them any harm.

It was the wind that did all the damage. The breeze picked up, but it was not a breeze so much as a gale. It was persistent, unwavering. It did not rustle the bushes, lift the tree branches, and then retreat. It blustered and bent the vegetation in its wake. They were a good ten minutes down the path when it began to pick up. Lucy rushed along, hoping to find the path turning ahead, and offering an exit from the wind tunnel. It did not. She hadn't brought her jacket. She cursed herself for this.

'Crumbs!' she called out, her hair blowing in front of her face she couldn't see him. He barked to let her know he was there. A young man with blonde hair in a red sweater was clinging to a tree nearby. But he was hardly struggling in the same way. In fact he only steadied himself against the tree, and he leaned out to see the girl coming along.

'Hey there!' he called to her.

Lucy could barely make him out with her vision obstructed by her hair and the debris in the wind. But she was certain she'd never seen this man before. Was he a tourist? Or passing by? Or new to town?

'You struggling there?' he called again, 'take my hand.'

Lucy stopped as she neared him, trying to scrape her hair away long enough to look him over. Her flimsy weight was shifting, and she kept losing her footing in the gale. Through the brief glimpses of him that she caught, he was still and calm, unaffected by the wind.

'Who are you?' she asked.

'Just take my hand,' he insisted. But Lucy backed away, alarmed and confused.

Hazy moments passed by and Lucy found the path descending steeply. Strange, as she knew the reserve to be fairly flat, although she didn't go there often. The descent brought some relief as the wind whipped over the top of her head and the micro-valley she descended into provided some shelter. But she was rushing to get away from the strange man, and in her haste she tripped on the wet crumbly slope, and fell to the bottom where she lay in a heap. Crumbs raced down after her. He licked at her cheek tenderly. The wind had suddenly ceased. Lucy coughed and crawled onto her knees. She dusted the dirt and clotted mud from her tunic. The tumble had not injured her. How odd that the wind had stopped like that.

Slightly to her right Lucy noticed a rusted copper plate in the ground. Its borders were obscured by the grass growing over it, while three handles spread evenly across the circumference seemed to indicate it was a hatch of some kind. It looked like a lid to a sewer main below the earth, but the fractures and rusted green casing suggested it was a remnant from a time long ago. Lucy had just enough time to notice the lettering across the surface; *E.W*, emboldened and raised up, though for the most part weathered away. 'E.W,' she whispered touching it, remembering the notes.

Suddenly the gale picked up with fiercer strength than before, now from the other direction. It raged down the opposite hill toward her, then up the slope she had just fallen from. Lucy was forced backward. The wind ripped debris and dirt toward her. She had to find shelter. From the forest beside the path the young man appeared again, this time he was struggling in the wind nearly as much as her. Forced to his knees he crawled along the ground on his elbows toward her. He reached his hand across the metal hatch, offering it to her again.

'Come on!' he cried through the roar of the wind storm, his other hand gripped the handle on the latch as though he knew it, as though he knew how to open it but only once he had her approval, 'it's the only way.'

Twigs, seeds and nuts blasted against her cheek. She could barely open her eyes to judge the sincerity on the man's face. But they just had to get out of this sudden hurricane. She reached out her left hand and grabbed Crumbs, yelping defenselessly beside her, and dragged him beneath her stomach, sheltering him. Then with her other hand, she reluctantly stretched out and grabbed the man's hand. At once she regretted it, but it was too late. The man grabbed her wrist and flipped her hand upward forensically. He began flicking through her fingers until he found the one that had days ago been wounded by his world's pin. He squeezed it sharply. Lucy looked on in horror, but she couldn't pull away, she couldn't even try, she was frozen. Another burst of blood broke through the wound and rushed down her finger. Only then did he lock his hand with hers, the blood running over both their clasped fingers. The wind now felt more destructive than ever before, as if at any moment they would all be ripped from the ground and carried off in its path. But the young man's other hand remained on the handle, and at his unspoken behest, the hatch began shifting, sliding into the earth to reveal a cavernous hole beneath it. And that's all Lucy would remember.

To those that knew her, or tried to know her, Lucy Crypt had been a gripping mystery, a provocative puzzle. Speaking little and absorbing much. Constantly sinking into solitude. 'Indeed a case…' agreed her teachers. There was a time in her earlier adolescence (about which some of the local nuns still gossiped) where she committed herself to silence for almost a year. Not a word was spoken. Her distressed mother had come to them for help, or comfort even. Alice, not being a local church-goer herself, was but a stranger to them, and they themselves had become estranged from such trauma in this dull and quiet town. Their ill-thought suggestions were naïve at best.

After a series of Bible readings and supervised prayer they had sent Alice away, unfixed. But they had remembered Lucy, the puzzle, and prayed for her soul. Softly she indulged in child-like hobbies. At times she hummed with innocence. Which was right; she was innocent. But it was a false innocence, outlined by an illegitimate polish. She was no child. Whatever she seemed not to know about the adult world was a facade, to her own self even. After all, she was no virgin either. It had escaped her that irreplaceable societal title - not entirely unwillingly. She hadn't necessarily wanted it. Nor had she objected to going along with it. She conceded. Submitted. Guided by what the obedience, bred strictly into her, compelled her to do.

He was older than her, by four or so years. The son of a teacher, and friends with the twelfth-grade boys. A regular visitor to the school grounds - but a practical stranger to her. She knew his name - Gerard…or Jarred, she thought it was, but she couldn't be sure. He had started a conversation with her one late autumn afternoon, as she trailed down the steps of the school library. This innately sharp boy of widespread popularity, had flashed his smile to begin a conversation… with her! Gosh that smile! She had felt both flattered and suspicious, but nevertheless her curiosity meant she failed to resist going with him when he asked her if she'd ever seen the teacher's courtyard. He later chuckled about it with the twelfth-grade boys, and they sung periodic taunts whenever they saw her. Nasty little vultures - but the story was so absurd and erotic to them. The beautiful girl that hardly spoke, could it be true? But they weren't worldly enough or wise enough to see that Lucy wasn't necessarily shy, or strange, or even sad…she was just lost.

Chapter 3

Archmond

'In their first weeks of life, when you hold your baby under the arms, she'll dangle her legs and push against the ground with her feet, as if attempting to walk. But this is just a reflex -- those legs aren't nearly strong enough to hold her.'

On slightly worn, slightly faded carpet, Lucy awoke face-down in the nook of her elbow. Her body was slumped slightly on its side, her other arm sprawled outward, her ankles crossed over on themselves. Crumbs was still sheltered below her waist, just as he'd been in the height of the storm. She lifted her head, letting her vision come slowly back into focus. She could make out her arms, and the green markings on the red carpet. It hurt. It hurt to see. It also caused a tingling sensation to run down her neck and spine, and her body began to revive its circulation causing an unbearable onset of paresthesia to run through her limbs.

As it ended, she lifted her torso and tried fleetingly to compose herself. Warm sunshine overwhelmed her. Was she dreaming or had she been poisoned? The shadows, shapes and scenery were all dauntingly foreign. The windstorm, the pushy blonde man, and the marshy wetland had vanished. Now the toasty sun glared over her, the sun of a sky she had never before been under. With just one breath of the heavy, spiced air, Lucy knew she was a long way from Scotland.

Beneath the rich blue sky, the street before her was perfectly flat. It was seemingly infinite. It stretched into the horizon until it was blurred in the distance. Stone terraces on either side of it overflowed with flowers. The red carpet that rolled out from under her, ran down the street until it too disappeared with the horizon. Ebony poles bearing pearlescent glass lanterns, frequented themselves alongside its path. Below the rug, the ground, a floor of polished timber, also stretched out and went on indefinitely. Multicoloured glass windows of terraces, speckled the sidelines with rainbow light. Lucy began to hyperventilate as she looked everything up and down, attempting to fathom where in the world she could possibly be. The closest terrace to her had an arched tin awning over a tiny rounded door, a row of potted tulips beside a pastel pink window, and a large sign marked CLOSED. Lucy sat. Her head still hurt, and a dizzy sensation made her nervous to stand.

It would be impossible to describe, by location, the reality of where Lucy was. What can be said is that she was certainly no longer in Scotland. The place, was Archmond, the westernmost kingdom of Escallia Wimbers. More specifically, she had found herself upon Archmond's Wooden Floor Boarders, (aka the WFB) the capital and city heartland. Archmond had a history of being a kingdom of considerable wealth, albeit a wealth that had in recent times deteriorated. But the streets reflected their prosperous past. This was particularly so across the arty streets of the WFB. Nearly every structure in the heartland was conceived with a certain stylistic aspiration - mere functionality of construction was not enough. In fact the prevailing architecture was quite unconventional; in multi-storey dwellings, spiralling peppermint or teal staircases outside the buildings, bypassed first floors to the second, the paintwork bright, as though new. Balconies overflowed with flowers, and ground floor patios were crowded with terracotta pots. The larger government buildings boasted over-zealous entrances; wide and narrowing steps were guarded by ceramic statues of ambiguous meaning. The ornate stone carvings that looped the top of their perimeter also advanced the status of these grander addresses. The incidence of glass, both stained in pretty pastel, and clear as air, was also a symbol of the capital's wealth. Archmond was known, and indeed named, for its rows of angular and arched rooftops. The unbroken terraces looked like a colourful quilt from afar, with the alternating shades of tin and tile (rust, navy, and iron). The entire city, neatly divided into a grid system of wide streets and slender laneways, stretched out for over five square miles, and all rested wondrously upon an unbroken foundation of varnished timber floor.

Lucy had taken in very little, if any, of such detail. The world around her was simply a dizzying onset of excessive vibrance and unfamiliarity. The warmth was something she'd never experienced at home, even in high summer. The thick blue sky and its burning yellow sun created more intensity of colour and heat than she knew to be possible. The lunchtime air was swimming with the pungent smells of sugared fruit, citrus, chilli and cardamon. Whatever had occurred between the windy parkland and now had upset her faculties, and the intensity of fragrance and colour only served to further disorient and nauseate her. The beauty of the opulent city, on its seemingly impossible foundations, was something she would only later come to appreciate. But in the moment she arrived she was a fish out of water, an abandoned kitten, a paralyzed mouse in a bizarre experiment.

'Crumbs…' she muttered drawing in terrified breaths, 'we are in so much trouble.'

The loud echo of trumpets being sounded prompted Lucy's attention in the other direction. The rug beneath her could be traced with the naked eye into the midst of a large crowd in a public arena. A stage and an open auditorium were the permanent placards of this public space. Beyond the crowd, the intimidating and imminent outer walls of Archmond Castle stretched outward and upward, casting the entire city in its glory. Angular towers of stone and cement peaked up over the curtain wall. The crowd below was half cast in the pointed shadow from the leftmost tower's arched roof.

The gathering crowd, and the event it related to, granted Lucy a fortunate and opportune moment to rush into cover. She had not been thrust into this place in full view of its residents in their normal day-to-day activities. She had arrived just when they were all distracted. But she could not yet lift herself. She felt heavy, heavy and hot. The shock of this awakening among inexplicable scenery was all but paralyzing her. All she could do was look on, and hope that none of the crowd turned back to see her lying there on the rug.

A person approached the podium upon the stage, causing the whispering and murmurings to cease. It was then, that even in her shock and distance, Lucy began to appreciate how impossible her situation was. The man at the podium exhibited features one would ordinarily describe as an abnormality. *Ordinarily.* But this was no singular peculiarity of one man. The others that entered the stage behind him, silent and in sage and bronze uniforms, exhibited the same odd features. Another at the edge of the crowd, a child perhaps, who turned around to scratch his ankle, was much the same. She was witnessing first-hand, a race of people she never knew existed. The peculiarities were slight rather than shocking: overly rounded faces, abnormally small ears, notably short, though not dwarfish nor disproportionate in stature, and abnormally large eyes, which perpetuated an innocent and soft expression. The other features, complexion, weight, nose, hair, varied from person to person.

As the announcements began, and the crowd became staunchly fixated on the podium beside the castle perimeter, the child who had several moments ago turned to scratch his ankle suddenly stiffened with awareness. He turned slowly, as he considered in retrospect, an error with the scenery behind him. He caught the error instantly with a ghastly squeal - the limp lanky body of a young but larger girl; characteristics of which were not pleasantly received. Those around the boy reacted, spinning and gasping, the wave of curiosity and panic spreading back through the crowd. The fear spurred on and tumbled into a ruckus of hateful shouting. But it was nonsensical; something about a queen, something about the borders, hiding, retaliating.

Crumbs began to snarl and growl as the threatening tones of their cries seethed toward them.

'Bash her head in!' one man cried out.

'Enough - enough!' cried Soleman from the podium, but nobody noticed him. Ron looked to his partner condescendingly, 'she's *eeeaaarly.*'

'I know,' said Soleman defensively, with irritation.

Lucy, unaware of the conversations about her on the stage, tried to stand, to run, as the men in sage uniform surrounding the perimeter of the crowd, were reacting fiercely: hands clutching at swords, marching toward her. But as she tried to push her heavy body upright, sweating as she did so, her palms pushing into the rug, a surge of pain springing from her finger shot up her arm. She looked at her hand. The pin prick had become a deep wound down her finger an inch long, and her finger was swollen and discoloured, with deep red and purple blotches.

'Ooooh, ghastly! Sorry about that. We...ahhh...We'll get it fixed up. Necessary rite of passage...so to speak,' Soleman said, reacting to her alarm at the injury. Lucy looked up. The conniption in the background had all but ceased, and a plump older man with a milky blue tunic, was leaning forward, offering her a hand; the man from the podium. He looked not nearly as old as his wispy white beard made him appear from afar. With sun drenched skin and brightly sparked eyes, Soleman's perennial optimism was immedi-ately apparent. For those that knew him, his eagerness and casual warmth came through in his gentle manner and excitable tone, and his face when relaxed bore a soft joyousness as though he couldn't help but smile.

Emerging from courtside in comedically stark contrast, his lean and tall counterpart, Ronald Tobias, moved and held himself in a state of careful reluctance. Head held high, he scanned the world in a constant scepticism. The contrasting nature of each of them was reflected across their respective facades; Ron was a moody palate of maroon, olive and grey, and Soleman was an uplifting palate of tan, white and powder blue.

The sage guards behind the two men stood stoic, heads bowed in apologetic posture. The crowd had been commanded into a muttering, whispering silence. Crumbs fidgeted back and forth with low snappy growls, unsure of whether to proceed or retreat.

'Where am I?' the most obvious question, as she stared upward with distrust.

'Deep in the heart of the WFB my dear, which is itself the heart of Archmond.'

Soleman retreated slightly, still smiling, but accepting she would not take his hand. He secretly chastised himself, considering perhaps he'd been too forward.

'She doesn't know where the WFB is, or Archmond, or anywhere for that matter,' said Ron, who had very slowly made his way forward to be in line with his co-ruler.

'I know that,' snapped Soleman, 'but a name is always a start.'

'It's irrelevant,' said Ron, who with much reticence also offered a hand to Lucy.

She hesitated; the last time she'd given a hand to anyone she'd ended up here, with a disfigured finger.

'Eventually,' said Ron dryly, examining her with none of the warmth and interest of his colleague, 'you will need to stand.'

Unwittingly, Lucy took his hand and allowed him to pull her to her feet. Soleman pretended not to be offended at what he worried might be the beginnings of favouritism.

'The point is you are not anywhere you know child. Nor can we tell you how far away you are from your home. Because we do not know,' Ron continued.

'I don't understand…' she uttered, signalling Crumbs to sit by her feet. Although bewildered and confused, she still understood that

there was more to know than what they were telling her. They understood something she did not.

Soleman put his hands on her shoulders. Instinctively she wanted
to shift away, but the heaviness of his hands was somehow comforting.

'You may not understand any of this for longer than you can
imagine,' said Soleman, as preciously as if he was consoling a mourner
at a funeral, 'but you may come to accept it. And that is at least…
the beginning.'

Lucy trembled turning this way and that, taking in broken
snapshots of the opulence and incredibility around her. The floor's
varnish was highly reflective, and sent midday glare bouncing off
windows, lanterns, and polished benches. The seemingly infinite
street was starting to speckle with other onlookers in the distance,
as the news had quietly spread that the person from the other world
had arrived.

She went with them. She followed the two men of the strange race.
She did it with little thought. But there was seemingly no other
option. Where else would she go? There was not a familiar thing in
sight. There was no way to tell whether they would hurt her or help
her. So she went.

The sage soldiers now became her escort, as she was led through the
crowd of peculiar people. People who had moments ago been reacting
wildly with fear and hate, were now gossiping with excitement, scrambling to get a look at the subject of the spectacle. The few that met
her gaze fell suddenly still, there was almost a reverence about them.
The details of her location were blurred in the impossibility of it all.
She was dizzy with disbelief. Had she needed to recall the streets, or
names, or landmarks to describe her location to a rescuer, she would
not have been able. She would only remember the grandeur of architecture, the doe-eyed marvel of onlookers, and a feeling of being led
that was more like tumbling down a thorny precipice.

When they made their way beyond the defensive walls into the luscious surrounds of the royal gardens, the silence and serenity invoked a new sense of urgency in Lucy. She began to ask them desperately if they knew how she could get home.

No, the two men had repeated.

And with each confusing, 'no', her heart pounded harder inside her chest. And the panic in her rose.

They told her that instead, they could try to explain what had led to her being here, that there was a story that could help her start to make some sense of things in her mind. Soleman had all but pleaded with her. There had been countless hours and precious resources spent on a project that had finally culminated in her arrival, it would only be fair, he had urged, if she would at least just listen, to what they had to say. But Lucy only rephrased and repeated her question again and again.

'Do you know how I can get back to Lockerby, in Scotland? I'm not in Scotland anymore, am I? I really need to go home.'

As she was more and more incoherent, the decision was made to leave her in the care of the maids, and return to her later. She then begged the maids all the same.

'Will you help me? I don't know how to get home. I have to get home. Can you help me?'

'Yes, yes missy, we help,' the old maid had said unconvincingly, leading her through the corridors of polished black stone. Glassy flecks in the stone began creating angelic prisms of light around them as they walked. The corridors led to stairwells and further corridors, taking her to the north-east wing of the castle where her room had long ago been prepared. As the maid had led her over to a four-poster bed Lucy refused to let go of her wrist.

'Please, please help me,' she begged, though unconsciously she let herself be gently guided to sit on its edge. Her eyes were welling with tears of terrified uncertainty.

'Let go missy, you lie down now, we'll come back later to check on you,' the maid had said as she forcibly removed Lucy's clutching hand. Behind her by the doorway the younger maid looked on tenderly, and two guards stood motionless. Helpless to do anything, Lucy sat back and rushed her hands to her mouth. Crumbs leapt into her lap. And then they left her there alone in the chamber room, until the daylight turned golden and then paled, as the world began to sink toward twilight.

Remaining on the edge of the bed, Lucy had stared at the fading light from the balcony window letting it transfix her, until it became a numbness that calmed her.

It was hours before she did anything else. When coherency began to sift back, with a deep breath, she took in her surroundings. She consoled herself with her observations. She was not in a cell, but in a grand room; a room of brassy candelabras, velvet laden chairs, silver framed mirrors and artwork. The high ceiling was painted with bluebirds and bell flowers and there was a fresh bouquet in every corner. From memory there were guards posted at the entrance, behind a large wooden door now shut. But was she a prisoner? Or were they *her* guards? The maids, (or were they *her* maids) had left her with water. A large basin of jade and glass affixed to the wall by the balcony had been filled to the brim earlier with two fresh buckets. She went to it to drink, and wet her face.

Her room faced directly east, and there was enough light left to see the sun setting in the distance. Past the sea of tin and clay rooftops, the orange ball was descending rapidly behind rows of olive-green hills. The distant ruggedness of the rural landscape almost looked familiar, but of course, it wasn't.

She stayed by the balcony windows vacantly, until the dusk gave way to night, and bright red embers drifted up in the breeze from the fires around the castle, and pockets of amber-light littered the city below.

'Miss,' a short-time after night-fall the young maid knocked and entered, heaving the wooden door open with great effort, 'supper for you,' she curtsied, leaving the silver tray on the side table by the door.

Lucy was out of questions as she watched the maid kneel and kindle a fire. The fireplace was closer to the door than the balcony, on the far wall opposite the bed. When the flames were licking at the logs, she dusted herself off and made to leave.

'Wait,' Lucy called, stepping away from the balcony, 'there are guards outside my room?'

'Yes miss.'

'Am I a prisoner?'

The maid looked shocked at the question, 'of course no, you are not.'

'So I can leave at any time?' Lucy asked.

'*Yes*,' an oddly insolent tone that implied the question had already been answered.

The maid curtsied again and left, before Lucy could ask anymore.

So she was not a prisoner. She returned to the balcony, and looked out into the darkness. But where would she go? Lucy sat on the rug that lay across the stone floor, and in the firelight she ate the meal they brought for her; pickled eggs, stale bread, and a fatty meat stew. She looked around. The flames sent dancing shadows across the ceiling. They were starting to stir her imagination.

'It feels as though this can only be a dream,' she said to Crumbs as she broke off bits of bread, and plucked out pieces of the gamey meat from the stew for him, 'but how can a dream feel so real…'

Crumbs didn't answer her, but he lapped up pieces of the meat and the bread.

'But if it's not a dream,' she continued 'then what are we going to do? I don't know if anyone here will help us get home,' she muttered softly, starting to tear up again. 'I don't know if they can't, or if they just won't.'

From somewhere in the castle below, the muffled shouts of celebration found their way through her window; flutes, a harpsichord, clapping, dancing, the beastly drunken elation of men.

'This is a very strange place. Everything is old. It must be far, it must be so far…' in thinking of home her eyes lost themselves in the ceiling again, as if nostalgically recalling a distant past. It was as her memory pieced it, only hours ago she was there, yet she felt herself distanced from Lockerby not just in space, but in time.

'If we're in the dream-world Crumbs,' she said sometime later, after letting the sounds of jubilation soothe her, and returning to the soft downy surface of the oversized regal bed, 'then when we sleep, we shall wake from it. I think that's a rule in dreaming. It's got to be.'

Elsewhere in the castle - a discussion ensues.

Soleman shifted wearily on his throne, as he nodded politely at another nobleman offering praises to his Majestic Eminence and Imperial Lord. The day had been testingly long, and yet the night continued. Before them the throne room chorused with blaring jubilation. Soleman silently noted that the evening's band, flute players and tap-drummers from the town, had not had a rest in performances since night fell, and that someone should fetch the choir to relieve them and soothe the evening into a more sober atmosphere. The firelight, permeating from iron pits in every corner, was creating an illusion of afternoon glow, and the people were still carrying on as though it was. And on a night in high summer the added heat from the flames was causing them all to sweat, which was especially uncomfortable for the men on the throne, who could not disrobe from the endless layers of royal silk.

'Enough, I will faint if this continues, how eminent will I seem then?' he said to Ron, reaching down and fetching his wand.

Ron took a deep breath. 'I hadn't thought it would go on quite so long. But if you're going to faint, by all means, you might as well.'

Soleman nodded, happy for the approval. He flicked his wrist and a heavenly mist of icy blue air surrounded them, and remained, hovering about the two thrones, cooling them.

'Ayerie!' Soleman called. A young girl draped in silks and jewels left her social circle and came to attention. Soleman wiped the mist from his spectacles and pushed them back up the bridge of his nose, 'put out some of the fires will you, our guests will melt into puddles in this cauldron. And switch the band for the choir.'

She nodded and set about doing just that.

But if the room was too hot, it hadn't hurt the ambience. The forty to eighty noblemen and women that remained, (although most had partially disrobed) were enjoying the wine, scooping up spoonfuls of the remaining lavish desserts, and twirling about ecstatically, drunk on good news as much as anything else.

'All this excitement, and she hasn't even come out of her room yet,' Ron snuck in the snide remark. He had been sitting on his preliminary appraisal for hours, but hadn't had the opportunity to share it.

'Well, what did you expect?' said Soleman, showing a little more spirit than usual. 'Eh? Her to get here, dust herself off, stand and salute, then pick up the nearest sword and off she goes towards Meta Emery, aye? That what you had in mind?' Soleman said mockingly, rising from his throne to imitate his impression of his partner's absurd expectations. Some of the guests noticed, looking back and chuckling. It was not uncommon for the two rulers to feud.

Ron rolled his eyes, 'sit down you old fool. No. Don't be so outlandish, you know very well that's not what I expected. Rather, what I *hoped*, is that there would be an initial display, or at least an inkling of, some of the characteristics we associate with someone for the task. Bravery, even a little curiosity. She's only begged, cried, and curled up in the dark like a…like…I don't know, a sick bird or something,' Ron retorted.

'Well, I say again, what do you expect?' said Soleman, 'she's a young girl. Young, seventeen is young in their world. And as we've seen, as we know, she's untried, untested, untrained…'

'Exactly,' said Ron, 'it's the lack of experience that just absolutely baffles me in your decision.'

'You're looking at it so narrowly, Ron. It's not always someone who has already had the training, who is going to be the best at the job. I mean…I mean…look at Catapol.'

'What?'

'*Yes!* Yes, it's like Catapol.' Soleman shifted into a sideways position on the throne, facing Ron as he began to delight at his own analogy.

'It is not at all like Catapol,' dismissed Ron unamused.

'It is, it is - more wine please Tammy - no hear me out. Some of the best Catapol players we've seen have come from families where there is no association with the sport at all. None. And yet, from someone spotting some knack early on, they've been rounded into the training schools, and they've come out brilliant. Records have been broken on the backs of young unassuming prodigies. And you would just reject them because they don't have the training to begin with? If you were captain of those teams, imagine all the victories you'd have missed with that attitude?'

Ron took a deep breath trying not to let his frustration overwhelm him, 'we've a lot more at stake here, than the cost of putting someone through a training school.'

'I know,' said Soleman flicking his index finger out with conviction as he took Ron's glass and his own and leant forward letting the aid refill them, 'that's why I did the spell. That's why I watched to see if it was right. I didn't make any mistakes this time, and all the other prophecies seem to fit with this girl. It might just…take more time, than we'd like,' he said pausing as he uttered the word time, a realisation only just coming to him. Ron nodded, he remained unconvinced, but his objections served no use now that they'd brought the girl here. Besides, it was late.

'Well, just don't tell them that,' he said indicating the gleeful crowd of their subjects dancing away still, even amongst the diminished light and now somber singing of choir girls.

'Yes,' said Soleman rubbing his beard as he allowed the first wave of anxiety and worry to flow through him. Ironic, in that it was his own words that eventually shed some doubt on the situation. About Lucy he was right, he knew that emphatically. But about how, and how long it would take, he had no idea.

Lucy's logic was that sleep within a dream, was in substance, a way to remove yourself from the illusionary surroundings, and go back into a more alert subconscious, where you could realise you were asleep, and then wake up. Lucy was not a dreamer. She could recall only a few restless times in her life, when she had been bombarded with nonsensical or frightening imagery, for what seemed like hours when she'd overslept. These were the times when she remembered being able to slip back from the imagery into the dark nothingness of sleep, and from there, she was able to wake up.

Her logic was still sound, but now the premise was wrong. This was not a dream. She realised this, and finally accepted that she was not dreaming, when she woke up the next morning *from a dream*. Suddenly the contrast of the two states - the dream state and the waking state - was now glaringly apparent. There could be no more doubt. The cream sheets in the stiff regal bed, the particles wafting through the sunlight in the hollow middle of the room, and the smell of ashes from the fireplace - this was not an illusion of the mind. Whether the dream she had just awoken from had been an illusion though was a different question. It was certainly not real in the way being awake was. But it had been less like a bizarre onslaught of faces and nonsensical happenings, and more like a delivery of information. In a dreamy narrative, a tale had been recounted to her while she slept.

She sat upright and adjusted the pillows behind her. Her hairs stood on end as she re-played it to herself, trying to memorise the scenes before they evaporated. Some of the details were grimmer than she was comfortable with.

The Dream

It began the way most dreams end, with blackness everywhere. But rather than this being the empty void of sleep's canvas, she had an awareness she was standing in a dark room. She was able to shift this way and that, but she saw none of her own self, as though she was completely covered in it. Not one speck of grayish light lit her limbs, or the boundaries of the room, to give any dimension to wherever she was. This period of unknowing had been fleeting though. The sound of a mechanical switch and a spotlight glared down on her from above. The bright white light made visible only the dust particles floating through the air; it gave not a clue to where she was, or what the dream was to mean. The sound of another powerful switch echoed, and another spotlight, not too far away, appeared. The dust floated through it unsuspectingly.

Moments later, a purple and green umbrella came floating down through the light as flimsily as a feather. And fading into sight, in the moon hook of the polished handle; a teddy bear.

It had the beginnings of a nightmare. The charred black bear had a blood red patch where the heart might be imagined in a child's toy, with rough stitching signalling a healed wound. The eyes were each made of two stitches, crosses, symbolising death, and adorned on his head, a shiny black top hat. Lucy remembered her breath racing and wanting to run away, but just like now in the chamber room there was really nowhere to go. The bear's soft feet touched the floor, and with his head tilted low, he ran his claws along the brim of the hat, as if he was about to break out in song. He broke out in rhyme instead.

'No need to fear, for I am sincere, just be wise, and open your eyes. Just open your ear and listen my dear.'

She had then found herself in a chamber room. But it was a different chamber room, and a different castle. It was grander and lighter. The sandstone walls cast a yellow hue across the floor, the ceiling was higher, and the windows angular. The daylight was almost blinding.

In the corner, a woman in the bed curled over on her side and groaned with pain. Servants (notably human and without the odd features of the strange people she'd just encountered) fussed around the room impassive to her feverous cries for help. Buckets surrounded the bed, while towels and discoloured rags were bunched at the base. The woman's hair was mottled, and the sheets were dampened and stained yellow with dirt and sweat.

The woman turned and the protruding bulge explained her pain, the woman was very pregnant. The bursts of agony vibrated across the gothic glass windows like the winds of a pipe organ. Watching the graphic yet dreamy scenes move past her Lucy pieced together that the woman was someone significant. Outside the room in the hollow hallways she saw the father pace impatiently.

The woman bore triplets, colour drained babies each with varying crowns; first an ash blonde baby, the next with cherry red hair, and lastly an ebony crowned child.

And the dream went on, and the children grew older. She could see that the children were all girls, and it was clear they belonged to a royal family. In several visions she saw the father that had been pacing outside the sunlit bedroom, this time robed, and crowned. He was the King. The lady pained in childbirth was his Queen. She saw visions of the children playing over the years. The gardens near the castle were rippled with veins of rushing green water, the melting ice caps from the summit above. The girls swam with other children of the castle, in a lake thick with mustard reeds. They hid in the fringes of the willow trees, whose silvery blue leaves dipped into the water. Beyond the gardens, the onyx cliff-face dropped down toward the city in steep rocky steps.

In another vision, an event, a celebration, below the castle. Streamers, flags, drums, and crowds of people filled the usually private grounds. The three girls, still very young perhaps five or six in year, were watching on from a terrace that overlooked some of the event from the south side of the castle. The Queen was there, as were several maids tending to them, and guards posted at the windows. But there was a call from within the room and the Queen and her maids rushed inside. A dark haired man with two soldier escorts of his own and sporting a sash with medals and badges, someone of apparent signif-icance, had summoned them in.

In the same moment, while the man had the Queen's ear, the ebony haired child grabbed her blonde sister and pushed her between the pillars on the terrace. In moments the child was a lifeless lump, pool-ing with blood on the grounds below. The assailant screamed, calling for help. The only witness, the other sister, looked on at the chaos that then ensued around her, disturbed but afraid to speak.

The frightening black bear came into focus once more, and the other imagery of the dream faded away.

'*The murder of a future Queen,*
concealed as accidental,
was not entirely unseen,
but the witness all too fearful,' he uttered, stretching the words to make his rhyme work.

In another series of blurry disjointed images, the black haired girl, older, ten or twelve, was being comforted in her parent's bedroom. It was just as bizarre and disturbing as the last incident of the dream. In what appeared later to be an almost overdone reenactment, the girl took a knife from under her nightdress and slit first her father's throat, then her mother's. The passive King and Queen both clutched at their wounds, and fell forward, bleeding out across the sheets.

'Dauntae' was one of the palace guards on duty that night,' the voice of the bear narrated in the background,

'he was hung for Regicide.'

In another vision the other sister was running fearfully through the castle gardens. Strands of her strawberry curls caught in the splits of the ferns, as she disappeared into the mountain fog. And that was it. Then Lucy woke up.

Lucy shifted in the bed, leaning her arm along the bedhead and resting her head on her knuckles. A convoluted story about murdered royals, and the pink haired sister who escaped into the mist, as narrated by a deathly teddy bear. Lucy exhaled with deep foreboding, but knew she should try and get up.

Meanwhile in the kingdom of the east, an artificially young Queen stirs.

The barely adolescent Queen burst awake, thrown from her own dream like a comet plummeting to earth. Her black hair fell across her face, and she rushed to clasp the pendant around her neck, the white sheets bunching around her.

'Thomas,' she called, panting to her fiancée, 'Thomas!'

A dark haired young man stirred next to her, he turned his head, squinting up at her with one green eye.

'They did it,' she gasped, her pupils wide with terror, *'they did it!'*

'Did what?' he groaned sleepily.

The young man rubbed his eyes and begrudgingly sat up.

'They're going to kill me,' she said, and began to hyperventilate, clutching at her throat. Her skin was whiter than normal in the panic.

'The wizards? Is that what this is about?' he put his arm around her, 'they're nothing. They're just bumbling fools. They don't stand a chance, and I will die a hundred times to protect you if I have to,' he kissed her forehead and stroked her hair back neatly.

She turned to face him and gripped his hand hard, 'they brought her here, the girl. I dreamt it. She's here. She's coming.'

Back in Archmond...

Lucy was still waking up, and still in a place more foreign than she could have ever dreamed up. Crumbs shifted next to her where he'd slept, lifting himself up he stretched his back and then began licking her excitedly. He was ready for affection, ready to be fed. He was oblivious to their predicament.

She could ignore the urge in her bladder no longer. She would have to do something. She found a metal bowl at the foot of the bed and sighed with unease. A bedpan. She knew what they were, but she'd never needed to use one before. There was no toilet in the room, it might be safe to conclude this was all there was available. She tried to bury her disgust. In this historic city, this was probably all there was anywhere.

Ahhh the clarity a night's sleep can bring! As she squatted in the corner behind the changing screen, feeling herself waking up, she understood now she would have to seek out the men from yesterday. She would have to hear this explanation they had been so desperately trying to give her. She rolled her eyes at the memory of her own idiotic delirium the day before. Why hadn't she listened? It hadn't helped anything.

Lucy found guards still posted at her door.

'Excuse me, can you get the men from yesterday? The men who escorted me into these grounds? One of them had a long white beard, the other one was taller and grey, with olive skin…do you know them?'

She gestured as she described them, but the guards only eyed her up and down with contempt. The hateful looks were reminiscent of the angry crowd yesterday. She stepped back a little, wondering if they were here to imprison her after all. But they were simply disparaging her appearance, her knotted hair and dress were still covered in dirt, her very light layer of mascara had run from her crying and was streaked across her cheeks.

'Do you know who I'm talking about? Can you get them for me?' she asked again.

'We cannot leave our posting,' the guard to her right eventually replied with a tone that matched the contempt on his face, 'but you're welcome to go looking. We'll follow after you.'

'I thought you couldn't leave your posting,' she uttered carefully.

'You are the posting,' the other guard replied.

That was when Lucy first began to understand her relevance in all of this. The men from yesterday knew *why* she was here, because they were trying to tell her. And she was important to them, because they had assigned guards to protect her. On the other hand, this also suggested she was in danger.

She wandered the halls with the guards following five paces behind her. She made her way half a mile down the marble corridor. She had no way of knowing how late it was into the next day, but the light rushing in from the windows was soft like morning. As her path turned, she saw a maid carrying laundry leave a room and continue into an intersecting corridor.

'Excuse me,' she said coming up behind her.

The maid was so alarmed at the sight she threw her laundry into the air, and spent the next few minutes apologising profusely while she gathered it all back up into the wicker basket. Lucy had never seen this woman before. She was not one of the women who supplied her with fresh water yesterday.

'I just want to find the men from yesterday, you might know them? The man with the white beard, in the blue dress?'

'I will send for Elotta. I am so sorry,' said the maid, she was still kneeling beside the basket on the ground, staring into the laundry, deliberately avoiding eye contact.

'You don't need to be sorry,' said Lucy not wanting her confusion at the woman's behaviour to turn into desperation. Despite her efforts though, she started to feel her emotions overwhelming her again, but she had promised herself she was done with crying. Her eyes watered, but she stopped them turning to tears.

'I just want to find those men. Do you know who they are?'

The maid nodded, and then shook her head again, 'I...I...I will send for Elotta. I'm sorry,' she said in a desperate rush, scrambling to her feet and hurrying off without having to look Lucy in the eye.

'Wait!' Lucy cried after her, 'What do I do? Where should I go?'

The maid turned, 'to your chamber,' she replied but nearly inaudibly, as if she was too timid to yell. She gestured with her hand, as if pushing Lucy back away.

Lucy was on the balcony when Elotta returned. She had gone outside to look at the vivid orange flowers spurting off a vine like jasmine. She hadn't noticed them in the chaos of yesterday. The vine fell from an awning above the balcony, zigzagged down a lattice on the left wall, and then looped around the balustrade. But Lucy's attention had since wandered upward, and she was watching a bulbous cloud pass over the sun.

'Dannis. It's a weed actually, we just haven't had the gardener up here for a while.'

Lucy turned to see the maid from yesterday had come into the room, and stood before the balcony watching her.

'Then why do you have the lattice?' she asked.

'Was meant for jasmine, but dannis suffocated it.'

Lucy studied the maid for a moment quietly, 'are you Elotta?' she asked.

'Yes, that's me. One of the laundry maids said you were after me?' She swung forward, hands clasped at the waist of her mustard uniform.

Lucy burbled with increasing frustration, but she wouldn't show it.

'I just want to find out why I'm here,' she sighed trying to keep from tears.

'The men, from yesterday, they wanted to tell me something. Where are they?'

'You wish to meet with them?' Elotta asked.

'I just want to know what's going on.'

Elotta put a hand to her chin thoughtfully and looked Lucy up and down.

'Okay, good. I will fetch the bath.'

'Bath? I just want some answers!' Lucy was becoming petulant.

'But you cannot meet the Eminence and the Lord like this. You need to get ready!' Elotta said defensively.

'Ready? Ready for what?' Lucy raised her eyebrows with growing suspicion.

At this Elotta was very amused, 'for the day of course. I hope you don't go around looking like this all the time missy? It is not very becoming for a lady. I would think you feel embarrassed?'

Lucy took a deep breath, she was a mess, but it was evident these people would not grasp how much she didn't care under the circumstances. But she was in their world after all.

The bath was an hour of sickly trespasses upon her privacy. A violation she was uncomfortably pressured into through the maids' motherly smiles and mockery of her prudish attitude. Lucy hadn't allowed anyone to see her undress since she was a young girl. Even the boy who took her virginity had only been able to get enough off to do the deed; she'd never been naked.

They had cleared the rug from the centre of the room as the guards brought in a metal basin, free standing on four legs. Below there was a space for a wood-fire, which Elotta set about lighting.

'I can bathe myself, it's okay,' Lucy had softly tried to suggest. But Elotta and the younger maid, Freriana, had only laughed and began to undress her.

'A lady doesn't bathe herself,' said Elotta dismissively as she unzipped the back of Lucy's pinafore, and Freriana peeled off her socks. Lucy would look back and wonder why she hadn't stood her ground more adamantly. But she would look back on much of the early days in this way, and pity her youthful self for being so meek and complacent.

Elotta's hands were much too coarse and weathered for a woman of her age. The clay coloured skin cracked from a lifetime of servitude; excessive submersion in soaps and chemicals, compounded by little self-care. The crackly skin had an exfoliant effect as she smoothed the soap over Lucy's body. But no matter how much she tried to ease her subject with a tender smile, the girl continued to quiver nervously and look away uncomfortably.

When it was over Lucy smelt like the summer apple fragrance of the bath water. They were kind enough to let her pick a dress, after she cringed at the first two voluptuous gowns they pulled from the wardrobe. Emeralds, rubies, frills, velvet, and long lace trails - Lucy kept pushing them back alarmed and repeating that she wanted to be simple, anything clean and simple would be fine.

Eventually she found a straight black dress the maids insisted was for only for mourning, but they let her wear it. They dried her hair and plaited it, and they dusted her face lightly with powder, the only make up she would allow.

'Can I please go and find those men now, whoever they are?' Lucy asked desperately. Freriana gave a look of pity, how sad that she was looking exhausted and the day had only begun! She pinned Lucy's fringe behind her ears, using a hairpin with a golden albatross, the final touch.

'There!' she exclaimed proudly, 'yes, now you may go.'

A Most Memorable Meeting

Escorted again by the guards, Elotta led Lucy and her little dog across Archmond Castle to the Southern Wing. In the far corner tower a drawstring bridge led them above the royal gardens, to the drawing room nestled into the southern end of the curtain wall. Soleman was alone and drowning in paperwork as his guard announced her arrival.

'Now?' he called from within. There was then a pause, and the guards shuffled them into the room without answer.

'Lucy, please come in, come in, I insist,' he said as he saw them already coming in. He was rushing from the far side of the room, arms filled with papers that he promptly slid into a large wooden drawer in a cabinet by the window. The room resembled a home office, scattered with lounges, wooden tables, bookshelves and desks, all cluttered with papers and open books and half melted candles in iron holders.

'Sorry about the mess. We have had quite a bit going on of late, with ahh your arrival and what not, and I ahh…wasn't expecting to see you so early,' he called gathering another bundle of papers from the round pine table near the lounge and hurrying back up the step of the split level room to where a basin had been gathering with empty cups to be washed. With the paperwork in his right arm, he leant to the left to allow the cups to roll from his left fingers and into the sink. He then hastily rushed down the step again sorting the papers onto a shelf by the wall near the door.

'Of course, it would have been nice if Elotta had given us some notice eh?' he called as he sorted out the last few items into a cupboard and then, after stilling himself with a deep breath, paced calmly towards them.

Elotta grew red and her head dropped to the floor.

'It's not her fault, I asked her to bring me,' Lucy said, pleadingly.

Soleman became embarrassed for his condemnation of the servant. He worried what the young girl would think of him.

'Of course, not to worry, not to worry, I'm glad you're here. You may go Elotta. Thank you kindly.' Soleman bowed most genuinely and Elotta left.

'Sebastien, send for Ayerie, would you?' he called to the guard outside the door.

The lofty room was nowhere near the comfort of the rest of the castle. The stones making the defensive perimeter were hard and fire resistant, but in such way cold and grey. A morning breeze broke through the gaps in the barred windows and balcony doors. Lucy shuddered momentarily.

'Are you cold? I will send for a shawl. It's oddly fresh this morning, not common in high summer I can assure you, but a nice change nonetheless. But I don't want you to be cold.'

Lucy drew back and waved her arms lightly in dissent, 'oh, no, no I'm okay,' she muttered softly. Her shudder may have been nervousness, or the residue of shock. The morning was heavily warmer than the world she was used to.

An awkward silence permeated between them once they were alone. Soleman's awkwardness was in part due to a deeply harboured and private guilt about the whole operation. It was in the simplest terms, kidnapping, what they had done. He knew that. He tried to discount this by reminding himself of the savage and violent home life they had taken the girl from. But this was always outweighed by the knowledge of the terrible violence and depravity he knew awaited her here. Still, if the prophecy was right this was part of her destiny in a separate force, and he couldn't therefore be entirely accountable. He could only pray as he always did, that the greater good would prevail. He'd never had any children. The celibacy was part of the duty imposed on Eminent leaders; their successors chosen for them. But he had cared for many children, his sister's included. And he would hate for any of them to endure what he knew Lucy would.

Soleman was fidgeting. His hands poked through the sleeves of his red tunic and clasped in front of him by his waist as Elotta had stood earlier. And like the maid, he too swayed backward and forward slightly, gathering the right words to begin with.

'You look well. I'm sure it has been a difficult evening and day. But I'm glad the maids have taken good care of you…or umm it seems they have…I hope they have,' he said, beginning to breathe rapidly in his nervous distress.

Breaking the tension, Ron marched into the room followed closely by Ayerie, their glamorous and dexterous young courtier. As if by practiced routine, Ayerie continued past Lucy and up the step to where spirits decanted on a shelf by the sink, and an array of marked metal boxes stacked on top of each other. Ron collapsed onto the lounge.

'Ron, good timing! You must have sensed it!' said Soleman cheerily, relieved to no longer be alone with the subject.

Ron made a face. 'I was there when they sent for Ayerie,' he said.

'I was just telling Lucy how lovely she looks today. Doesn't she look lovely? As if brand new! The maids did a fine job.'

Ron glanced at Lucy taking her in for the first time. Disappointment. Not at the girl, but the maids; how could they have let her out in a mourning dress when they had stocked her room with so many beautiful gowns? He made a mental note to raise it with them later. But for now he feigned a smile, trying not to let his lack of regard show through. But even the forced smile was bare.

'Yes, lovely,' he said, and nodded to her respectfully.

'You must want a drink, can we get you something? Tea? Wine? Sintep?' Soleman offered, strolling to join Ron on the ruby lounge.

In the background Ayerie shifted attentively, ready for instruction.

'No, I just want to know…' Lucy paused, she couldn't quite phrase exactly what she wanted and needed to understand.

'Of course you do. Come sit, child,' said Ron calling her over.

There were two moon shaped lounges facing each other. Hesitantly Lucy sat herself across from the two men. A small round coffee table was all that bridged the gap between them.

Soleman shuddered. 'I'm a bit cold,' he said, 'maybe there's a shawl somewhere in here? Ayerie, do you have a shawl?'

Before he could finish speaking the aide was draping his shoulders with a fine mohair blanket.

'Thank you Ayerie, thank you,' he said most genuinely as she rushed back to her station.

'The first thing you should know,' said Ron, sensing his partner was stalling, 'the unpleasant truth - is that *we* brought you here. I want to get that out first. It was no accident; quite the contrary. It involved an excruciating amount of effort.'

Soleman's heart raced as he watched the girl's eyes morph from merely confused to a fixated glare that was both fearful and hostile.

'And this was not random. Please understand also, that there are things pre-dating our lives that have led to this,' Ron went on. He stood, went to the drawer by the window, and retrieved a paper larger than the coffee table. He handed it to Lucy. It flowed across her lap, the edges curling up again by her thighs.

'There has been told for generations, a time would come that would fork the destiny of our world-'

'Escallia. Escallia Wimbers, that is our world,' Soleman interjected. Ron regarded the interruption contemptuously but went on.

'-into two possible paths, continued peaceful co-existence, or the domination of a self-serving and vacuous force -'

'An evil force. No use sugar coating it. A depraved, violent and narcissistic force would come over the world in its entirety… that is the prophecy,' Soleman cut in once again.

Ron levelled his fixated look toward Lucy in a bid to ignore the distractions of his over-excited co-ruler. 'This fork in destined futures can only be corrected by the same fibres that created the tear in the fabric. Or in other words, only the same force that caused the tear, could mend it,' Ron said, and leaned back into the couch.

Soleman took deep breaths, watching Lucy look over the paper in a daze. Her eyes flitted up and down it. She was trying to interpret calligraphy that meant nothing to her. Just like the notes that had chased her through the breeze in Lockerby, the words were illegible to her eyes.

'You sent me those notes?' she asked, almost inaudibly. The two men looked at each other puzzled, neither knew what she was referring to.

'Ahh, the prophecy,' Ron went on, ignoring her question, 'if that's what we call it, was not understood correctly, nor given any weight, until the turn of the last decade.'

'I was never taught it, growing up,' Soleman added, 'even now, only the Archmonders really consider its significance. I'm afraid the rest of the world seems trapped in oblivion,' he said, and sighed woefully, as though unravelling a personal problem to an old friend.

'Where did it come from?' Lucy asked, still pondering the familiar style of the text and its connection to the notes that led her into the wetland.

'The prophecy? We don't know exactly. We'd heard of it. Vaguely. But it wasn't until the announcement came from the east - regicide and a new queen - that things started to click,' Ron said.

'The new Queen was only a child! Instantly we knew something was wrong…' Soleman threw in, leaning forward, the shawl slipping back behind him as he fervently relived the memory.

But the two leaders drew back somewhat, as they noticed their last few words giving rise to a new interest from the girl. The confusion from her delicate face had dropped.

'You seem suddenly intrigued?' said Ron

'That word you said before…regi?' she queried

'Regicide?' Ron offered

'Yes, what does it mean?'

'The murder of a king or queen, but in this particular case it was both. Why do you ask?'

Lucy twitched.

'What is it girl?' Soleman pushed.

'And after that there was a young queen?' she asked, her face all the while tinkering with recognition.

'Yes, and still is. She is the youngest of triplets, Abigail. Her coronation took place when she was eleven in years,' said Soleman, 'the eldest died young, and the second eldest went...ran off, a little while after they executed a guard for the crime.'

It was patently clear that Lucy was processing something more distant than the story she'd just been told. The two men lurched forward, eager to get something from her.

'What child, what? What do you know?' Soleman placed a hand on her knee.

Lucy pulled back ever so slightly, 'I think I dreamt it…last night. There was a little girl with black hair living in a palace. But she was very bad. She threw her sister off the balcony. Her sister was blonde haired. Then later I saw her kill her parents… in their bed… the king and queen. She slit their throats!' Impulsively she rushed her fingers tenderly to her own neck remembering the vision. 'And then the pink haired girl ran away…' Lucy's head dropped back down again, and she stared into the curly letters on the parchment once more, trying to make sense of both the dream and the words.

'Well that's it! That's why you're here…Ron, tell me that isn't something?' Soleman gasped, 'it's what we've always suspected but you must admit…well just tell me that isn't something!'

Ron shrugged, 'it is telling,' he conceded.

Soleman addressed Lucy once more, 'that black haired child from your dream is Abigail, the current Queen of the Eastern Kingdom of Meta Emery, or as the last decade's events have seen it referred to - Murder's Echo. Queen Abigail is the dominating force from the prophecy. Her ways are at odds with all the peace that holds our world together. Liberty is not a value she honours. She has waged wars, severed alliances, and even her own people suffer under her rule…this is why you are here.'

'You say the black haired girl killed her parents, in your dream?' Ron posed, alarmed.

'Well of course she did! We've always said that haven't we? It makes sense doesn't it? A dominating force does not sit back and humbly dwell in the privilege it was afforded,' said Soleman, impassioned, 'they take it! They take whatever they want. It was never an unfortunate accident, her early ascension.'

'And her sister? She killed her sister? Gloria, the blonde princess?' Ron asked, as he cocked his head. Scepticism was oozing from him.

'Well she was the youngest, Ron. Killing her parents would have been futile should her older sisters ascend to the throne,' Soleman said, rushing out the words in haste, irritated by the doubt.

Ron pressed his hands flat together letting his index fingers rest against the tip of his upper lip. He leant back, taking it all in.

'I'd just like to understand the origin of this dream before we make any conclusions, there could be a number of things at play here,' Ron said without taking his eyes off the fearful child before him.

'Let's put the dream aside for a moment,' Soleman went on, addressing Lucy once more, 'the prophecy's legitimacy started to become apparent when the new Queen began expanding her army beyond its normal boundaries. There were assertive claims suddenly being made about new lands and territories, and most significantly in terms of conflict, the resources within those territories. And when we voiced our concerns, we were attacked. There was no warning. There was no negotiation. There was simply destruction. The *murder* of our people. Eh-hem, anyway, *Murder's* Echo is the largest kingdom, and we are the second largest. We each mark the furthest points east and west across the world, see?' Soleman indicated a map painted across the floor beneath the coffee table.

'Between us…' he continued, the coffee table grating the stone as he moved it, 'sit other kingdoms, of varying sizes. Once we were attacked, other kingdoms were forced to choose a side. Some are still trying to maintain an air of impartiality, but with trading rights, resources, and the Queen's powerful army to contend with, that air is becoming increasingly thin.'

'And she wants to expand her control, we've seen evidence of this. But if what she has done in her own city is any indication of what she intends to bring to the other kingdoms, there is much to be concerned about,' Ron added, 'her rule insists on a level of obedience that goes well beyond general oppression. Her controlled subjects have little say in most matters of their lives. The only ones who live freely are the extended families and confidants of the Dynasty behind the palace gates.'

Soleman gently took the paper from where it rested on Lucy's fingers, 'so you see, this is most certainly the dark and dominating force the prophecy foretold.'

Soleman lightly rolled the paper back up again and handed it to Ron who returned it to the drawer by the far wall. A small green bird landed on the railing beyond the frosted window and let out a series of reverberating high-pitched trills.

'Oh,' was all she could comment on their story. There was a tense silence that lingered for several moments and the green bird took flight before she eventually drew the courage to ask, 'but why am I here?'

Soleman's eyes cracked at the sides as he smiled, 'you are the answer my child. You are part and parcel of this mysterious but ever accurate prophecy. Abigail is the tear in the fabric. And you are the thread that can sew our world back together.'

Lucy swallowed and her chest rose and fell more quickly.

'The prophecy tells that only the same intervention that led to the chaos, can resolve it.' Ron was gesturing as he spoke, his hands randomly waving this way and that not adding to the explanation at all.

'There is speculation, well, more than speculation, there are a number of witness accounts that attest the late Queen Laura, Abigail's mother and predecessor, had some well-hidden peculiarities. Some people say sparks flew off her when she was distressed, other accounts state that the edges of wings could be seen from underneath a coat she wore. They say she healed at an accelerated rate and her hair took on strange shades of varying colours,' Ron said, and then paused to smile in light-hearted appreciation of the absurdity of his words, 'this is of course……all rumour and conjecture…but we believe there is something to it, and an explanation.'

Ron reached his hand into the air holding up his index finger. At once Ayerie brought a decanter of Sintep (a nectar drink) and goblets to the table.

'We can appreciate your confusion. And your apprehension,' said Ron offering Lucy the opportunity to weigh in, but she gave nothing, so he went on.

'Your world and our world were never meant to overlap. But it has happened before. Our understanding is that if someone from your world and someone from our world were to…ahh for lack of a better word…*breed*…there is much to suggest this would lead to deformations in the offspring. Deformations of alchemy and voodoo.' He stopped while Ayerie distributed the partially filled bronze cups. The young aide and protégé stole one quick glance at the prophetic heroine as she slid the heavy goblet toward her and disappeared. Her doe-eyed Archmonder features hid the jealously in her expression. Lucy was too distracted to notice her completely, but a snapshot of her face would filter into the depths of her memory.

'This would explain the abnormalities in the former Queen. We believe part of her ancestry is not of this world but of *yours*. How this happened we have no idea…but what we also believe is that when she went on to have children with the former King, the life split. Three children, triplets, all with varying colourations. And we believe…cascading levels of morality,' Ron said and eagerly brought the goblet to his lips.

Soleman's face lost its cheerfulness. 'That's how the world ended up with this third child, the black haired girl… the current Queen. Born with no moral compass she was. No moral compass at all. An unleashed psychopath, and now ruling the most powerful kingdom, if we want to be honest about it.'

'But you,' Ron finished his drink, trying to ignore how overzealous his partner had become, 'you are what the prophecy says will mend this. The interaction of someone from your world and ours, led to the birth of an enchanted girl. That enchanted girl became Queen, and the last of her offspring is the bad seed the prophecy predicted. Only someone from your world can restore the balance again. The final words of it say, I think it goes… *the blood she carries will suppress the powers of the sorceress.'*

Lucy blinked at them, 'me?'

She hadn't the confidence to appear arrogant, but the question all but implied their stupidity. Why in heavens would that person be her? Why would anyone wanting to save a world bring in a meek adolescent? She knew her own worth. She was of little help to anyone. Let alone what they imagined.

Soleman smiled again as if amused by her self perception, 'it may be pointless to go through it all. But the prophecy is complex. We've studied it for years. What I can tell you though, is that it does tell of an adolescent, dark in hair and clear in eyes, from a small kingdom long conquered by another. Blind to her uniqueness. Surrounded and yet…alone. It says those that bring her here will know her for her misery, for she will be plucked from a harrowing history and vicious reality. But under our sky she will restore not only our balance, but her own. Through our world, destiny will see her fulfilled.'

Yet another awkward silence. But the little green bird did not return this time to distract them from the tension. The day was becoming warmer quite rapidly. Soleman discarded the shawl and loosened the mustard collar of his tunic.

Lucy was not taking to the narrative with much enthusiasm. It was clear the men before her were quite delusional, victims of hopeful desperation. Whatever their prophecy supposedly said, they were mistaken. They were mistaken about Scotland, about her life, and about her. Yet, she was here, nonetheless. She shifted warily on the sofa. Even underneath the heaviness of the black dress, her rapid breath was apparent. This morning she had come to accept that she was in fact, not dreaming, and that something unimaginable had happened to her. It was difficult to accept, because it could not be understood. No memory could be dragged out from the depths of her mind that could help explain how she got here. There was only the cruel and sudden wind, a sinister stranger in the wetlands, and a hole in the earth.

Now she was being told to accept that she was not in some distant country of Victorian practices and peculiar people. She was in another *world*. And even still, she could not properly grasp what that meant.

Another planet? They hadn't said.

Another dimension? They didn't say that either.

Just another *world*, another reality. And as she tried to piece this logically into her mind, the transcript of yesterday was repeating like a soundtrack in the background.

Do you know how I can get home? No. I have to get home, can you help me? No. No. No. No. No.

She glanced up. 'So you can't get me home? Or you won't let me go?'

Soleman sighed, his face cringed at the question he knew she would ask but had optimistically hoped she would not.

'We ehhh - ummm - it's - ugh - eh, Ron? Can you?'

'It is not that we won't let you, *truthfully*. We do not know how,' said Ron in a somber tone.

'But you brought me here? How did I get here?' Lucy persisted, feeling hot and flustered again. The panic of yesterday was slowly returning with heavier frustration, but her thirst for knowledge today was greater. So she tried to subdue it, pushing it back inside herself. She needed to get to the truth today.

'Yes, we brought you here, yes. That is true…' Soleman's expression froze as he struggled to find the words to explain the complexity of the concept, 'but we didn't pluck you. We've not been to your world and we don't know how. To bring you here was a complicated spell, and I'm afraid one that we haven't the power, at this stage, to reverse…If that is even possible.' Soleman cracked out the last few words.

Lucy drained of colour. The room began to spin. She felt faint, but she was frozen, '…I…can never…I can never go home?' she choked out as her crystal blue eyes glassed over.

'Not necessarily,' said Soleman, quickly trying to prevent her oncoming tears. 'There is a way. Well, we suspect it. But it's not been tested…'

'Just give her the key,' said Ron shaking his head.

Soleman nodded. The plan was to wait until she'd accepted. Or until she seemed to grasp the concepts they were imparting upon her. But the girl was distraught, and he couldn't bear to see her cry again. From the desk in the far corner Soleman retrieved a twisted iron pendant, a tube linking back over itself, much like the infinity symbol. He handed it to Lucy. She examined it carefully, but wasn't sure what to look for.

Ron then explained. 'Gloria's. The little blonde princess you say you saw in a dream? We believe this used to belong to her. We're told after their birth, each of the princesses had one made for them. A symbolic gesture, that they held the key to the future and so on. But, rumour has it the pendants are bewitched, impressed with a magic that operates like a key. This…then, perhaps, could be a key to another world…maybe to your world,' having never fully understood the explanation in his own mind he found it difficult to put into words. It wasn't something they were very certain of. Lucy rubbed the metal pendant between her finger and thumb. It was rusted and old but otherwise ordinary.

'But where's the door?'

'We don't know,' Ron shrugged.

'Another rumour, is that, on Meta Emery, somewhere deep within Verity Palace…there's a…a. Apparently…Rumour is, there's a door that guards a well…or a fountain…or a gateway…which leads to another world. Your world perhaps. If this does what we think it does, it could be the key to that door.'

Lucy looked doubtful. None of this made much sense.

'Where did it come from?'

'We believe the late King had them made, with influence from the Queen no doubt. We…' Ron paused unsure of his next words, 'if the rumours about them being bewitched are true, we *think* the idea was that should the palace be under threat, and the gateway or the fountain, if it exists,' he choked on those last few words but it was too late, 'I suppose provides…an escape from this world altogether.'

'Why are you giving it to me?'

'Well aside from the obvious reasons, it's unique,' said Ron sitting back, 'instantly recognisable to most people. Should you need to identify yourself, prove yourself, this…this will give you some legitimacy.'

'Spare you from inter-kingdom conflict perhaps,' Soleman called from across the room where he was looking for something on the shelves. He gave up and returned to their conversation. Lucy was no more than a trembling child lost in an unfamiliar market. She crossed her arms over themselves and rubbed her shoulders, 'I don't understand.'

'As would be expected. But I'm afraid there isn't the time to take you through this in the appropriate stages, and I can imagine if I were in your position, I wouldn't have the patience,' said Soleman.

'So, the only way home is through a well, in a palace over in the east? With an evil Queen?'

Soleman shifted his head left and right indecisively 'ahh yes… possibly.'

'But what is it you expect me to do? I don't understand what you want from me,' she begged meekly, without the confidence to raise her voice.

'The pink haired girl you saw running away, that was Princess Cherry, she was the second born and thus after the death of her older sister, the rightful heir. She initially went as far west as she could, by some divine mercy, and ended up here. Bless the child. She was a caring and placid thing with a fervent view of right and wrong. She lived here in the castle for a time before we were attacked. We haven't seen her since. She was about your age, perhaps slightly younger, at the time. But we believe she is out there somewhere. We need, rather this world needs, for her to overthrow her sister and become the Queen of Meta Emery. That is the restoration of peace and balance the prophecy foretold.'

'How?' she asked.

Soleman threw his arms outward, 'you will need to figure that out along your way. We don't have all the answers. If it were that easy there wouldn't be a prophetic heroine needed. But the prophecy says *it will come to her…providence will guide the way,*' Soleman smiled.

'But where? Where do I go? I don't know anything about this place,' Lucy protested.

'Our people will see you safely to the border of Archmond. They will give you whatever you need; food, accommodation, clothes…they will guide you and you will be taken care of along the way.'

Lucy let out a gasp of anxiety, 'I can't stay here?'

Soleman and Ron exchanged a glance. 'Only for a few days. Our understanding is if we keep you here, it may be damaging. You have to find your own truth out there, in your own way. We don't want to influence you. In a few days, it will be time for you to make your own way through Archmond,' Ron said.

'My own way? How? How will I know where to stay, or who to trust?'

'Dear girl, you are a long-awaited hero in the eyes of our people. No one here will do you any harm,' Soleman said dismissively.

'What about after Archmond, you said there were other kingdoms? That they're picking sides…I don't -'

Ron cut in, 'you'll need to learn to survive on your own, Lucy. Everyone does, eventually. For you this has just come on sooner, and in many ways much stranger, than you expected.'

Under the flourishing crystal waterfall, Crumbs pranced in and out of the water as though the marine life were bountiful only for him. It was as though they were home. As though the tiny fish, the water, and all of it were ordinary. It wasn't, but it might become that way.

This is what Lucy considered as she watched him in the stream, a small entourage of servants close by, short in stature but not in eagerness. They treated her with no less reverence than the Eminence or the Imperial Lord. For the past three days the maids had brought fresh water and emptied her bedpan, they had changed the flowers in her room and bathed her. The guards had escorted her to the dining hall where she now ate her meals.

But like a child, she was restricted and protected in being tended-to. The western gardens where the source of this stream originated, along with other parts of the castle, were off limits to her. The guards would not give a reason. Their commands came from above. No explanation was necessary for them, so it shouldn't be necessary for her. By the time she saw Ronald or Soleman each day her questions had piled up so much that restricted zones were a forgotten problem.

But when she wanted to sit in the gardens, the eastern gardens where she was not just allowed, but *encouraged*, to go and 'meditate', the maids would bring blankets, cushions, food and wine. Though she didn't drink the wine, Freriana kept bringing it, just in case. It would have been flattering, if she didn't recognise the expiry on such servitude and adoration. For the last hour she had sat on a cushioned swing chair beneath the pergola by the stream. A collection of crisps, nuts and dry roasted vegetables, sat untouched in a wooden bowl on the creamy metal table beside her. Pushing her toes against the limestone she rocked herself back and forth. The gentle sway was soothing her anxiety. But she was no longer a nervous wreck. A new wave of calm had come over her.

This was her fifth day in this world. After she'd returned from the meeting to her chambers several days ago, she'd been inconsolable again. Desperate tears had flooded onto the pillow as she softly wailed and choked with the possibility that she may never return home. But time had brought a shift in perspective. For the last two afternoons as the city glowed in sunset, she had watched with curiosity and enchantment, the peak hour bustle just beyond the castle walls. And as she did, she imagined the cities beyond this one. There were cities where the people looked like her, they'd said. Was it possible, she began to consider, that she could make a life here? Was it even possible, she wondered, remembering a time when her father had slammed his fist into the mirror and screamed out in agony as the blood and splintered glass fell to the floor, that she could have a better life here? A better life than the isolation of a small cold town? A better life than a school where the girls mocked her for being poor, and the boys mocked her relentlessly for losing her virginity? A better life than being scared to go home, not knowing if this night would be *one of those* nights? A better life than the inexplicable poverty they always lived in?

Lucy looked up. If she squinted, she could still see the orange flowers on her chamber balcony high in the distance. The balcony looked over the sunflower garden to the north, separated from this one by the narrow and fern-lined gravel path that guided the way in from the curtain wall. The iron gate within the archway (the only entrance through the curtain walls) was having the same problem with the orange flowering weed that her balcony was. Did it say something about this place, she wondered, when even the weeds were pretty?

The archway was a meagre hole in the curtain wall that locked in the castle and its garden surrounds. The exterior walls were daunting to her. In several hours as the sun crept lower toward the eastern horizon where it set, the walls would see the garden fall into shadow. Lucy fell into a different shadow momentarily, that of a large bird flying overhead. The same giant white bird, or others like it, visited the castle twice daily. They swooped downward as they crossed over the walls and landed on a terrace before waddling inside. She wondered about them, but it never stayed on her mind long enough to ask anyone.

Soleman was feeling ceremonious today. He had worn his gold overlay, a heavy tapestry that draped over his shoulders and fell down the back of his cream robe. He all but complimented the scenery, pacing toward Lucy in the limestone features of the Southeast Waterfall garden. The garden was a pasture of tapered lawns spotted with serpentine firs. In the centre where the land dipped and the stream rolled down a rocky crevice, a thought-provoking courtyard had been built for exactly these kinds of meetings.

'I suspect your little dog won't want to leave,' he said, surprising her. But she stirred only slightly; she had heard the swishing layers of his fabric as he came toward her. He was disappointed to see her still in the black mourning dress she'd worn every day. He hoped it wasn't some deliberate symbolism on her part. Certainly others at the castle speculated as much. The maids had said she was very stubborn about it. But even under the thick layers of black plaid, her pretty charm could not be drowned out.

'Why would he? He's never been so well fed in his life. I can see what he likes about it. It *is* quite beautiful here...' she muttered drearily.

Though the rapport between them had been steadily growing over the past few days, awkwardness remained in some topics. The point of her having to leave was a difficult one to reconcile harmoniously. She didn't seem to accept their mantra about her needing to go on her own, as soon as possible.

What a stupid way to begin, Soleman cursed himself. He put his hands on his hips appraising the landscape, 'yes, we are afforded a great many luxuries in this role, and I have to say, the time I am able to spend in these gardens is certainly my favourite of those.'

Soleman observed her to ensure his comments were well received. Lucy was still watching her dog jumping through the stream, chasing fish and shadows beneath the rushing water. She was smiling slightly, albeit sleepily.

'Are you really a wizard?' she asked eventually. A kind of new, frivolous and childlike joy had come over her. Soleman laughed robustly. He was glad there was some intrigue left in her after all the shock of the last few days.

'I suppose you want me to do a trick?' he asked, grinning.

Lucy nodded enthusiastically.

Raising his wand lightly from his side, Soleman focused on the stream. As he rose his wand incrementally higher, the stream changed colours, from orange, to yellow, to green, to purple and back to blue again. Lucy laughed, delighted, and then clapped. It was amazing, but when all of this already seemed not to be real, sorcery didn't shock her the way it might ordinarily have.

'One more,' he said, encouraged.

Directing his attention now to fruit trees beyond the shiny lacquered bushes by the stream, he flung his wrist around as though conducting an orchestra. In time small pink fruits floated up from the branches of three close jek-wood trees. They hovered in the air, suspended by his will. With another flick to the left, he liquefied them mid-air, and then directed the liquid to the empty glass on Lucy's table.

'Juice,' he said, giving a half serious bow, 'seeing as you won't drink the wine.' Lucy laughed again, delighted by the trick, and took the glass, drinking from it.

'May I?' he asked eventually, indicating the cream table and chairs near to where she sat.

Lucy shrugged, 'sure.'

'I don't mean to interrupt your meditations...'

Lucy recognised his carefulness at that point. He was clearly frightened she would burst into tears at any point.

'It's okay I'm not upset today. I am feeling a lot calmer,' she reassured him but then looked away, 'but I am still in a bit of shock. I half expect to wake up any minute now...' She felt more strongly about it than that. She was angry at the way she had been ripped from her life. But she still felt too afraid to say so. They had taken extremely good care of her, but admittedly it seemed it was for self-serving reasons, and she was still entirely at their mercy.

Soleman nodded, also unable to face her as he replied, 'yes, I suspect you may feel that way for some time, I'm afraid.'

Lucy sat up straighter and squinted at him. She was becoming more direct as their relationship had grown, 'it's this princess you want me to find and put on the throne...*somehow*,' she couldn't help but let out a small scoff of disbelief as she said this. It was hard to fathom how strongly they held on to such an absurd idea.

'Isn't it likely she's already dead? So who am I meant to...who is going to...?'

He took a few minutes to consider his answer. It was a legitimate question. Even he had trouble maintaining this hope that the docile and bendable Princess Cherry could be the next ruler of the most powerful kingdom. She had been harboured in their care, the city was attacked, and no one ever saw her again.

'I believe in my heart that she's out there...she just...she just has to be. But if not the Princess Cherry, then someone. Someone else from the bloodline must take the throne...nothing can ever be good again otherwise,' he said eventually and sighed.

'Who? How?'

The questions distressed him. 'I'm sorry but I just don't know at this point. But it will come to you. It will become clear.'

Lucy gave a look.

'I know, I know, I know. It must sound crazy...it must all sound completely and utterly stupid to you. But I hope you keep faith. Because it will. If you can't find her - there will be other opportunities for us to discuss an alternative. I will see you again.'

Lucy sighed heavily. She reminded herself that it was futile trying to get reason from them. Their explanation in that first meeting had relied on a vague prophecy of darkness, and some convenient theory about a dead queen's ancestry being from her world. Somehow, they claimed all of this had something to do with her. But their explanation left of lot to be desired.

'Why wouldn't you search for the Princess yourself, or get someone in… umm…your castle…or in one of the other kingdoms? A friendly one of course. Wouldn't that be better? I am no good at finding lost things I can assure you,' she said.

Soleman only laughed at her joke, but ignored largely, the rest of her question.

Lucy wanted an answer though. 'Really, why would a *foreign* girl be able to help with getting rid of a queen? I can't fight. I don't know anything about this place. I've never even survived on my own.'

Soleman laughed again. 'Oh, you have, you just don't recognise it.'

Lucy stared blankly, still waiting for an answer to her question. Soleman took a deep breath preparing himself, realising his jovial attitude could not quell her confusion.

'What I want you to realise is two things,' he said, 'the first is that this can be an opportunity, not a tragedy. I know only a little about your history and your home and I can see much despair. I suspect there are things about your past you don't even remember. Perhaps because to remember would be too painful? In Lockerby, there was nowhere else for you to go but home time and time again. There was no pathway out of that house in the near future, and the continued years there would have only made things worse. There's only so much people can take…' he paused to stop himself. A heartbroken expression was pained across her as she stared away into the stream as if hypnotized by the rhythm of the waters. He realised his interpretation of her life was obviously much more grim than her own. Not only might he be severing the rapport and causing offence, he might be forcing a self-pity on her that would not be helpful at this time.

'The second…thing that I want you to understand,' he moved on, 'is that the prophecy is like a recipe in some respects - Ron hates this analogy but it's true - it takes all the ingredients for the recipe to work, but you are the only ingredient we've been missing.'

Soleman stopped as Lucy's posture shifted up in alertness toward the castle. A slender young man with dusty blonde hair in a teal robe was crossing the path and strolling down the hill toward them. He had caught Lucy's attention first. She saw the reflection of his shadow flickering across the stream. She recognised the face. She had seen him in the hallways, but they'd never been introduced. She had a feeling he knew who she was though.

'Aramor,' Soleman stirred.

'Lucy. Your Eminence,' he said, and bowed slightly to each of them in respect. 'I hope I'm not interrupting anything, but I have been looking for you for hours Eminence.'

'I'm afraid you are. What is it? Is it urgent?' Soleman scanned the subject's temperament.

Aramor cupped his hands together and shut his eyes apologetically.

'I'm afraid it is. Supply issues again from the hills. The council wants a meeting at once.'

'Since when?' Soleman became irritated, 'we got to the bottom of that several quarters ago?'

'No,' Aramor shook his head 'the issue subsided, but it was never resolved. We haven't had full quota for some time. But they're pushing it to new boundaries now. We've just been issued the latest delivery report from the border. You may want to have a look before you meet with the council.'

Soleman heaved with frustration and fidgeted for a moment indecisively.

'I'm sorry, Lucy, but this is important. I will try and meet with you again at dinner. Please, try and think of any other questions you can before then, it will be the last chance we have to talk before you leave.'

The two men walked away silently until they'd crossed out of the boundaries of the waterfall garden and onto the steps of the castle veranda.

'I thought the Easterners were a lot taller? She's more-or-less as tall as me.'

'Well she's not really an Easterner, Aramor, you know that. And yes, she is small among her own kind I believe,' Soleman replied.

The two men said nothing again for a few moments.

'Why do you say? What are you getting at?' Soleman pushed at him, eventually considering a hidden undertone to the comments.

'Oh, no, nothing…' Said Aramor. But he changed his mind several moments later and quietly added, 'I suppose I am still getting a tender vibe from her.' He was rather nervous after he said this. The implication of doubt was clearer than he'd intended.

'You've said barely a word to her. You're just looking at those pretty blue eyes that's all.' Soleman waved his hand at him.

As he wasn't furious at the doubt Aramor became more courageous and went on, 'I admit she is different to how I pictured her. A pretty young girl never came to mind when I imagined the saviour who would set things right in the east.'

At this Soleman laughed dismissively. 'And in thinking of the east, if being a pretty young female meant you couldn't do any damage, we wouldn't be in this mess to begin with.'

An *opportunity?* Lucy thought about the word in this context as she watched the two men meander back across the supple jasper lawns. Another shadow passed over her as the giant bird now departed from the same terrace he'd earlier used as a landing pad.

Opportunity? She took in the world around her again. The colours, the flowers, the sky and the castle, the timber and tin city beyond; she could barely re-create the vibrant landscape in her mind. Even in the detail of small things, there was a strange allure that reminded her she was a long way from home. Trailing down the crumbly platforms of the small waterfall before her, a violet flowering plant was but one example of this. The texture of the petals was such that they all but glittered under the spray of the water. Several low-lying trees up and down the stream, whose branches stretched outward like performers bowing, had small leaves that shone as though coated with lacquer. Beyond those trees, scattered across those soft misty lawns and leading back toward the castle, the ripe fruit of the jek-wood trees was canvassing the air with the same sweet smell as the juice in her glass. The little lilac birds, that teased Crumbs and bathed in the white waters, were darting back and forth to these trees, bringing back the fruits and breaking them open on the rocky banks of the stream.

Perhaps this wasn't the prison she had immediately seen it as. Perhaps, she thought as another small lilac dove carried a branch of jasmine to her nest beyond, this could be paradise? And yet, there was still something about not having any choice.

Chapter 4

Go with God

'The best thing about the future is that it comes one day at a time.'
Abraham Lincoln.

On her sixth morning in the new reality, Lucy was ushered into her future; beyond the castle's walls. The ceremony to see her off had been hardly ceremonious. With some basic supplies bestowed upon her, they'd simply walked her out.

Now on the other side of Archmond Castle's iron gate, she rubbed at her forearm watching the doves skirting from rooftop to rooftop. They shot across the sky in rows of twelve, perched motionless upon sculptures, and noisily played in the red foliage of small trees. The mark Ron had left on her forearm as he'd said goodbye had something claw like about it. She hadn't seen what did it, and he had apologised as though it was an accident that he'd cut her, as though he'd merely brushed past her. It was clear to her that it had been deliberate though, and the cloth he rushed to the site of the scratch sent tingling sensations through her nerves. No one had seen, and she'd pulled away, and not made a fuss.

She glanced over her shoulder at the castle behind her, looming. Deep down she knew there was so much more to all of this than what they were telling her. But it didn't really matter, she thought soberly squinting in the sunshine. They were behind her. It didn't change the view in front of her. She sighed with the weight of the acceptance, but rushing through her was also this wonderful electricity. The rush of anticipation.

Along the street, ebony poles lined with glass beads glistened on either side of ebony benches. Eateries, small shops and homes, all boasted exquisite marble finishings. The varnished wood floor was without creak as Lucy and Crumbs walked along it, and she wondered to herself what might lie below these fine timber panels, to allow it to support such weighty stone buildings.

'Oh my lord,' Lucy remarked, some distance on. She stood motionless in amazement of a structure she thought she should have surely noticed by now. On the other side of the wide street, lodged along the pointed tips of terrace rooves and chimneys, was the remaining structure of an enormous sea-vessel half eroded away. Tilted on its side, it had been eclipsed from view until now. On its strange angle, it would have blurred into the sea of rooftops from her chamber window at the castle, but now its angles and edges caught the sun and exposed it. What would have been once a glorious ship was now a teetering oval of rusting steel panels stretched laterally for a daunting half mile. Neither the mast, or bow, were in her periphery. Lucy scoffed, what and why?

The royal war vessel, Annaluxa, was displayed boastfully as a reminder of a deserving victory they had once had against the (now extinct) city of Mandoo. One that had been separated by seas before the land changed. But history records it had been conquered and destroyed long before that geographical change. Lucy later learnt as much by reading the inscription on the marble plaque, which stood at street level, centred horizontally between both ends of the ship. She later supposed, after initially deducing a vanity from this, that perhaps they had nowhere else to keep such a sizeable trophy.

The people largely left her in peace, but the stares were intense. People moved out of her way as though she were diseased, or dangerous. For a long time now to local Archmonders, Easterners had been considered the enemy, and she looked very eastern. Word had fast spread that she was no Easterner; she was the girl from the other world here to fulfil the prophecy. But people maintained their natural scepticism and caution.

'Come along, Fred,' a woman whispered hoarsely to the child who had stopped still on the rug; awe struck. Needing more of a nudge she grabbed the boy by the collar of his shirt. Groceries in the one arm, head down, she shuffled them both away as quickly as she could.

As Lucy went on, the shadow of the castle started to become fainter behind her, and she grew less cautious. Scratched font on the window of a dark store appeared to say, 'maps and supplies', although it read M_PS & SU_PIIES. As she heaved her way in through the framed glass door, a bell rang out and a cloud of dust arose around her. Her wheezing attracted the attention of another. A man standing in the far corner cried out directly, 'two, two bits. No, no, no, three, ahh um seven, yes, that's it, seven bits each.' The shop's window frames let in little light, leaving the room quite dark. It was lit only by horizontal stripes of white light from the slender gaps in the blinds, which fragmented across the corners of the room.

'What is?' asked Lucy. Crumbs left her side and began sniffing around the shop, inspecting it, security detail routine.

The man turned around still dusting his hands. He was short like most of the other Archmonders, and had unusually large hands, but his eyes were grey without dimension. He was practically blind.

'You're wanting a sunshade I presume? That's all anyone's come in here for these last few days.'

He put his hands on his hips, scrunching them into his floral shirt, which was both collared and faded. The shop around him was cluttered. Stock half unpacked in boxes, shelves empty, and others gathering dust as though it had been shut up for a decade.

'No,' she replied, although she wasn't sure what a sunshade was.

'A trophy then, do you want something made up? You'll have to run it by me first - what do you want to have won?'

'People buy trophies?' she asked.

'Who's asking?' His stance turned defensive.

'No…' Lucy said, and shook off the digression, 'I thought you might have a map?'

'A map!' he exclaimed amused, 'goodness, a map of what? I can't remember the last time anyone's bought a map off me. Before the attacks, I guess. No one has any use for them anymore. Unless you mean of the WFB? You don't know your way around your own neighbourhood? It's not that difficult.'

'People don't need maps anymore?'

'Not when they can't go anywhere, don't tell me…you're not? Are you planning on leaving the territory?'

'I think I'm being kicked out actually.'

He then surmised her. He was very nearly blind, but he could make out shapes, figures. He sensed her proportions were odd.

'I can't see child, so I don't read the news - but I hear it. Something tells me you're not from around here.'

'No,' she agreed hesitantly.

'From the other world?' he postured. She needn't answer. 'Well, this *is* an interesting day.' He sat down on a chair behind the counter to steady himself from the shock of it. There was a stand to the left of him, which had numerous bundles and booklets. Lucy went over to it and began examining them.

'So…' he went on, 'so you've agreed then. You're going to do it?'

'Do what?' asked Lucy, although she thought she somewhat knew.

'Kill the Queen? Isn't that what they want you to do?' but he doubted that very much as he said it, the girl before him seeming so meek and mild.

Lucy frowned, 'I'm not sure,' she said. She was speaking very slowly and carefully.

'But you're going there?' he pressed, 'you're buying a map.'

Lucy spun the stand around. On the other side there were bundles labeled, '*Coby and the Eastern Coastlines*', '*Que and beyond*', '*Gemini, Que and Trimany*', '*Rumustica Region*'.

'Well I can't stay here,' she replied, but she said it so uncertainly he'd be forgiven for thinking she was asking permission to do just that.

'You think you'll find a gateway then? Back to your world?' he offered, not sure if she knew about it.

She looked him up and down, hearing it from some common store owner was encouraging, 'I hope so…' It was clear in her voice how frightened she was about that now, 'is there one?'

He shrugged as if to say *who knows*. But then sensing her unease he went on, 'but if there is one it's not in Archmond, so a map probably is a start.'

She smiled.

After he'd sold it to her and she was zipping up her backpack (her original school one) he asked more softly this time, 'so are you going to do it? Or is it…is it you haven't made up your mind what you're going to do yet?'

Lucy drew breath, 'no I haven't. I don't…I don't really know what to do…'

They were silent for a moment with some sort of unfinished business before he said, 'you know - there's someone you should meet, someone a bit more enthusiastic about this whole thing than I am.'

The curious case of Pepper.

Pepper was in every sense, a horse of a different colour. These small rounded people close to the castle and its surrounds all had an air of haughtiness to them. They regarded this tall, lanky, Easterner girl with fascination and wonder. They were courteous and hospitable but largely they saw no reason to engage. Toby, the owner of the dusty supply store, was the first person to interact with her in a way that wasn't overly stifled and cautious. So Pepper's familiar nature was more welcome that it otherwise would have been.

He was this mousey-haired boy, barely adolescent, slumped against a wall in a laneway, where beer and grease from the tavern leaked out and stained the wooden floor. Partly covered in soot, in a grey uniform, he was chatting to a cook who was shovelling pasta into his mouth from a container, leaning on a door that swung open back into the kitchen. Their dreary conversation was coming to a close as she approached; sentences ending with those melancholy tones of winding up. Her shadow actually announced her arrival before she could say anything. Crumbs hid between her calves. Pepper kind of shifted in shock, shamefully. He stood up and bowed and looked to his peer, the cook, a young man, who simply froze and kept his gaze on Pepper with equal unease.

'Are you Lucy?' Pepper said breathlessly, his dilated pupils still examining her.

'Yes, how did you know?'

'Bleakers! Squid, it's her - it's her - it's the girl!' he yelped, hopping about, looking to the cook with amazement. The cook nodded but like all the locals she'd interacted with seemed uncomfortable in her presence. He bowed lightly and headed back into his kitchen, leaving the excited boy to his find. Pepper continued to hop around.

'Oh bleakers, bleakers, bleakers,' he rushed his hands to his gaping mouth as his sparkling young eyes traced her up and down, 'bleakers, I...I can't believe it's you. I can't believe it's you!'

'I was...' as she addressed him, she wondered about all the possible ways this random boy might know who she was. She remembered there being an announcement, and tried to steady herself, 'I was told to look for a Pepper here...a boy called Pepper.'

Pepper's eyes widened more, as though he had been bestowed the greatest honour known to man. He started to come forward but then stopped, his hands went in front of him about to explain some proposition and then he stopped again.

'That's…that's me!' he eventually exclaimed, but then his face turned to alarm, 'wait. Wait…why do you want me?'

He had something warm and Scottish about him. Although he was now very riled up by her presence, there was still a cavalier air of confidence about him. Perhaps that was just his youth not succumbing to any boundaries.

'Me? You've come for me? Why?' he cried but with eagerness, not hostility.

'I was just…' Lucy didn't know how to explain anything lately, least of all this, 'a man called Toby…from the supply store…he said maybe I should meet you?'

'Toby?' Pepper said, and sighed with relief. He re-examined her briefly, and then started laughing, his hand against the wall. 'Oh, Toby sent you,' he chortled, 'oh ha ha! I guess now he knows I was right!'

Lucy looked around and then looked back at him puzzled.

'What?'

'Shouldn't someone be chaperoning you or something?'

'There's no one with me,' she responded in an inquisitive tone, and then wondering if there should be, asked, 'should there be? Am I in danger?'

Pepper laughed. 'Nah! No, no. Not here, we're all your friends. Especially me!'

He came toward her dog then, 'hey come here, come here you lil woofa. Woofa, you're alright,' he said, kneeling down. He coddled Crumbs with his mouth, swarming him with kisses and the like. Lucy looked on in silence. He wasn't as rounded as the other locals, and had a pale, shadowy look of malnutrition. She couldn't really place his age yet, but he was young, adolescent maybe.

He bounced back up. 'I still can't believe it!' he began, 'but I knew it all along, everyone else was wrong, not me!'

'Is that why Toby wanted me to meet you?' she asked, pushing herself back against the grey wall.

'No! Not just that. He knows that I...me...I'm the best tour guide there is for this place.'

'Really...'

'Yeah! Definitely. No one knows the WFB like me. No one. All day I'm exploring.'

She nodded. Crumbs yelped up at him excitedly, and began bouncing around the boy's feet, caught up in his whimsy.

'So come on then, don't you want a tour?'

His prelude statement was a way for him to ask permission, and when Lucy didn't reply, within a moment he had grabbed her wrist and was starting to lead her back out to the street and eastward along its central carpet.

'You can't know this city until you've been shown it by a local,' he explained.

'Oh...I see,' said Lucy tentatively. She was caught between her natural reticence and her curious inclinations toward this forward and provincial child. But Pepper remained completely oblivious to her hesitation, and kept tight grip on her hand.

'Look just there!' he said jerking her to a halt some eighty metres on, 'that's the best jewellery store in the city, need a lot of bits to shop there. They sell rubies and diamonds from the depths of Chupner's Chasm.'

'Chupner's Chasm?'

'Yeah,' he said cheerily, 'it's in Chupner's Forest. Well actually there's lots of them. There's tunnels in the ahh, in the ground and stuff. Some tunnels lead to these caves, and in the caves there are these endless holes in the rock, the chasms that is, but some,' he paused to stare at her intently, 'some tunnels just open up and you fall right through the ground and off into oblivion. A lot of people have just disappeared down 'em! Actually, I think the tribe throws people down there, when they've been bad. But some people say the chasms go on forever and ever. But they used to send people down with ropes and stuff, to look for rubies and stuff. My friend's cousin, his dad used to go, back before. Don't know who goes there now. Probably no one.'

Lucy mulled over his description sceptically, while Pepper was roughing up Crumbs. But it was the second time she'd heard someone mention the chasms. She had overheard discussions about them at the castle. Discussions that had hushed on her arrival. The subject made her nervous. She looked then to the store he'd been talking about. It was a rather majestic building, even for WFB standards. The opulence around her was continuing to surpass itself at every turn.

A seed was planted in her head at that moment, which morphed over the day into a confusion; what kind of problem was the kingdom trying to solve? She glanced down; by the side of the carpet Pepper was tending to his laces. They were still across from the jewellery store and it was the first time in several minutes that they'd stopped even briefly

In that moment she considered that she probably could use a guide. From whatever ramble he'd told her so far, she had gathered there was so much to learn. And it only gave her an insight as to how much more there would be to learn, how much she'd have to learn, ultimately, before she could begin to decide what she really was going to do. She sighed and heard her grandmother's voice telling her she should be so lucky - and hence grateful. Why would someone want to help a perfect stranger from another reality? '*Yes*' she thought '*why would they?*'

'So, might I ask, why are you doing this? Showing me around?'

'Eh?' said Pepper screwing his face up at her, 'what you mean?'

Lucy sighed, he was just an excited kid. Even in her scepticism she had overestimated him perhaps. So they continued eastward. Across the hustling city, she occasionally spotted handsomely clad citizens, floating about majestically with royal aura. They were conspicuous amongst the hurrying commoners. They flashed their layered silk skirts or golden walking canes and oversized headpieces, in bundles of colour-coordinated dress.

'Who are these people, the dressed-up ones?'

'Eh - various odd bods,' he chuckled and nudged her. She blinked impatiently.

'Oh, some you can tell are part of the castle folk. That chap there - with the red note broach on his robe - that's the castle symbol.'

'What about those ones there?' asked Lucy pointing to a trio of women that had particularly caught her eye. They wore matching feathery coats of jasper, and blue feathers poked from their floppy green hats.

'Just rich bleakers show'n off,' he paused to stare them down, 'but the colour means... the green...ummm...I think they do the agricultural stuff, they manage it from up here. Getting all our food and stuff.'

Upon realising they'd caught her foreign eye, and knowing exactly who she was, they began to dramatise their own role, noses high in the air, with a catwalk strut. They let their coats blow open in the wind, almost suggestively. Of course, none of them went so far as to acknowledge her. This plain and constant display of stature was feeding that seed of doubt and confusion.

'What is it that is so wrong in the kingdom that people need saving from? What do they want out of bringing me here?'

'To get rid of the evil Queen,' he retorted quickly, tipping his hat to a girl, and she understood then that she wasn't going to get any added insight from this child.

While sitting on a bench to take a rest, a short breeze broke down the main street, rippling through the waxy leaves that dangled from the coolabah trees. Both the fresher leaves of teal hues, and the crumpled older ones of midnight blue, had a dusty aniseed fragrance that filled the air with the wind. The same scent would fill the whole district as they blew around on the slender grey branches all the way up and down the miles long main street. The small red trees were less frequent as they went along, and really only served to mark out the grounds surrounding the castle.

The wind dangled chimes hanging from awnings all around, and the soft clanging of thin metal and glass woke Lucy like a delicate alarm. She wasn't asleep but now felt as though she'd been in a heat induced daze. She was suddenly alert to the cooling sensation of the breeze, the reprieve it brought as it rushed across the sweat beads on her face, neck and décolletage. The chimes, hearing them she now realised they were in a more residential area. The castle was barely visible on the horizon at the end of the seemingly endless street. She tried to calculate how long she'd been walking down it with this young boy, but she couldn't quite tell if it had been minutes or hours. The heat daze was not completely dispelled. She realised Pepper was still talking and she hadn't been listening for a while.

Squinting up at the sun, it having moved only slightly from when she last checked, Pepper paused his monologue to comment, 'it's always sunny in Archmond.'

She heard that, because it resonated with how hot she felt. She registered too that smells of bread were still rushing by her. But she was once again struck by her situation and overcome by it. She took in again the blue trees, the round people, and the varnished wooden floor.

Pepper stopped talking, and eating. He'd been biting into some doughy snack from his knap-sack, 'hey, you're shaking, are you alright?'

Lucy lifted her forearms and realised she was.

'I'm…I'm okay, just a bit tired,' she said. She leaned forward over her legs; the safety position.

'You're probably just hot. I don't know why you're wearing that mourning dress, you look weird walking around in that. Maybe you can fit into some of my clothes. You're pretty small.'

Lucy didn't reply for a moment, she heard the footsteps of people rushing by, of dogs barking, cart-wheels turning heavy pressure on timber panels, and children crying out in the distance. 'I think I need to lie down.'

'You can lie down at my place… it's not very far away. I only have one bed but if I nap too, I can sleep on the floor. Then you can see if you fit my clothes too!'

Lucy's head was spinning, but that suggestion shocked her, and she sat up a bit, 'what?'

'Don't you need somewhere to sleep tonight? You can sleep at my place tonight, and have a nap there now.'

Looking at this malnourished, dusty boy with a uniquely unpleasant body odour, she could not think of anything she'd like to do less, but she was tired. Sensing her discomfort, he added, 'unless you've already got somewhere to stay?'

Lucy realised she hadn't, and that this kind of thing may be something she would have to get used to.

'No,' she replied, and he shrugged in a manner of which said, *'hey how about it then?'*

Lucy didn't really appreciate how unkempt and at odds with the landscape Pepper's place was, until she woke up. She'd unconsciously taken stock of things in her daze as he led her inside, and now, having woken up from a nap to feel the air had cooled slightly to an evening temperature, she blinked at the flaky ceiling and reflected.

He was living in some kind of room, that they entered through a rusted staircase behind a trio of shops, some blocks away from the main street. The room had a sort of balcony, which was really the metal platform where the stairs met the door, and only one small window that was stained amber with grime. She was on his bed, a lumpy mattress with little support, and she could hear him doing something on the balcony, chipping away at something and then banging it against the wall, blowing on it and beginning again. It dawned on her that he lived here alone. Alone. And he couldn't be more than fourteen. The room had a table in the far corner with a lantern on it, a trunk overflowing with clothes, and some boxes scattered around, some open, some stacked on top of each other.

She sat up, and he was instantly alerted to the sounds of crumpling linen, sticking his head through the open door, 'sorry, did I wake you?' He had some small smooth wooden object in his hand.

She blinked for a moment not saying anything. 'No, I've rested enough,' she muttered softly. Crumbs stretched out by her feet where he lay. She reached down and petted him, letting her finger glide through his chocolate fur.

'You're here,' she said, 'you're here with me.'

'What?' Pepper called out.

She walked to the open door. He was working away.

Sitting on a square of cloth, his legs stretched out in front of him and a metal file in one hand, he added another piece into the basket of wooden carvings between his legs. They were small, some angular like tiny door stops, some bulbous like bottle stops. She looked beyond him into the laneway. The adjacent building was tall with large windows. An office or a factory, but there was no one in it. The windows were empty. Everyone had gone home for the evening.

'I've got to drop these to Michael,' Pepper held the file in his mouth as he picked up another piece of wood beside him, it was already triangular, this one he just had to sand down a little. The wood was soft and malleable. 'Maybe you should stay here though, and see if my clothes fit, I don't want to see a girl getting dressed. Then when I get back later you can have dinner with me and my friends. They'll bring something extra this time. It's Hult's turn. I think I've shown you enough for one day. Tomorrow when it gets to night-time, I might be able to take you down to the Clink Gates.'

Lucy blinked at him, her mind racing with questions. She didn't understand what he meant, or why some child was here alone living practically out of a storeroom, or who his friends were and why she would be having dinner with them. But all she said was, 'okay.'

'You really should try some of my clothes,' he said a short while later as he left, 'it's weird you wearing that stupid dress. You look crazy.'

Lucy did try on some of his clothes eventually. Being left alone for a while she felt she might as well. Most of the clothes were piled in crates by the wall and smelt of mildew. She perused them, mostly long swishy trousers, flowy shirts, and variations of that grey uniform she had met him in. But there were other strange garments; robes, colourful pants, sparkly hats, silk shirts with large engulfing collars. It was soon apparent from the wide discrepancies in sizes and styles, that what Pepper owned was a random collection of second hand, potentially donated, garments, that made in their own right, an expansive ensemble of dress-up costumes. But Lucy eventually found a pair of mid-length shorts she could squeeze into, and an oversized blue shirt. It was cooler than the heavy plaited black dress, but having not seen any women in shorts, she knew she didn't look any less strange.

A final box in the corner of the room was smaller and painted with shiny lacquer. Inside it were hats and scarves, belts and buckles, pretty chains. She toyed with them for a while, smiling to herself, teasing Crumbs, wondering about the bizarre people of this world that had worn them. What would their days have been like? What problems and dreams do their days consist of? She was letting the thin iron chain run back and forth through her fingers. It was rusty like the pendant key they gave her. Which generated a thought. Where had she put it? Frantically searching around the room and in her school bag, she located it with great relief in the pocket of the black dress she'd so casually discarded into Pepper's pile. Clutching it with relief she looked back at the chain, and immediately threaded it through the loop on the pendant. She clipped the chain together and slipped it over her neck, as she expected, it hung low enough that no one would ever see it.

Pepper referred to the place they were going to meet his friend as, 'Backwater Square', but they headed uptown toward it, into the more ostentatious areas. They went west once they emerged back onto the main street with its endless red carpet, in the direction of the now distant castle, the sun setting behind them. They turned off down a side street near rows of prominent stores and shiny new buildings, and wandered, for a time, down the laneways of boutique markets, all closed-up for the night. The evening was still warm but there was a strong intermittent breeze. This is what allowed her to smell the aromas of Backwater Square still blocks away, the smoke of burning herbs: spicy, earthy, and sweet. In this quiet business part of the city there were not a lot of people, but she could hear the murmurings long before she arrived; the chortled murmurs of a crowd.

Backwater Square was an opening - a courtyard - encircled behind several large buildings; Eltress Hospital, Wellard School of Arts, and the Treasury. In the dim dusk light you couldn't identify any particular significance to the structures, but like much of the architecture around this part of the district, the prominence was apparent.

Once they emerged from the small alley that allowed access to the square, under its floral hedge overpass of sorts, they were instantly immersed in Backwater's bustling night scene. The courtyard was dotted in the centre with wooden tables, fire pits, and cylinder stools that held the leaves of the burning aromas she'd smelt. Orange, emerald, and grey smoke was curling up into the sky from three distinct locations. Around the borders where the edges met the backs of each of the three public buildings, crates and baskets of food were piled on benches beside fruit trees. No one was manning them; people helped themselves. The square was crowded, a hundred or so people gathered in small groups around the tables, eating and talking. They found Pepper's friend Hult, in the far corner, his teeth ripping eagerly into a fried wing of a bird. He was older than Lucy expected; later than middle aged, grey hair, missing teeth, prickly white beard coming back.

'This is Hult,' Pepper said introducing them. Hult looked up from his wing and examined her, momentarily unimpressed with a look that was near scornful, before continuing to devour the poultry. Pepper seemed unfazed, instead keen to move things along, 'sit down. I'll get you some grub.' She considered offering him some of the money she received when she left the castle, but it didn't appear as though anyone was paying for anything here.

A variety of birds sat atop the poles of the iron fence that encircled the square. Twitching and squawking they watched the people as entertainment, all the while waiting for them to let their guard down, swooping in for their measly share. Easing the coarse sound of eighty or more boisterous conversations across the square, was a group of young girls playing flutes near the entrance. A few people who came through dropped coins onto the velvet cloth they'd laid out.

'How do you know Pepper?' she asked. She felt her voice catch in her throat as she did. Hult gave off a hostile air. He had barely looked in her direction in the moments that had passed.

'From the same district,' Hult answered matter-of-factly, tossing the bone over his shoulder. If he had meant for it to land in the bin behind him, he failed. He belched loudly and tore into a loaf of bread. It was stale, and it took his wide jaw much effort to pry it apart. Yet even in his vulgarity he kind of glimmered in the fire light. His old, bearded, grease covered face, sparkling away.

'What do you with yourself, Hult?' she asked, straightening her back against the wooden crate behind her.

'Pipes.'

'Pipes?'

'Bend pipes, fix pipes, clean pipes,' he spat out between mouthfuls. He still hadn't once made eye contact. He swigged something from a canister beside him as Pepper returned.

'Got you something,' Pepper said presenting Lucy with some items he'd foraged from the crates around the perimeter. Wrapped in a chestnut cloth were some fruits, bread pieces, cheese, and a piece of red meat.

'So what is… what is this?' Lucy gestured around the square. 'It's where we come to eat. Hult and I come most nights, sometimes Squid comes. It's here every night, these are all leftovers from shops and taverns and yeah and stuff. So anyone who doesn't have food at home can come here and eat for free!' He gleamed telling her this. Lucy took in the crowd again, they looked to be a variety of ages, statuses. There was a real cocktail of people. Lucy noted that a good few were very young. She was impressed by how well the city took care of these people. It didn't even occur to her at that stage to ask why all these people were here…with no other way to eat.

Squid did come that night after all, arriving just as Pepper was off to scour a second helping. It turned out he was the young cook with curly dark hair she'd seen leaning casually against a kitchen doorway earlier that day. Even that memory as it came to her, seemed so long ago. He recognised her, too. He seemed surprised that she was there.

'Hey friend,' he moved on, greeting Pepper by gently knocking his shoulder.

'Was just telling Lucy you have dinner with us here sometimes!' Pepper exclaimed.

'Sure do,' he locked eyes with the foreigner dubiously, 'better get some grub before it runs out, hey,' he gestured, and the two moved off leaving Lucy alone with Hult again.

'Rich boy,' muttered Hult. He glanced at Lucy but looked away again quickly. Her face, it was too angular and strange to him. The face of an Easterner. *Enemy.*

'What?'

'He's a rich boy,' Hult said, singing out the words. 'Went to Myzarad. That's a rich boy school. So he's a rich boy.'

(Later in the night, when they walked back to Pepper's tiny room, Lucy accidentally tipsy, having not realised the sweet drink was alcoholic, she asked him what Hult meant by that. Lucy got the impression the people at Backwater Square were all in some sort of difficulty. Pepper then explained that Hult was right, because Squid (they thought his real name was Daniel) *had been* quite wealthy. His family had owned a lot of farming land in the Hills, and he'd been a boarder at a prestigious school called Myzarad. But during the attacks his family's lands were all destroyed, and when the Hills were cut off from the WFB, Squid was out of the school and on his own. He had then managed to get some work as a cook.)

When Pepper returned with food and sat down beside Hult, Lucy decided that Squid seemed threatened by her. For some reason - even without knowing him - she thought he seemed more defensive in her presence than he otherwise would have been, when it was just him, and his unfortunate friends. As the hours went on, he let slip once or twice that he'd attended Myzarad. It was obviously meaningless to Lucy, but in his new life it was clearly something he still clung to as part of his identity.

'You're a cook?' she posed at one stage, trying to create a dialogue. He nodded.

'Where'd you learn that?'

He took the question very seriously.

'My dad,' he answered solemnly.

In that moment there was a thunderous crackling in the sky, deafening almost. Crumbs whimpered into a corner and Lucy jolted. Bright colourful lights were exploding across the sky.

'Fireworks?!' Lucy exclaimed. She, like most, but not all, of the crowd in Backwater Square had stood up to observe the sky show.

She spun around to Pepper, 'what are they for?'

The boy threw his hands out in front of him without answer, but his eyebrows were as raised and excited as hers.

'I don't know,' he exclaimed, his head bending as it tried to take in all the sky.

'Maybe they're for you,' suggested Squid.

On the way back to Pepper's, as they had nearly reached Barthlow (the quasi market / quasi manufacturing area where Pepper lived) Lucy tried to push Pepper again about his situation. They had just finished discussing Squid, and she was aware that the sweet purple syrup they had been given at the square was alcoholic. 'Where are your parents?' she asked, her voice trying to be quiet, mindful the streets seemed mostly asleep.

Pepper just shook his head at first, but eventually opened up, 'down in the Hills. They're down there so, yeah, I don't see 'em.'

Lucy pressed on, 'but why, why are they down there - and you're up here on your own?'

'I was up here when it happened, I was with my grandma.'

Lucy's pace slowed unconsciously, and her head tilted as she tried to decipher what he was getting at, 'the attacks?'

'Yeah, I was up here, staying with my grandma, just lucky I guess.'

'Your grandma?'

'Yeah… she's dead now.'

Lucy went to say, 'I'm sorry', but he gave her a strange glance and she thought she best not say anything.

'But why are you still up here. If your parents live down in the… in the Hills?'

'Because I can't go back there. No one can go there now. It'll make you sick, everyone knows. The best thing we can do for them is stay up here and work hard to help get them better again,' he said that last bit with such conviction it made Lucy reluctant to go on, but she did ask.

'Have you heard from them? Are they okay?'

Pepper started walking faster. He kicked at a discarded half-eaten apple furiously, flinging it into the gutter of a building. 'This is stupid I don't wanna talk about it!' he snapped.

She hardly slept well in Pepper's room. She slept on his bed. Somehow the lumpy, foam or hay mattress had been much sweeter when she'd napped on it. Meanwhile the boy curled himself up in the far corner. That was really what kept her awake. He insisted, in his stubborn child-like way, that she had to sleep on the bed. But she felt horrible for it, and the guilt disrupted her all night.

The next evening before the night fell, they set off toward the Clink Gates. The day had felt fast, now that she was more comfortable with being here, now that being outside the castle and in this world seemed less daunting. The moments weren't dragging on so long, now that she didn't feel stuck outside them looking in. Now, more and more, she felt wrapped up within them, and going along with their current.

They'd visited the school he talked about, Myzarad, its cornered boundaries marked by several man made streams, winding basins slotted between gaps in the floor boards, that all eventually found their way in beyond the gates to a small lake within the school's gardens. The sun was intense, and correspondingly the world was intensely colourful. The scenery was no less vivid than the day she arrived. But the heat wasn't bothering her so much anymore, which gave her more room to appreciate it. Pepper walked her through the city's urban orchard, in the far south. Two 'urban farms' housed several dozen rows of various fruit trees, growing in submerged trays wedged into the floor. Vines in above-ground potting lapped at the lattices of the buildings all along the edge, and soil dusted across the ground. At the entrance and exit large oaks based in enormous garden beds overhung it all. An unconventional orchard, but an orchard in all respects; miles of nature, persisting impossibly on wooden floors. More than once, she looked back at Pepper, and wondered if he could ever possibly appreciate the surrealism she felt.

On the way back to his room they'd gone through Dwellon Lane, a street exclusively populated with bakeries and patisseries. She'd heard people mention it, in passing. In various crowds she'd heard children begging to, 'go to Dwellon'. Archmond was famous for its cakes. Another testament to its opulent past. The wizards had given her some money, not much it turned out, as she watched Pepper count it. Probably only enough to survive the one night they expected she'd spend in the city before continuing east. The currency was no good anywhere else, so she used some of it to buy a sugar loaf to share with Pepper. It was in one of the simpler store windows; a store without the pastel ribbons wrapped around its entrance, without four-tiered sponges rotating on an axle in the window, glimmering with pearlescent candles. But the loaf from the simple bakery with its wooden doors, was delicious, nonetheless. Gooey vanilla cream melted from between the layers as they split it between them.

It was in that sweet, colourful street, amongst all that joy and frivolity, when Pepper turned to her and said she should probably go down into the Hills now. That he would take her through the Clink Gates tonight, so she could get down. The whimsy of the day was instantly vanquished.

Now, that evening, they were lingering in the last few moments of twilight on a street corner. The sun had set less than an hour ago and yet there was no one around. Another empty evening in the WFB. As they waited, though Pepper wouldn't say what for, a cart rolled past them and stopped again several feet up. Two men launched out of the back in opposite directions and lit the lamp posts on either side of the street, bouncing back in again. The cart rolled on a few feet and the men repeated their actions with the next pair of lamp posts. This procedure continued until the cart faded into the darkness. Flickering specks of light emerging in the distance, remained the only indications it was still there, the work ongoing.

Pepper whistled and waved his hat down a crescent to their left. Lucy blinked at him. There was no one there. He turned to wink at her confidently. A moment later, a carriage came bopping blissfully from the shadows. The moment it fell into the light she could see it was the most outrageous violet colour. Made of paper, the seams of the carriage narrowed together toward the top like an onion. A purple, paper, onion carriage - balancing on two wheels - led by a man on a pony. 'Up to the Clink Gates, my friend,' said Pepper dropping some change into the silver bucket at its front. Lucy's look of incredulity remained as Pepper casually clambered into the carriage through the opening, Crumbs following excitedly after him.

'Come on,' he called impatiently, and Lucy had no choice but to once again, shake off her reticence and follow.

The journey to the Clink Gates was long. Nearly an hour went by and she could see the fringes of the city in the distance were speckled with white light. Industry. 'Ridgeton,' Pepper explained. Lucy broke from her trance realizing he had been oddly quiet the whole journey. Aside from a few mumblings as they settled in about being hungry, and that Hult owed him money, he'd hardly said a word. The carriage had rolled on to the rhythm of its rickety wheels, with the occasional murmur from the world around them.

'Ridgeton?' She asked.

He cocked his head toward the window, 'it goes Ridgeton, Brackenstien, Illian.'

'Right,' Lucy digested. She was tired. She had felt the early buoyant mood of the day continue to slip away as night fell. And now as he recited the names of suburbs to her she could only stare back blankly and wonder why it is he thought this information had any use to her - if she was never supposed to come back here again.

'What are the Clink Gates?' she said later. The question had been on her mind from the moment he'd said it, but other questions had always been more pressing. Pepper strained his voice with irritation, 'aww, like a border…I guess, you know. Like that's how we know where our bit is, and on the other side it's only meant to be the Illian workers.'

Lucy considered that Pepper's incomplete explanation simply suggested he was perhaps too young to fully comprehend the meaning of these 'Clink Gates'. Further on, after a significant reduction of street-lamps began to concern Lucy, the onion carriage rolled to a stop. They stepped out. Cold winds were blowing in from the east. Two towering floodlights, the first electrical lights she'd seen, blanched their immediate vicinity making anything beyond consumed by an ebony abyss. Between the flood lights a lengthy queue of a hundred or so stretched out before them, facing the cool night in an effort to pass through the gates.

'The Clink Gates'; a fifteen-foot high barbed wire fence aligned with the familiar khaki clad military at its base. Cavalry and infantry alike were sweeping back and forth along the endless fence. Instinctively Lucy grasped Pepper's arm. Her breath steamed through the crisp air. 'Yeah - Clink Gates,' he said, then laughed and edged her to join the queue. Lucy fixed a worried stare on the stillness of the soldiers at the checkpoint. Statues.

Pepper tried thoughtlessly to ease her. 'Illian,' he said waving his arm around theatrically, 'last district on the WFB.'

She should have gathered as much. The cemented scent of heavy industry was everywhere. It was like they were in a completely different city; refineries, the cylinder containers, the ghostly warehouses, all cluttering like rubbish on both sides of the now widened street. Pollutant clouds of brownish smoke rolled through the flood lights cyclically. Broken down gravel piled here and there down the cluttered lanes either side of them. 'Charming,' she muttered rubbing under her nose, wondering how far back the beautiful city had left them.

'Move along, move along - eh single file, SINGLE file,' a toughened woman in a grey uniform with proud gold brooches passed up the line with a baton in hand, and a whole belt of other paraphernalia ready for use. She was official, but not military. She hadn't yet reached as far back as Lucy and Pepper, when someone back at base called out to her,

'how's it looking Madge?'

'Clear up this end, but got another eighty or so to go. Another few carriages expected before shut off,' she called. Her partner was on the other side of the line, a few yards back. She leapt up and signalled the same information to cohorts back at the barricade, making the numbers 'eight' and then 'ten' with her hands.

'Pepper, where are we, what is this gate?' Lucy's tone changed then, she was feeling her heart start to rush with panic and his lack of explanation thus far didn't help.

'It's like I said, the gate for the WFB, I told you that,' snapped Pepper with frustration, 'it stops Easterners and Hills folk from getting in. But we workers…we just show our cards and they let us through.'

'Cards? I don't have any *card*, Pepper.'

'Course you don't! You're not an Illian worker!' He sighed then as if Lucy's ignorance was unmanageable.

'Okay - so how will I get through?'

'They'll just let ya' I reckon. They have to - if they know who you are. You have to go through. You're Lucy, isn't that the whole point, that you…you know…go onward?' He gestured into the distance and she looked down at him with annoyance, but then her lips curled upward slightly. He had a point. Being flustered melted the cold off her, she fanned her neck while sucking in long pipes of air. Pepper was kept most amused by this.

'Makin ya a bit hot under the collar is he, love?' a cheesy accent from behind snorted. Lucy flipped around, more startled than offended.

'Gauwww!' the greasy old man exclaimed, a face weeks unshaven, and clothes waxy from weeks without wash, 'you're an eastern miss!'

His eyes were being unsavoury, and he leant forward reeking with a sickening cocktail of body odour and petroleum. Lucy pushed back, moving as far away as she could without falling from the pedantically straight queue.

'Don't flatter ya'self miss, I'm not about to be fornicating with the enemy. More than I can say for your boyfriend *heya*,' he indicated Pepper. Lucy was too confused to respond, she couldn't imagine why the man thought she was involved with this child.

Pepper responded for her, 'for your *information*,' he uttered with a fair degree of attitude, 'I'm escorting our future heroine to the border. And I'd be watching your tongue if I were you. I could report you for that. No way to treat our guest, is it?'

The man quickly slunk back and remained silent, one position behind them, while the queue shuffled gradually along. The military had become especially tense as they first laid eyes on Lucy. All jumping to attention from somewhat restful postures, edging forward - ready to act on target. What an Easterner could be doing right-side of the restrictive passage was beyond them. But there was light-hearted humour at their absent mindedness when her identity unraveled. *Oh of course! Lucy, the matriarch to be! Of course, of course, come through young one!* Curious whispers spread through the dying queue of tired workers behind her, as the guards close by, tipped their hats well-wishfully.

Green and red lights flashed at her body as she passed through the single and only exit. A rouse of shouting erupted as they were walking off through the other side of the barricade; the guards were forcing the greasy man behind them to the ground, and bagging objects they pulled from his jacket. The mendacious old sod he must have been, sending one last glassy eyed glare in her direction, as they wrestled his chin to the floor.

Pepper eventually explained, as he began to lead her down unsightly streets into the thick of the industrialised Illian, that he sometimes worked in the area with his friend Hult, which was why he was allowed to pass through the 'Clink Gates', as they were colloquially referred to. Following Pepper's bizarre story of separation from his parents, the Clink Gates were another indication to Lucy that Archmond's state of affairs wasn't necessarily as simple as had been storied to her. The Kingdom of Archmond, as far as she understood, extended beyond the WFB and into an area called 'the Rolling Hills' below. But for some reason, after what had loosely been described as an 'attack' from this eastern Queen, the leaders erected a fence to separate the city folk from their rural counterparts. That made no sense.

It was an unruly sort of world that collaborated in the periphery just beyond the 'Clink Gates'. Dingy taverns of lonesome labourers spilled liquor to customers until the wee hours. The intoxicating after-spray of beer and spirits, was riding gauchely on smoggy midnight drifts. The spurious sounds of pleasure were blaring from the venues in the form of bouncy music, or moaning out the windows of upstairs guest rooms. It was a completely different world to the pristine and proper avenues in the suburbs before the gates. Probity was long eradicated in the prostitution capital of the city. A truth about the kingdom that seemed almost blasphemous to repeat some yards back - was all but non-contentious here. The women, the men, they had nothing to hide. The area was full of working men who often stayed on-site for months on end, and regulation was lax when the imperial government wanted very little to do with the daily life of the second-class citizens of the industrial edge. Of course the true extent of this wasn't apparent to Lucy, or her child guide. Leaning against a wall in an outrageous yolk gown a pretty woman winked at Lucy. Her overly lacquered chocolate curls were balancing carefully in the air above her shoulders with some sort of product - whatever it was they had here. Lucy looked down uncomfortably, noticing as she did that the girl's dress was already sticky with grime at its lacy finish. Pepper led her on.

'Hult's place's got none a them around,' he said, embarrassed, leading her away. She was relieved to hear him say that. He was too young for that. But she remembered disconcertingly that he was too young to be around any of this.

The noise and ambience, (if you could call it that) near the gates was quickly behind them. They entered a silent world of factories, warehouses, and uniformed accommodation blocks. The handful of people she happened to see, looked to be wearing the same grey overalls of Pepper's she'd seen, presently tucked away in his knapsack.

'That's it there,' he said some while on, pointing to a wobbly metal tower in the distance. It was right out of a fairytale. Lurching disjointedly over the sea of tin-rooves and factories before them. It was an opaque black spike against the varying shades of charcoal in the night. Lanterns and such amenities didn't qualify as worthwhile use of imperial ministry funding here. The night cleaners with their scouring machines, that took to emptying the gutters of the day's waste, were only necessary to prevent the outbreak of disease. (As had happened in the past.)

They hurried down the street before the tower, a low-lying street of adjoining dormitories. Identical, simple, lifelessly cold sheds.

'This is where all the permanent trade workers sleep,' Pepper whispered resentfully. 'It's why they're so well built. Government looks after 'em.'

Lucy appreciated nothing enviable about them. Their structure was simple and devoid of any finishes, but they were newer and more solid than many dilapidated structures she'd seen this side of the gate so far. There were very clearly two classes of people who lived on the WFB.

The cool night was suddenly colder with lashing icy winds. Pepper reasoned this with the nearing of 'the drop'.

The drop. As Lucy looked out across its vastness, it was as if she were standing on the edge of the world. The floor beneath her feet finished and eternal space went on in its place; a universe missing its starry constellations and planetary configurations. That's the best analogy she could muster, as she lulled a poetic fascination with the drop. Mystified by its vastness, yet too timid to approach it completely. She didn't trust herself to move any closer, to front herself on the un-railed edge. Perhaps she would lose all reason and consciousness, become drunk on the wonder of it all, and throw herself suicidally into oblivion. So several metres back, near the foot of Hult's tower, was close enough. But she could see the splintering floorboards give way to a galaxy of darkness.

'Come on, its bloody cold, you comin' in or what?' Pepper said impatiently, with all his weight pushed against the iron door.

Lucy flinched, 'Hult lives here?' The tower was tall and exquisite, a stony sort of lighthouse for the land, but what a lonely place to live, 'how?'

Pepper shrugged. 'Hurry up the door's heavy!'

Lucy obliged. By the time she entered the tower's top and only room, Pepper was settled into conversation with Hult already. He was laying casually with his hands behind him supporting his torso, behind them both the fire flickering. Hult flung his head in her direction with a crazed eye as if an intruder had burst in, Crumbs barked but she shooshed him. Hult then grumbled something to himself before drawing in from a pipe in his left hand.

His small loft was not unlike Pepper's room, if maybe slightly larger. Floury coughs of sawdust filmed the air faintly. His belongings piled up chaotically against the walls without shelves or cabinets to categorise them. The piles fell into each other with their own weight and imbalance, the uncared-for things being moulded into new shapes under the pressure. An earthy coloured rug with white markings appeared to be the hide of some sort of mythical beast. Waxy piles on windowsills and around the room, the memories of candlelight.

After a deep inhalation Hult fetched a satchel and began counting out some coins for Pepper, there was only a small pile. He gave Pepper four or five, which Pepper delighted at.

'I can go back to Dwellon tomorrow!' He winked at Lucy, shoving them in his trouser pocket, 'good to have some bits to spend.' The light from the fire between them cast great shadows across the room as if they were all puppets in a play.

'A shared treasure?' Lucy asked, looking between them.

Pepper's eyebrows furrowed with confusion, 'it's from our business,' he corrected, 'Hult and I sell stuff, so we have some bits to spend in the city.'

'Don't you get enough money from the work you do here…'

Hult had drawn back on his pipe again but at this comment from the girl he began choking. Pepper launched up to pat his back down and the old man coughed out plumes of thick grey smog. He looked at Lucy with glassy eyes, all red from the sudden deprivation of oxygen, but he was grinning with amusement.

Pepper widened his eyes, 'we don't get any money from this work. We don't gets bits and coins from being in Illian,' he informed her rather condescendingly.

Lucy felt suddenly fractured from them, and nodded softly, instead of asking any more questions. In the same moment Crumbs began chasing Pepper's shadow hand puppet across the near wall. His moment of carefree joy was sufficient to change the direction of discussion.

'Get comfortable!' Pepper encouraged and threw a pillow her direction. She had so far knelt awkwardly a distance away from Hult, on the warm edges of the beastly rug, but distant enough to convey polite objection.

'Do you smoke?' Pepper lit up Hult's pipe and drew in. Seeing Lucy shake her head he added, 'have some of this mafvja,' and shoved a metal canister in her direction. She didn't know what mafvja was, but she drank it anyway.

It was an unconventional and somewhat awkward evening. She moved in closer, positioned herself more loosely across the pillow to give the impression of being at ease, but nevertheless remained on the outskirts of their chatter of mutual associates and work. But Hult at least was asleep quickly. At that point Pepper's youthful energy began to evaporate, succumbing to the lateness of the night. He was all talked out, and they both found themselves fixated on Crumbs as he tried to sniff insects in the rug, and rubbed his nose into fluffy patches, rolling on his back with huffs and puffs of joy. They could hear the steady breeze outside, the winds that whipped up from the Rolling Hills far below; the geographical anomaly behind the micro-climate that made the air so crisp at the WFB's eastern fringe. Pepper's frame was cocooned in a blanket. His small, rounded, freckly head was popping out at the top, staring at her contentedly but with nothing left to say. She couldn't help but look past him, at the myriad of stars beyond the tower's elliptical windows. In one window she could see the moon, and she realised she hadn't studied it with any intensity the nights before. In the castle she could never see it from the chamber room she was ushered into at night. It wasn't full, but she couldn't say if it was waxing or waning. But what she realised as she now took it in, was that it looked no different. No different to the moon she used to stare up at back in Lockerby.

'I'm so hungry,' muttered Pepper, his lips chapping together. They'd only had some stale bread of Hult's. He had a jar of some beans, but they weren't appealing to either Lucy or Pepper.

'Me too,' Lucy said watching his cocooned figure snuggle into a pile of clothes in the corner. She wondered how he got by like this from day to day. Why there wasn't anyone to take care of him.

'I should get fed in the morning,' he muttered, 'at the depot, they should feed us before start at the depot.'

He was all but fast asleep as this last delicious thought filled his mind. Lucy sat up a while longer, looking at the stars, drinking this majfva, whatever that was, thinking about the possibility she would never see her home, or her mother, ever again. By the time she let herself lie down to sleep, her cheeks were wet, her eyes red.

Chapter 5

The Rolling Hills

And now the background of this troubled world was spinning vigorously away from the archetypal narrative laid out for her introduction. It began moulding into an ugly world of competing insidious political rulers.

The morning summer sun was strong, but it was competing with a wild white haze of industrial pollution. The sky and consequently the light that filtered into the tower was bright, but eerie. The mechanical workings of Illian were grinding away down below the tower. The sequential sighs of steam engines, the crashing of heavy metal, carts rolling upwards on chains, the grinding of saws on wood, and the racing commands of the foremen, crowded the air.

Lucy looked around the room. It was empty.

Hult's pipe still lay in the spot where his body had been. But Pepper's knapsack was gone. A sense of anxiety came over her, adjusting her garments back into position, (the shirt's collar had become twisted around her neck) she told Crumbs to stay as she hurried down the stone staircase to the tower's vestibule. The jacket hanging on the hook by the door told her nothing. She heaved the door open, in the street ahead there were a handful of small round men in grey overalls moving about. None of them were Pepper. Pensively, she fetched Crumbs and her bag, and they left.

As soon as she was several feet from the doorway though, her concerns about where the boy and man had gone became sidelined by a sudden awareness of her surroundings. She stood stoic as she took

in the horizon. In the night she hadn't seen them. But now, what in
God's name were they? An almost sinister procession of enormous
vents or silos straddled themselves along the edge of the drop into the
horizon. Each silo was several stories high, resembling a wide, grey,
water tower. There were at least a dozen in her view. Some nearer to
her had scaffolding surrounding them and stretching part the way up.
Between each silo, and between the lofty warehouses beside each silo,
were wide pipes of varying sizes, often several metres wide. Many of
the pipes and silos emerged from lake like hollows in the floorboards,
originating far below. For as far as she could see along the drop looking to the south, this reflective network of pipelines and warehouses
smothered the landscape. Above them, against the deep blue of the
morning sky, rusted red cranes twisted and turned, moving cargo and
equipment to new sites.

The clanking of construction echoed all around her, crashing platforms of iron, grinding of wood and stone, and the clunky motors of
very basic machinery. The theme of industry was clear, but it was not
clear exactly what she was looking at. She could only appreciate that
it was beyond her. She flinched in disarray as lightning blue rings of
electricity flashed up the exterior of the nearby silos, and crackled as
they charged into the warehouses. It was a jungle of metal, almost
blinding under the solar surplus, unconscionably extensive, and today
there was no small boy, itching to explain.

There was no discernible passage from the drop down into the Hills
below. Such a presentable escape would make redundant all the effort
to constrict the inter-flow of the population. But she eventually found
herself a way. She knew she had to keep going forward, and that in
her case, forward meant downward. She wandered around, ignoring
the looks of surprise from curious workers, until she found a group
of sheds that had that familiar look of abandonment. There were
grasses and vines that covered some of the signage, yellow from the

summer sun. The grass poked through some of the gaps in the floor like a weed, and broke free into bundles in soil patches by the edges where potted plants used to neatly present the buildings.

Inside one of the buildings, whose door had long ago come off, a tunnel had been left unlatched. What filled the crates and space within the tunnel, unbeknown to her, was a stockpile of new and old pressure vents and their parts. This particular shed was once the depot for the water-ways council, which had long ago relocated closer to the Clink Gates. It was therefore likely the tunnel she'd found was an old workman's entrance down into the guts of the sewage system below the city. The meagre gate that prefaced the tunnel was itself rusted, a sign reading 'WARNING' but with the first N and the G missing. The tunnel plummeted endlessly down into darkness, but a few faint electrical lights buzzed around several rungs of the ladder. The fading lights illuminated the hanging platforms branching out on either side, upon which workers would sit and inspect the pipes. There was lime build-up on the rungs, which fell short of concealing its long vacancy; many rains had come and gone. High above, the warehouse roof was scattered with missing sheet metal and rusted holes.

There was no way to know where the tunnel went, but for some reason she understood that it was where she should go. With Crumbs under one arm, and trying not to take in too much of the air, thick with rusting aluminium and oxidising iron, she descended. Her bag was heavy, but the weight of Crumbs helped keep her balance forward. She began to imagine as she went, while simultaneously struggling to maintain balance between each rung, the lives of the people down below. But of course she had no idea. Not even the citizens of WFB really knew, or could have imagined, the ruined world that survived below them. But she would see it, through her raw, foreign eyes.

It became clear that the tunnel had been meant to be accessed easily once upon a time. Maybe in the time before the Clink Gates existed,

a time that Pepper might have told her all about, had he not disappeared. After what felt like an endlessly perilous descent, she at some
point had caught glimpses of the ground beneath her. Her eyes having
adjusted to the dark could make out the rough patch of dirt - the
ground - not far off, and she relaxed. At the last rung there was a drop
of about six feet to the ground, which she managed to land without
much affray. It was dark. Looking straight ahead was an endless chasm
of darkness that became too deep for her vision to grasp as it went on.
The pillars and poles supporting the ground above became enveloped
as the shadow thickened into the distance. She was after all, standing
beneath a city. In the other direction some thirty yards on, the sunny
world of the Rolling Hills broke the shadow like a beacon from where
the floorboards above her stopped sharply. The contrast of the outside
world was so bright she could barely focus on any one detail.

Closer in the sounds muffled around her as though they were
underwater. The creaking of wood was clear and sharp, but in the
distance there were voices, their words indecipherable. High above,
small gaps in the floorboards allowed finite beams of light to cascade
down, like sharp shards of sunlit glass. She put Crumbs down and he
stood by her feet, silently waiting for her lead.

They were not alone. She could hear the murmurs of people
working, in the distance, their words indecipherable but the tone
monotonous enough to be consistent with labour. Soon after she
could see them, her eyes readjusting again after the shock brightness
of the open world nearby. She focused on where the light fell and
saw it curve around corners and edges, realising there were sheds
and warehouses down here too, and the bulbous little people were
carting things in and out of them, down tracks that were almost
invisible in the dark. As she focused on them more, she saw that the
sheds were just as numerous as they were above, but comparatively
they were modest in size. The activity began a few yards to her
right, and where it became more crowded into the distance there

were multiple posts of gates and soldiers, monitoring the passage of goods. Fortunately, where she had landed, she would be able to bypass all the security and the attention it might have brought, by simply going straight ahead.

Once drenched in daylight, her direction suddenly felt so unclear. But the land before her ascended sharply. It was chaotically divided, broken into a number of small hills. The part of the underworld where she'd landed aligned with one small escarpment, and it was, very conveniently for her, separated by a sudden dip, from the escarpment upon which much of the underground activity seemed to culminate. Several busy tracks used to cart goods and supplies wound their way through the valley between her hill and this other one. Part way up the hill she could see that the various tracks all led to a checkpoint, where armed guards at boxy booths oversaw the handover. The stock and machinery changing ownership once it transcended into the shadowy workplace below the city.

She made her way along a track she found at the crest of the hill. It was nearly moist in the humid day. Between the overgrown blue-green grass, it led her down into the valley where the rural industry thickened, and meandered up and down until the industry started to give way to a condensed expanse of run-down dwellings. The landscape stretched like an impressionist painting; one where the slums of Columbia had been juxtaposed beneath shadowing figs and Canadian maples. Blue-green grass grew richly unattended between the ramshackle factory mills here, in what would have been the most operational area of the region. There was an immediate distinction in the atmosphere here. Although her presence was noticed, and not met with warmth, it caused no stir.

As she turned off the track into a village street, she noticed a girl with a bucket, taking water from a stream. At the end of the stream the water wheel from a mill was churning through the water. The wheel was clearly at the end of its life. The water looked soil laden; brown, sloppy. Homes spread up the hillsides on either side of the track. There were large dwellings that looked as though they were once grand, but now faded, and somewhat reclaimed by nearby forest. The girl saw Lucy and regarded her with a kind of curious annoyance, before walking back up the hill to where she'd come from. There were few people around in this first village. Largely it was older men. As she moved through its centre she saw several men wheeling carts - separately. A middle-aged man was rearing horses into a pen, and a group were tinkering with an old machine outside a large shop resembling a barn. The street was partly pebbled, but opened up to large patches of dirt in parts.

As she continued on there were open stables with repairs being undertaken, and animals being rounded up onto carts. As the street moved around the bend of the hill, a large fenced area came into view several yards along. It sat beside the street with a sign on it long faded. As she passed it, she saw that beyond the fence piles of wood were being fastened, filtered, and moved into positions, presumably also ready to be sent away somewhere. As she went on, the street then began to narrow and once again met up with the stream. Then the nature of the world down here became more apparent.

The homes that crowded around the stream and continued upward on the hillsides had once portrayed an image of uniformity. Once, the townships of the Rolling Hills had their own distinct style; curved rooves had sat upon light and dark wood homes. But there was a considerable amount of repair work that had been done in the last few years, since the attack, and that repair work was so haphazard and makeshift that nearly all the homes had developed their own unique ramshackle appearance. A tent cloth here, a tree log to hold a roof in place there, hay barrels in place of a wall there, and a sketchy extension made of metal crates and machinery scraps. The people had made do with whatever limited resources were available to them, after the government turned its back and the rural half of the kingdom became its own world. The stark display of poverty was a marked difference to the prestige of the WFB. It was an awakening.

Crumbs kept close to her as the hours went on, this dense new township lacking the safe welcome that the WFB had offered. Things were slower here, but they were slower in a calculated and cynical way. The light-hearted glee had disappeared. A tension of anxiety and distrust filled the air. But it wasn't directed her way, she simply moved through it. The path steered them upward, and the homes eventually gave way to a small marketplace of sorts, that stretched across what was somewhat of a plateau, littered with smaller fairy hills. Whether it was a marketplace in the way she knew them remained to be seen. Machinery and impoverished huts, stalls of unappetizing produce and primitive knick-knacks, colourful gypsy tents and rusting unfinished construction, crowded uncomfortably together amidst bustling hoards.

The atmosphere finally seemed less tense, with people buzzing around and folk music echoing from somewhere nearby. As she passed a rectangular tent of burnt orange cladding, mud splattered up its side, a lady, seemingly from nowhere, linked into Lucy's elbow.

'You're the girl from the other world aren't ya?' she asked. Lucy went to answer, but noticed a fierce greyness in the woman's eyes. She yanked her arm away.

'She's here!' the woman called, attracting only a mild amount of interest from passersby. She was middle to late aged, with light coloured hair wrapped into a bun, and a breezy white blouse over a patchy purple skirt that dragged in the dirt. She held a pipe in her left hand that she puffed from periodically. A ring on her right hand she rubbed over her cheek again and again.

'You can all relax now, she's here and everything's fixed!' She cried out. The people largely ignored her, but her own amusement at her mockery was evident, as the woman let out a hearty laugh dripping with sarcasm. Lucy stepped back. Mirroring, the woman stepped back from Lucy, relenting.

'Can I get a juice, of something, and ahhh…what's good to eat?'
Lucy asked as she presented several coins to a man behind the bench.
She hadn't eaten anything all day or much last night. This stall appeared
to be trading in fresh produce, as well as various ready-to-eat to foods.

The store-man rolled his eyes at her, he closed her palm and leant
in close, 'we don't normally trade in silver.'

Lucy was confused, 'what do you trade in?'

'Something you probably don't have.'

'What?'

'How much of those do you have?' he asked looking at her satchel.
But she was too skeptical to show him and went to leave.

'Wait, wait, come back,' he called, 'for ten bits, you can have sugar
juice and a lukso.'

'Ten bits!' Lucy exclaimed. Back up on the wooden floors she'd
bought the gourmet pastries on Dwellon Lane for one or two. But
he simply shrugged.

'Up to you, not many people around here will have use for your
money.'

As she sat on a bench eating the strange concoction of mushed
vegetables with the occasional animal bone cracking in her throat, a
band of young people began to perform, gathering a small but docile
crowd. The men played flutes and the women danced around them in
a silly fashion almost designed to be absurd; knees rising high, goofy
looks on their faces. The crowd were neither enchanted or amused.
Most of the audience took the charade as an excuse to rest, and sat
on the grass encircling the band, talking amongst themselves, paying
limited attention to the performance. The young she thought, seemed
less bitter, or at least less fazed by their own bitterness and resentment.
She watched and absorbed the dancing. The dancers had a group of
friends in the crowd, who were occasionally clapping along in support.
There was potential there, in their cheerfulness; a potential that these
carefree people might help her. But she was too shy to approach them.

She was aware her shyness was the cause of her isolation, at times a great and unnecessary burden. But it couldn't be helped either way.

Lucy began to notice something else about the people and crowds. The general lethargy here, was more than a cultural difference. If studied, many of the people presented as quite ill. Stumbling or limping as they walked, clutching their sides occasionally and coughing into handkerchiefs. More than the odd one or two had a complexion which was pale with a jaundice yellow. Having spent time amongst the Archmond people in the city above, she knew this wasn't their natural complexion. Crumbs leapt onto the bench and began nuzzling into the bowl in an effort to share in what she was eating.

'Alright, hold on,' Lucy said edging him away, but then she looked into his eyes and the realisation again hit her. Her stomach dropped.

She clasped her hand behind his ear, taking half his fluffy head in her grasp, 'where are we?' she whispered, but gave him the rest of the food all the same.

She waited for things to quiet down at the stall, and then went back to return the bowl. The man was youngish, heavy-set with a shaved head. He had offered no olive branch, but his apathy had more hope of generating help than the disparaging looks she got from everyone else.

'Thank you,' she said as he took it from her. He gave nothing away, putting the bowl in a pile of other dirty bowls and returning to face her.

'So, do you mind telling me what you do trade in down here?'

The man unfolded his arms and looked around. He seemed to want to be sure no one was watching him talk to her before he went on. He unhooked a cloth from his belt and began wiping some of the bowls.

'Clorix,' he put the clean bowls in a new pile by the pot of vegetable mash, 'it's a quasi-medicine, quasi-vaccine they make upstairs in the WFB. And nearly all of us here really need it.'

'Medicine? Why - what's it for?'

'Miss…we're trapped in a toxic wasteland.' His tone was sharper now.

Lucy glanced around, but he brought her attention back to the ground they stood on.

'You're basically standing in poison. Since the attack around ten summers ago, it's in everything. The soil, the water, the air too, probably. They don't know how to fix it. So the longer anyone stays here, the sicker they get.'

The corners of his thin mouth lifted slightly, enjoying the concern this stirred up in Lucy's eyes.

'That's right. If you're planning on settling in for a while, I'd be careful what you eat and drink, and where you sleep.'

Lucy tried to bury her alarm. This was a test. If she reviled, the details would dry up.

'If it's so toxic here,' she said after a moment of casually adjusting her backpack, 'why don't you leave? Why does anyone stay here?'

'Leave! Didn't you just come from upstairs? Don't suppose you happened to notice the big long armoured fence they got?'

Lucy shut her eyes, *yes of course*, but that's not what she meant, 'not up then, just *away*. Away from here. Somewhere else? Wouldn't you all want to move to a new land that's not toxic?'

'We're surrounded by forest on all sides. Chupner's Forest. Most of us folk won't go through it. It's dense, and weird tribes live in there. Not safe. Besides, even if you get through, beyond the forest there's a frozen plateau. We'd have to go to the other side of the world to live. No one here wants to do that. We're Archmonders. Archmonders are a particular people, there's no one else in the world like us. We can't go traipsing off to some distant kingdom where people *like you* live.'

Until he spat out those last few words she had almost ceased noticing the peculiar features and figures that made them so foreign to her, and her so foreign to them. But she wouldn't go unnoticed. Not in a xenophobic society where she resembled the foreign enemy.

The young man at the stall was called Jock. After she let out a little of her plan, he told her if she was determined to go on, the only way was through the forest. Helpfully his Aunt Andy lived in a cotton field in the arable lands, close to the edge of the forest. He told her his cousins had gone hunting there when they were young. He offered up his Aunt's wisdom, in that she might at least be able to steer her away from some of the chasms.

He went to draw her a rough map of his Aunt's house in the field - and gave it to her with a note to pass on to his Aunt. Later when she opened it, it simply said, '*hello can you help this girl out? Thanks - Jock*'.

'How long will it take me to walk there, if I keep going east?' she asked. That was the general direction he'd given her when she asked about the arable lands.

'Oh…you'd be there before nightfall I would guess,' he said but then a thought came to him and he called to her as she walked away, 'wait at the intersection just after the bottom of the hill, where the horses come to drink, you might catch a ride at this time.'

Strangely conspicuous was this intersection at the bottom of the hill, after the land dipped down from the hilltop market, and the edge of the village again met the river. It was just before a flat bridge across the stream, and an intersecting road going both north and south. A hobby farm was on the corner, just by the bridge. In front of it was a sign marked, 'Water for Horses', and several troughs. Before the troughs five people sat waiting with baggage or baskets. Two women, whose faces were more or less hidden beneath bonnets, and some men of varying levels of cleanliness.

She watched the farm for a moment trying to figure out if it was somehow connected to the signpost that gave water for the horses. Beyond the flimsy wire fence, young men were turning the soil in one half of the plot, having just planted new seedlings in the other. It was a miserable image; they looked completely depleted. Across the pregnant field an old woman - their mother perhaps - sat in the rickety wooden doorway to her home looking bitterly disappointed at their work. She curled her legs under and pulled her head scarf tighter at the unfamiliar sight of the young Eastern woman. The sun helped her out by hiding behind the clouds. The day was becoming cloudy.

When she sat down, more or less joining the end of a queue, a man with no teeth in an oversized sweatshirt leapt from his place. He grabbed a rock from the road and stood over her, gesturing it threateningly above her head.

'What the heck does an Easterner want here? You want a free ride hey, free ride to the grave?'

Crumbs rushed forward in defense, but the man was pulled back by another.

'What are you doing?' An overweight large boy yanked him back by the hem of his shirt, 'she's sent here from the wizards, don't hit her, they'll get us all. They got spies everywhere.'

'Wizards? Wizards…' The man groaned and threw the rock away but regarded Lucy with disgust before returning to his spot in the queue.

'He's easy riled,' said the fat boy, older than boyhood, but not much older than adolescence, apologising. Lucy simply nodded, and kept her head down while they waited for whatever it was that could take them east.

Before the cart rolled up, a procession of five beasts looking like cows or buffalo wandered by. Their faces were rounded and their heads horned. Their torso and legs were stumpy, and their coat was mottled shades of mustard and brown. Riding several of the cow creatures were a trio of little girls, grubby looking, grumpy looking. The eldest steered the other two unridden beasts with chains that linked them all together. She had a muslin bag filled with tiny grey feathers that bounced rhythmically up and down against her as the beast ambled along. Handfuls of feathers spilled out into the air every few feet as the group passed by. The girl's rounded red face stared at Lucy in shock. She wiped the sweaty straw hair from her eyes in disbelief and disapproval. As she moved on, Lucy watched the feathers land on her lap and on Crumbs. He shook them off and pinned them down pridefully, before licking them over, as though they were prey he'd caught.

Two ponies yielding a large hollow cart were steered to a stop just before the bridge by a man at the helm with a large brimmed hat.

'Cotton fields! One way no return. One-piece entry,' he announced. The five or so people gathered by the bridge began to shuffle behind and up onto the cart.

The cart was wooden with a metal grate dividing the space into a two-tiered crate. Top seats and bottom seats.

'Top's better, you get a view,' said the fat boy climbing up ahead of her. She followed, unable to think of a good reason to be sitting underneath people looking up at their bottoms through a metal grate.

'First time on a clink cart?' asked the fat boy once everyone had taken their positions and the cart had made some progress eastward. The seats were positioned so you were forced to face inward, at whoever was sitting across from you. The fat boy was just opposite her. He was resting his arm along the top of the cart, giving an impression of ease that was entirely disingenuous and transparently so. It had been a bumpy ride so far and Lucy was forced more than once to clutch onto Crumbs, whose tiny legs kept slipping through the holes in the grate.

'What's a clink cart?'

'This is. Can't you tell?'

'Okay…what does a clink cart do then?'

'You know,' shrugged the boy, his arm slipping off the edge, 'odd job deliveries to the pipes and up to the clink gates. Bits and pieces. It's a private cart that can have all kinds of things in it - as oppose to a government cart just for one field. So sometimes it's not full. And when there's not enough stock to fill the cart, or when it's just returning, you can catch a ride. This one's one way, only going back to the cotton fields today, would've been full on its way up. Full of cotton bags.'

Lucy noticed the soft white fibres caught in the corners of the grill and on splinters in the wood.

'Yeah I only need one way cause I'm staying at the cotton fields for a while. I got a job out there,' he looked eastward to where the fields would be, but they had gone down into a gully and to the east were bulbous green hills with patchy fields, and brown huts with curls of grey smoke spreading into the sky.

Lucy wasn't sharing his dreamy distant gaze. She was taking in her immediate surroundings. In some ways, the landscape was not so different to the countryside back home. Although the land went up and down at a dizzying rate, and the homes were rounded and rustic. The cart was presently sweeping by trees with floral yellow chains, catching in the updraft of its velocity as it rolled speedily downward. Yellow petals soon covered the cart's top floor, but they were steadily lifted again by the wind as they tumbled down the next hill.

'Yeah it's a guaranteed job,' he continued as if she might be likely to doubt him, 'I met a lad the other day who was going down. Need at least ten more he said. Ten more! And he reckoned they were look- ing for people just like me, strong, you know.' He lifted his arm to demonstrate and to Lucy's amusement was not being ironic.

'Lots of cotton this season so we'll get a good amount of Clorix for that. And I can move a lot of it fast, because I can carry a lot, so there's definitely a job for me. It's a guarantee.'

He offered Lucy some water and she reluctantly accepted.

'Is that all you get from the WFB? Clorix. That's all you trade in?'

'From upstairs? Yeah. Oh…well,' he paused, reconsidering, 'some- times I think we get things that we can't make down here. Maps and charts and books. Sometimes Newscasts, but they won't often give us the Newscasts. It's like once every few moons, but sure they get one nearly every day. They don't want us to know what's going on.'

'Newscasts?'

'You know - news - what's happening around the world. Don't you keep up to date where you come from?'

Lucy nodded, but then shook her head. 'I think I know what you mean. But no, I don't keep up to date.'

'Anyway, mostly we just supply upstairs with produce, and they supply us with this medicine they make - this Clorix.'

'Does all the fresh produce go upstairs?'

'Well not all of it - only what the farmers don't keep for down here. But most of it yeah,' he paused for several moments then. 'All the cotton does.' He was more confident about this fact, 'no need for fancy cotton clothes down here.'

'How does it get up the pipes, all the produce? How does it get up to the city? Do the people carry it up, the ahh, the trade workers?'

'It's electric,' he said with a good deal of pride, 'do you know what that means?'

'What?'

'Electric. Do you know what electric is?'

'Well…yes…' She wasn't sure exactly what he thought it meant.

'Yeah not many people know,' he puffed out his chest, 'but there's a generator to the far south under the pipelines. I used to work on it. That's how I know. And that's how everything gets pushed up. No good job that was,' he shook his head at the memory of it, 'gets real hot down there. And I get sweaty.'

'So why isn't there much other electricity up on the WFB then?'

The boy shrugged. 'I don't know. But probably…probably they can't make enough of it to give to everyone. I think the generator only makes enough spark to send everything upstairs. And that's a lot of work, think there used to be eighty of us working on it. Can't imagine any of them up there wanting to work like that. I had to stop because it just got too hot. I don't like getting hot.'

It felt hot enough on the cart, bouncing around on the metal grate seats, under the warm but increasingly cloudy afternoon sky.

'So what's with all the fires?' Lucy piped up some time later, after having pondered on it for a while. She indicated the several chimneys she could see on hillside, 'isn't it a little too warm to need a fire going? It is summer isn't it?'

'Smoke houses,' he said, as the cart slowed while it rolled through yet another village, some of the villagers scurrying inside like little mice. He laughed at this display, commenting to Lucy, 'the towns-people think cart riders are trouble. That's why they run off.' He laughed heartily again, leaning menacingly forward in the direction of a windowsill where a woman who had run inside now stood, 'but that's silly. We're just travellers. Nothing wrong with moving around. Some of these folk have barely ever left their front garden.'

Lucy nodded to be polite, 'so…why are there so many smokehouses?'

'Eh? Oh. Nearly everyone has a smoker. It kills the bad stuff on the food. Everything here is smoked before it's eaten.'

'So how do they eat the food up there?' she asked, tilting her head in the direction of the WFB, having seen no smoke houses up there.

'Ummm, yeah, hmm. They must do *something* to it,' he said. Then they both stared silently for some time at a lizard that climbed up from the bottom floor of the cart and now waited patiently for a time to make its next move.

'You know, no other kingdom in the world has electricity,' he said, livening up again after the cart had left that village, having picked up a few more travellers.

'What?' Lucy wondered why were they back onto this topic.

'Well no, except for Murder's Echo,' he reconsidered, 'but that's something really. The Westernmost Kingdom, and the Easternmost

Kingdom - are the only kingdoms with electricity. That's kind of something isn't it?'

'It's something,' she agreed, but she wasn't sure what something was.

As the sun lowered itself further into the final quarter of the eastern sky, and the imprint of the metal bars on her thighs started to ache, she realized the pastoral and arable lands were much further than Jock had made out. She would not have made the journey by nightfall had she walked. It would surely be nearly evening by the time they arrived at this rate. The cart had stopped several times, for the horses to drink water and for more passengers to board. There would be about twelve of them now she figured, most were huddled beneath them on the bottom row, for reasons that she would never understand. The halfway checkpoint they had passed a good while ago was a place called Gathgate, *where the poor bathe in dirty masses'* the fat boy described it. But he seemed poor - so she found it hard to place the tone of his commentary. It was a large lake, supposedly an iconic divide between the confused gypsy land, and the world of extensive pastoralism and arable farming.

The emerald landscape was now becoming repetitive, and her fascination was waning. The hills on the horizon were ever changing, but they were starting to all look the same.

'Oh my!' said the fat boy miserably, 'can't wait to get off this cart. They say things are quiet at the cotton fields. But that's okay. I'm sick of the hustle. I reckon I'll be a good cotton picker. What about you, where you headed?' he asked her.

'Somewhere east,' she said, being deliberately coy.

'You're going through the forest then are you?'

'I am told I must? Isn't it the only way?'

He largely ignored her question, 'Chupner's Forest,' he said its name forebodingly, 'blimey. Well, gee, be careful of those chasms. You go the wrong way and you can just fall down one. It's dark in the forest and you can't see 'em. Oh! And the tribal people. Be careful of them too. They're cannibals.'

When they disembarked, at dusk and seemingly in the middle of nowhere, but by the side of a tavern with a sign that said 'locals welcome' the simplicity that this journey had about it disappeared.

'A piece each,' the driver was there with his hand out as she climbed down, she looked at him confused, unsure of what that meant.

'A piece of what?' she asked, straightening her backpack.

The fat boy climbed down after her.

'A piece,' the boy echoed.

'A piece of what?'

'What do you have,' the boy somewhat whispered to her, trying to help. The driver was starting to stroke a whip he had rolled up against his belt.

'Nothing…I only have the currency from the WFB,' she whispered back at the fat boy.

'How much you got?' asked the driver.

'But what's a piece? A piece of what?'

'Could have a piece of you if you're not in business to gimme anythin' else,' the driver responded.

The fat boy pulled a satchel from his pocket. In it were some peculiar looking smoked vegetables.

'Here - I'll pay for both of us,' he said.

Lucy's eyes widened, she couldn't possibly let him. 'No,' she said, touching his hand kindly, 'you mustn't.'

'One for the mutt as well,' said the driver.

'Cattle gets no price!' the fat boy retorted loudly.

'He is not cattle!' Lucy reacted.

'He sure isn't,' the driver agreed, 'a piece for him too.'

The fat boy grumbled but eventually took out another smoked vegetable and handed it to the man. The man stroked his moustache and left off.

Crumbs weed up the side of the cart before running back to Lucy.

'I'm so sorry. But I can give you some of these coins,' said Lucy when she caught up with the fat boy and the cart had rolled off.

'It's okay, I got no use for bits,' he said examining the silver pieces in her hand, 'just take it as a good favour. Maybe me helping you, will bring me some luck somehow. And…' he added, 'don't forget I saved your life earlier.'

She laughed. 'You did. Thank you.' He saluted her, not even ironically, before turning away, in the direction of the cotton fields down the hillside where he hoped to find work. Promptly at the edge of the tavern gardens, cornfields stretched into the distance on either side of the road, dipping down as the land did into yet another valley. There were homesteads in the valley in the distance, their thick figures loomed amongst the shifting cotton flowers of the fields. It was light enough that she could still see, but dark enough at dusk that the lanterns along the roadside were starting to glow, the yellow light from their flames cutting through the shadows. The large figure of the boy cast a long shadow behind him as he disappeared.

'Wait!' she called as he hit the crest of the road. He turned back.

'I didn't get your name,' she said.

'Dario.'

'I'm Lucy,' she replied with a curtsy.

He laughed, 'I know'. Then he turned away from her for the second time, galumphing off down the road.

Lucy followed her own set of directions, taking a left after the tavern, where a small laneway bordered by the corn on one side, led her past tiny cottages and other small and dilapidated dwellings. She found the next proper carriage road, and followed it down a ways, taking the second fork in the road, where she found the third large homestead in this part of the valley. It was surrounded by corn and wheat fields. The driveway was marked with something like a scarecrow, but it seemed more decorative than functional. A display of personality from the owners? There was a ball with a face on it, and all kinds of plant material (long dead) making up the hair. Other random sachets and ribbons draped over the arms which were more or less just a branch tied to the post. There were no legs.

The driveway was wide, the ground beneath it kind of sandy and pale in this part of the world, and the fields stretching higher than her on either side. When she followed its meander, she could see the timber house. It was large and properly put together, with a veranda running the edge. A man was scattering feed to a number of chickens in a pen by the house as she approached. He caught a glimpse of her, and then did a double take. He dropped the rest of the feed back into the bucket and backed up a bit, stopping on the first step up to the veranda.

'Andy!' he called out, and that's when she knew she had arrived at the correct place.

Mr Tunnable, as she later learnt him to be, remained on the veranda dissatisfied and annoyed as his wife took Lucy inside, the two of them linked arm in arm. He had always known his wife to be too trusting, it was something that put them at odds regularly, yet she always got her way. She hadn't even asked who had sent Lucy. Lucy had barely got the words out of her mouth when Andy Tunnable's hospitality compelled her to beckon the girl inside out of the warmth before she spoke any further.

Sitting on a crocheted cushion that stretched across the elongated fallen-tree-come-lounge-chair, Lucy watched the woman very casually put some water in a kettle over the small stove fire.

'You say you know a nephew of mine?' Andy asked.

'Only met him briefly, ahhh...Jock.' Lucy found the note she had forgotten all about and held it out for the lady. She was middle aged at least, but her features still seemed young; her eyes were joyous, her cheeks were rosy. She had wavy blonde hair cut short to her shoulders the same colour nearly as the sawdust scattered across her overalls.

As she started to acknowledge silently in her mind, the woman's relative beauty for her age, Lucy surprised herself. She realised she was becoming immune to the unusually rounded figures and faces of the people in this world's west.

'Oh Jock!' Andy said and laughed, her eyes disappearing into crescent moon shapes on her face, 'bless that ambitious young thing. I haven't seen him in years, or my sister Sandra mind you,' she uttered the last comment through hushed tones as though it were a secret.

'So what did he think I could help you with?' Her voice had a twang to it that Lucy hadn't heard before; it was somewhat nasal.

'Well I am from…' Lucy paused suddenly wondering how to explain her predicament to a lady who seemed to have no presuppositions about her. Andy sat down on the opposite log sofa, placing Lucy's tea down, and blowing on her own in an effort to cool it.

'Well the wizards from the WFB brought me here, His Imperial Lord and His…'

'Right, the wizards, yes,' Andy said, smiling.

Lucy examined her for a moment, her docile expression. *She doesn't understand*, Lucy thought.

'I'm supposed to go to find some Princess, through the forest, and well…I'm not sure exactly but …'

Andy laughed. 'Oh I know, I know. They want you to fix everything here, reinstate a new government in Murder's Echo right?' she asked, and shimmied her head seemingly trivialising it all, 'did you think I didn't know who you were? We're isolated in the arable lands but it's not the Alexandria Plateau…we wouldn't miss news like that…I mean an Easterner stands out anyway.'

'Oh.' Lucy was taken aback.

'What, you think I didn't know?'

'Well it's just…you…you didn't say anything.'

'I treat everyone same. Doesn't matter who they are, Imperial or peasant.' Andy nodded assertively, 'as long as they're a friend. And if you're sent here by one of my kin, well you must mean well. My family have a way of reading people very quickly.'

'I'm not from the east,' Lucy added, only just picking up on the last comment 'unless it's like, really really far east. Really far.'

'Either way.' Andy shrugged, 'might sound crass but you all look the same to me. How's your tea darlin?'

'Good,' Lucy lied.

'And your little woofer, he, want anything to nibble?'

Crumbs had been obediently lying at Lucy's feet since they sat.

'He's fine.'

'So, what did Jock think I could help you with, is it a bed you need?'

'No, I'm told I need to get through the forest, I mean I can't stay here…'

Andy's tone and expression became solemn then, with only the hint of a smile, 'no, you can't.'

Mrs Tunnable suggested they relocate to the veranda, as the sun had not long set and it would be pretty. The veranda looked over the fields, but at the back of the house the land dipped sharply down toward where the crops of neighbouring estates slowly dispersed into uncultivated meadows. The meadows continued in a steady decline to where they met with the boundary of Chupner's Forest. It loomed, forebodingly tall, a deep emerald boundary between the lands.

Lucy had been fixated firmly in that direction for some time before Andy remembered her earlier query. 'So it's a safe route through the forest you want help with?'

Lucy nodded.

'That's no bother. I can draw you a map that will set you on a reasonably safe path. But that's not all you need help with is it? Really?'

Lucy looked puzzled.

'Let me put it this way then, is that all you need to know about?' Andy's head was leaning to one side.

'No. It's not,' Andy said when Lucy's puzzled expression remained, 'there's a lot you need to know. Whether you've heard it all before or not I'm going to tell you some things. For one thing, if you're going to Murder's Echo, you're not going to get there in a day, or even two days or thirteen. After the forest there's a plateau, there's mountains and a jungle, there's miles of pastoral land and kingdom after kingdom…you're in for a long journey if you think you plan to go the distance. Once you've crossed all our lands Murder's Echo is a good three-day journey by sea, off the coastal township of Coby. Coby is back and forth with its alliances, so you don't trust anyone you meet there, okay? But, if you intend to go, you'll be on the road a good few moons.'

Lucy nodded, 'I don't know if I will go to Murder's Echo. I think…' she said and then stopped. She was rightfully careful about expressing her point of view but felt comfortable confiding in this woman, 'I just want to try and find a way home.'

'Well,' exclaimed Andy incredulously, 'I certainly can't help you with that.'

'No, I know, I know.'

'But if you do go to the infamous island kingdom, and bear in mind it might be the only way you get home, the magic on that island is far stronger than anything on the mainland. You have to appreciate what you're getting into, even by setting foot there. And there's a lot you need to know about the history, the politics, the dynamics. God knows I am no expert, I'm sure in your travels you'll come across wiser folk than me…but just what have they told you about this Queen you're supposed to help overthrow?' Andy, having finished her tea was more attentive now, leaning inward.

Lucy sat back and tried to recount all the miscellaneous facts that had been relayed to her in the short time that she'd been here. 'That she's very young, was the youngest of triplets, but the other two girls are missing or dead…she's changed everything in the kingdom since she acceded, and she's been aggressive with other kingdoms since she took over…'

'Yes well…'

'Oh, and the attack here, of course.'

At the mention of the attack Andy took a deep breath and looked across the veranda into the changing hues of the sky. Stars were beginning to twinkle along the perimeter of where purple dusk encroached on the retreating orange and pink blushes of sunset.

'What was that? What do they mean by an attack? No one has really…' Lucy tapered off, feeling impolite to make enquiries about such dark things.

'It was a ferocious explosion of light; green and yellow and white,' Andy whispered, 'it hit here in the Hills, but closer to what they now call the drop, where ramps nearly as wide use to lead up to the city. But its effect was strange…or…sporadic, I mean. In the place where it hit the hardest, still, not everyone was killed, and not all the buildings were destroyed. It was strange. Some with minor injuries, others dead, others unscathed altogether. It was the same closer to these parts, some homes were wiped out, and others beside them not affected. Just bizarre how speckled the damage was. But it was afterwards, it was the sickness. Trees, animals, people. Again, not all but, thousands began to get violently sick afterwards, as the days went by, and slowly died. That's when they realised the real effect was not immediate - it was ongoing. A curse almost, they began to say. A curse on the land and everyone on it. Much more apparent back toward the townships. I'm sure you saw.'

'I'm sorry.' Lucy looked away uncomfortably.

'Don't you be sorry. Anyway, at least that is nearly behind us. It's getting better. I can see the difference in the younger generations. Myself and Steve, well, we're lucky, it hasn't affected us at all. Because, as I said, it was closer to the WFB that it hit. But people down here have this fixation on it being a permanent part of our way of life now, that it's something that will be here forever. But really, well it's actually disappearing as time goes on. Less people are getting sick, the crops are getting better. But I get the feeling the Wizards want to perpetuate the idea that we'll always be sick, because I think they've gotten used to this split-kingdom system of things. I mean, we're all basically trapped here working for nothing. But,' she stopped to sigh, 'it will have to change. It will all have to change. The young folk will get strong and healthy, and when they realise they're not as sick as everyone expected them to be, they'll rise up and want no more of this enforced agriculture, you know what I mean?'

Lucy nodded, but she of course did not fully grasp all of what the woman meant. How could she possibly? But she followed to some extent her sentiments.

'But anyway, with Murder's Echo, and you know of course its proper name is Meta Emery, what you have to appreciate is that the new, I mean she's not really that new, but the young Queen is not who rules the kingdom,'

'She's not?'

'Not really. In title yes, but in reality, if you ask me, it's the Dynasty that run the show. They're not actually a dynasty per se,' said Andy, and paused to point Lucy to a blanket draped over the back of her chair, noticing her shiver in the sudden change in temperature as the evening breeze began rustling around them. The fields in all directions swayed creating a very faint melodic rustling of their papery leaves, and the spindly pot plants on the veranda bounced around flimsily. Lucy wrapped the biege shawl around her shoulders and pulled Crumbs onto her lap as Andy continued.

'The line of succession for the throne is the heir of the Winters family and this, well this has always been the case for as long as anyone can remember. And the King or Queen is the head of the Dynasty. But the Dynasty is not necessarily the family of the monarch, rather a bunch of powerful representatives from the kingdom. They hold certain seats of power if you could call them that, and those powerful positions have been passed down, and continue to be passed down to future generations. I can't remember how many are in the Dynasty, but they don't all have blood ties to the Queen, is what I'm trying to get you to understand.'

'Right,' was all Lucy said. As her eyes gleamed over the manilla haze of the Tunnable's wheat fields, and then focused in on the dark haze beyond them, it was clear she couldn't understand the significance of the information. But Andy was intent on communicating it nonetheless. It was not so much an endeavour on Andy's part, to educate this young foreign girl. Afterall, why should that be the responsibility of an ordinary farmer's wife, who only happened to be the aunt of a boy the girl ran into. Rather, it was Andy's delight, at having a foreign ear to hear all her opinions without any adulterated preconceptions to taint them with.

'Her uncle Norton is a strong figure in the Dynasty. Everyone's heard of him. He gained a lot by Abigail's accession - that's why people don't trust him. They think he might have been behind it, his brother's death. Of course, *no one* can *prove* that. I'm sure that sort of comment would be considered traitorous in any kingdom aligned with M.E so be careful who you repeat that to…But nevertheless he's one to watch out for. He exerts a lot of influence over his niece, if you can believe all that they say. But maybe these rumours are just spread by other jealous Dynasty members who don't have the same relationship with the Queen that he does? I don't know. What would I know? But there are a lot of messy and dubious alliances on that island, more than you might expect. Just be ready for that.'

Lucy's focus was waning, but Andy seemed more than pleased to have a fresh ear to yarn to. Her husband walked by the garden bed below the veranda, peering up at them suspiciously, and then disappeared off somewhere again. Andy continued to ramble at Lucy until a crescent moon was glimmering high above the corn fields. She then remembered dinner and later made Lucy up a bed for the night.

'The night got away from me I'm afraid, but tomorrow, tomorrow we'll get to talking about these chasms in the forest,' Andy said leaving the room, but Lucy was already asleep.

The next day Lucy awoke on a tiny bed in damp sheets, her torso and legs sticky and wet with sweat. The daylight poured into the colourful wooden bedroom intensely through an open window. The air was dry and the room was hot. She threw off the sheets. She was perplexed as to how she could have slept so long, noting how high the sun was, and took Crumbs to find Andy. But the house was empty.

Lucy eventually found Mr Tunnable mending a trellis in a pokey vineyard not far from the house.

He regarded her, then turned back to his work.

'Hello. Ahhh, where's Andy?' Lucy asked.

'Headed out to the market. Won't be back til this evening.'

He spoke without looking up at her. A vine had grown entangled around a post and he was hoping to untangle it without damage.

'Oh, umm. Ahh… she…she said she would draw a map for me, for ummm, for the forest,' Lucy asked awkwardly, cognisant of his disinterest in her and her problems.

'She'll be back this evening. You can wait in the house,' he replied.

As she turned to walk away, he added, 'you can feed yourself I take it?' He was inviting her to help herself to his home and food, and yet it still came across as an insult.

'Yes, I can,' Lucy let out in somewhat of a stutter.

'Well after you're done helping yourself to our hospitality perhaps you can make yourself useful,' he looked at her then, for the first time, letting the tools fall out from his thick soiled gloves, and tilting his head up, straining to see her from under the brim of his large hat. So after feeding herself with bread, tomatoes, and something with a texture like butter, but a taste much more pungently gamey, she went back out into the fields and let herself be set to work. Feeling somewhat overwhelmed and intimidated by his authority, she stayed out on the fields until the sun set again and he suggested they wait for Andy back at the house. To Lucy's relief when they got back to the house he made some comment about something in his room, and left her alone on the veranda, watching the grasses near the corn bend and sway along the edge of the sandy entrance path.

'Hope you haven't been sitting there all day!' cried Andy valiantly as she limped eagerly down around the bend, rousing Lucy from her slight slumber.

Lucy blinked and it took her a moment to recognise the galumphing figure, face hidden by the shadow but her white linen shirt catching the early light of the moon. Lucy looked around, realising with some disappointment that it was becoming dark; she would have to wait until dawn again to move.

'So much happening at the markets today, I had to get out early. In the rush I forgot all about the map I was ganna draw ya. Showing my age I guess. But I thought Steve might have drawn you one, he used to take our boys hunting in Chupner's all the time,' she said cheerily as she unloaded herself of all the baskets. Lucy realised with some disdain, that Mr Tunnable had seen it to his advantage not to draw her the map. Andy told Lucy it was imperative the chickens be fed before complete darkness, or else they get too spooked. So Lucy helped her feed them and Andy told Lucy all about her day.

'…but Fieria, she's got no hope of it you see. Her husband has no business getting into cattle. They don't have the land for it. They don't know what it takes. My uncle was in cattle, but that was back in the day. I mean the land's healed somewhat, but you have to be able to manage the feed of them, and keep them off the noxious grasses, and if you don't know how to herd cattle in normal conditions well you're a fool getting into it when the soil and the feed are still questionable…'

Lucy nodded, concurring, but tried to steer things back to the present, 'there was a lot of farming back home. We didn't farm. But my aunt and uncle, my cousins, they all grew up on farms. I hope I can find a way to go back.'

'I hope you can too dear. As I said, I wish I could help you, but…I know as much about the ethereal as the crows that pester my fields.'

Andy thought about this a moment more, 'hmm, they probably know more actually.'

As if to tease her, a number of crows appeared, swooping down from the darkening cerulean sky before resting on the rafters above.

'Oh, piss off.' Andy spat at them and waved her hand around, but in jest. They were out of feed and the chickens were eagerly pecking away, their food barely visible as twilight quickly departed.

'Just…ahh…you give me a moment would you,' said Andy watching the chickens pecking at the soil in satisfaction, before placing the bucket on the porch and ducking inside.

'Now, the forest, the chasms,' said Andy coming back down the steps into the coop. She had a piece of paper in her hand, 'I did start to draw that map but I…I wanted to tell you also…' began Andy but she was sharply interrupted.

'Hurry, hurry! The mistress is at work in the sky again! The gravestones are being destroyed!' cried a young man who'd come running up the drive.

'I've told my parents, they've gone to fetch the shaman.'

'Oh no, not again!' said Andy in an irritable fluster, hurrying off after the lad as quickly as her limpy leg and breathless lungs could take her. Lucy and Andy followed the boy down the road to an empty grassy hillside, where above them tiny dark clouds had gathered, and light in the space of the valley emitted an almost imperceptible red glow.

The three of them halted in a row at the top of a nearby hill. They were strangers to her, but the air around them, the intensity of the electric energy, somehow unified them as kin. There was some sort of unnatural connection. The air dampened, the glimmer of evening vanished behind clouds and fog. Lucy's eyes fell eagerly down the hill, this small micro-valley held a gathering of graves. The small storm was condensing above them. It was initially raining very sporadically, the way it does in summer storms, before the droplets fell hard and heavy and saturation was instant. Lightning emerged from the storm and frizzled down with increasing animosity. The crackle of the bolts was felt through the air as the thunder erupted.

'No, no! Begone you wretched wicked witch child!' the boy screamed to the sky.

'You let their spirits be, Abigail!' Andy wailed out loudly. The storm lasted only a few minutes, with the boy and Andy shouting out various curses at the sky.

'This was a school when the attack came. Strangest thing… like I said it hit hardest near the border, but for some reason this spot, this spot…they were all wiped out. Every one of them. Two teachers, nearly fifty little ones,' Andy said with resignation as her and the lad regained their composure while the mini storm rolled away.

'If you listen…' said Andy with a soft peril in her voice, 'you can still hear the children's screams.' Lucy listened, but she was certain it was only the wind, screeching through the trees.

'Andy!' a hoarse voice cried. A man with a scratchy beard was running up the hill behind them.

'Oh Jeyma, thank the skies! You're here but…' Andy turned back to the field where the lightning had stopped.

The man grabbed her hands, his own reaching from under his rust coloured poncho, 'I know. I know. I missed it. But still, it being so close, there's no time like now. We should do it now!'

Andy almost began to cry, but the scrawny man with the beard shook her somewhat, and she wiped her eyes before the tears could roll down her blotchy cheek. 'I know, you're right. Of course you are. Yes, now. Yes, now!' Andy replied.

And in another moment the two of them were charging away down the hill, the young lad racing after, and onto a path leading them north, the opposite direction to the Tunnable estate.

Lucy stood there alone for several moments, watching as their figures got smaller before disappearing around a bend. She took in the air, its metallic whiffs of petrichor, and stared at the empty space where they'd been. Very slowly Lucy began to sense that they weren't coming back. Whatever the local significance of this storm, wherever they were going, she would never know.

Turning back around, by some stroke of luck she caught sight of a corner of cream paper jutting out from the dark grass. Instantly she recognised it as the paper Andy had, the map she'd been about to give her back at the house. She picked it up. It was fairly detailed, not to scale, but there were notes and descriptions along it. It would be a useful guide.

The rain started to come back, the sky sputtered. Lucy made her way back to the Tunnable estate, only to find it vacant. It was unlocked so she went inside and sat with Crumbs at the table near the kitchen, lighting the candles when it got too dark to see. But as she waited around in the candlelight - and no one came - and the clammy night air filled with a sense of anxiety, she fought against a growing urge to head out and examine the periphery of the ominous forest-scape.

There was no doubt something odd about Andy's rushed departure, but it was the way she hadn't said goodbye, and the intensity of emotion during that short storm over the graveyard, that made Lucy uncomfortable about staying at their estate.

While Crumbs paced around the empty farmhouse, she tilted a candle over the map examining it, being careful not to drip wax. There was a path Andy had indicated - seemingly not that far from the graveyard - that seemed to lead to a conventional entrance into the forest. There were other, seemingly less favourable entry points that Andy had marked up with deterrent crosses.

Something close to an hour went by and the darkness of night had well and truly set in. She couldn't bear the anxiety anymore, and convinced herself there was nothing wrong with simply going down to the forest entrance and examining it. The impression everyone had given her was that it was more than a day's worth of hiking to get through it, so she would have to see through a night there in any event. There was no harm in investigating, she reasoned. But in actions that seemed to contradict this plan, she took not only her bag, but a blanket she could roll up easily enough and stuff in it. It would likely be too hot for a blanket for some time, but it would also likely be the only thing between her and the ground.

Chapter 6

Chupner's Forest

"The clearest way into the Universe is through a forest wilderness."
John Muir

Lucy stood looking up at the dark treetops; smooth brown trunks met emerald green foliage some forty metres above. Just as Andy's map indicated, the three paths from the northern farms, had joined to one, and led to the forest's main entrance. The only real light was moonlight now, but it was a very bright moon, and her eyes had adjusted to it. The hills behind her were sparkling. The languid moon having still not fully risen, looked enormous, its bottom half still hid behind their curves. Ahead of her, engulfed in the vegetation, the brown path turned black twenty metres ahead, where the darkness of the forest swallowed it and the lanterns ceased. Lanterns, just like the one she stood near. Amber flames danced from within frosted glass, hanging from a smooth green pole. It shed light on the sign below, which read:

Chupner's Forest
All beware his deadly glare

A disconcerting message. Particularly when it dawned on her in a rather sudden chilling moment, that no one she'd met had ever explained why it was called *Chupner's Forest*.

'Where is that music coming from, Crumbs?' she asked pensively. Amongst the chorus of crickets or cicadas or similar insect, there was a very faint underlying rhythm to the forest. Drums were pounding somewhere far away.

Lucy heard a noise and looked behind her, hoping to see Andy, or Steve, or even the young lad whose name she never got. But there was nothing but the hills, and the shadows they cast. She turned back to find another light, a lantern she hadn't noticed before, lighting another wooden sign by her ankles, which read:

Follow the Blue Eagle. Watch for the Yellow Eagle. Beware
the Red Eagle

Lucy whispered the words, wondering if it was some kind of town joke, or whether it had any actual meaning. It had the feel of a colloquial slogan rather than anything substantive. The sign was very low to the soil, almost completely hidden by the leaves of a fanning bush. The writing looked drawn by either a youth - or someone with a shaky hand. She crouched and held Andy's map under the lantern's light - just to double check - but there was nothing about either eagles or Chupner.

Lucy stood up with a deep sigh. Her hands trembled, probably because somehow deep down, she knew this was a bad idea.

She would not go into the forest tonight though. She merely needed to get a feel for how it looked and felt. She now knew it felt stern. It had its own sound, its own dense aroma of damp vegetation and animal matter. Lucy thought about trekking the distance back into town. She could find the Inn the cart had dropped them off at. She still had money after all, if they accepted it, and Crumbs could stay outside if they had an issue with dogs.

But a bright light from above disrupted her train of thought. It was almost as if a star had dropped out of the night sky. The twinkling diamond shone fluorescently, floating closer and closer, getting bigger and bigger, brighter and brighter.

When the light paled, and faded into nothing, there he sat; the black bear from her dream at the castle. He was sitting iconically in the handle of his purple and green umbrella, floating slowly down.

Red cross stitches for his eyes, blackened fur almost invisible against the night sky. He had a cigar in his mouth and as he floated nearer, he hummed a little tune, one that was more sombre than upbeat.

'I recognise you!' exclaimed Lucy. She caught herself then, a splintered recognition that she was saying this to a stuffed toy. But she couldn't help but continue, 'I've seen you before…in a dream…'

'Have you?' he said, feigning surprise, unconvincingly.

'But you know that, don't you?' She stepped back a little.

He shrugged. 'It was your dream. How would I know who was in it?'

'Yet you're here now…'

'I am,' he agreed, 'say, what are you doing here?'

'What are you doing here?'

He laughed at this.

'You're a good sort, not letting anyone else run the show.' A subtle dig. He was scanning their surroundings as he muttered it.

Lucy let her look of suspicion continue for some time while Bear floated softly, his umbrella rising and falling with the gentle night breeze. He was like some sort of storybook character, his tattered fur and missing eyes, his face never taking on much expression.

'Well, as a matter of fact I am here for you,' he said and put out his cigar on the side of the umbrella, 'I am providing some necessary assistance. You should be going through tonight, which I see you've realised.' He meant the forest.

'I was going to head back to town actually…'

'No. Not a good idea.'

'Why's that?'

'The town folk, they're…' he struggled to find the words, 'they're in a bit of a… It's become somewhat of a momentous night for them all of a sudden, and they're likely to make more of you being here than is necessary.'

Lucy felt no inclination to place trust in the talking toy, but as he said this a chill ran down her spine.

'What do you mean?' she asked slowly.

'It's hard to explain - there was - there was that little storm earlier. One of the gravestones was damaged. There's a lot of emphasis on symbolism in the Hills, and they're not if you've noticed, politically aligned with the, how do we say, the *visions* of Archmond.'

Lucy followed some, of what he was saying, but would not have imagined the ruckus going on back at the town hall. Andy standing beside her receding witch-doctor friend, vehemently slamming down suggestions that this foreign girl among them was either a treacherous tie to the east, or a dangerous act of provocation that, either way, needed eliminating.

'The forest is no more dangerous at night than during the day, just go slow, I'll help light the way.'

Lucy looked back over at the hills. The moon had risen somewhat, taking the light from their grassy curves further into the town. She heard faint rallying in the distance. She looked back up at the bear.

'I have a map but…these chasms I've heard of, are they off the path?'

'Way off!' he said, but in truth he did not know, 'you'd never find one even in the light.'

The enveloping darkness below the canopy created a contrast that made the sky seem a misty and star-sputtered charcoal grey. The night forest was black…but wide-awake. The birds were crazed with excitement; their strange gossiping calls to one another intensifying the atmosphere. In distant camps, sticks rapped drums as they had before, sending rhythm through the forest with their continuous beat. Other noises, echoed too, here and there. Noises that couldn't be accounted for, at least not by any *known* species.

He sensed her presence first as a disturbance. Her frame and image did not come to him straight away. The knowledge of something foreign, the knowledge of this alien presence stirred brightly in his mind like a small chemical fire. The potency of it was at first a light, a mere spark in the far abyss of space. But it grew. His people sensed this alarm within him in moments of time that connected them to him and to each other. They were connected to his mind so keenly and obediently, just as he connected himself obediently to the infinite.

He lay in the centre of the tepee, upon the podium, and focused on the visions that came before his unconscious mind. He was in slumber, but not asleep. His mind was roaming through the subconscious world of infinite knowing, and yet was still loosely aware of the shapes formed by the mallow wood smoke curling up near the pinnacle of the room.

His disciples held their posts at the periphery of the tent, watching over him as they did every night, but now sensing this emergence, and awaiting instruction.

The smoky incense created by the burning mallow wood in the corners, was starting to fall back down toward him, but it lifted again as if injected with life. He lay in this new understanding with his eyes shut, and he spoke not a word, but his voice began to etch its way slowly, into the minds of his beguiled followers, like water flooding their camp.

Desees, it is night, it is night. But the forest stirs. It is not at peace. An intrusion from the east weaves its way through our world, and it disrupts the Amoritai. What world will we wake to tomorrow? What blood are we willing to shed for the trees that guard us and our spawn?

The Amoritai is upon us. It must always be. We will not let intruding blood overplay what is and what must be.

This intrusion is human. It is female. It is Eastern in essence. Find it, and bring it before me, before the sun can rise on its betrayal. Together we will protect this camp.

When they seized her, she was a good half a mile from their camp. She was tired, and struggling to manoeuvre in the dark by her lantern-light (having taken the small one from the ground). It made it easier for them, but it was always going to be easy. Their feet were agile across the coarse and cluttered terrain of the forest floor. The forks in the undergrowth were memorised by their souls. She, a feeble town girl, was no match for them.

She had been travelling for nearly an hour, it had taken them some time to locate her. Though scattered, they stopped often in unison to receive the updated instructions from their master, *go north*, he'd said many times, *she is north*.

When they set upon her, Bear was shocked but not completely surprised. He withdrew, in disappointment, having been convinced they would have avoided this enemy. But there was nothing he could do but watch while she screamed and was bundled up along with her little dog into a sheet and onto a stretcher. He rose higher, into the canopy, and followed the procession from above.

Lucy recalled having walked for some time in the dark. Bear claimed to be leading them to a clearing where a stream ballooned out into a creek, and the forest parted to reveal the starry sky above. Against the rocks up the bank from the stream, he painted a picture of tranquil anonymity, where she could rest, safely hidden until dawn. But the longer they tried to find this place the further away it seemed to be.

It was when she was very weary that she noticed, in a dreamlike way, the sense of being watched from many angles.

Whether they had drugged her or whether she was simply so over-come by the tiredness already creeping in, and the lack of oxygen in the tightly woven cocoon of the sheet, she lost consciousness.

When she came to, all she recalled was her arguments with Bear about where they were going, and how irritated she had become with him. It was several moments, while her eyes struggled to flutter open, before the memory of her capture re-emerged.

She was struck first by the smell of sweet earthy smoke, the mallow wood burning in the corners of the tent. The rich light was flickering and hard to focus on, the darkness in its vacancy was dancing all over the room. She felt in that moment that perhaps she had been drugged after-all; she was dizzy, and it felt heavy to move.

As her vision came back, she realised that the room she was in, was part of a large tent; fabric walls, dirt floor. In the far corner, by one of the fires letting off plumes of powdery pink smoke, some women were examining a scroll. They muttered things to each other, pointing at parts of it, in words too quiet for her to hear or understand. She squinted for several moments, realising then that she was restrained; her hands were behind her, wrapped in rope to a pole.

Below the women, she saw her backpack; open, contents sprawled. She recognised the scroll they examined as the map she'd bought from Toby's shop.

'Hey,' she called in dreary confusion, 'what do you want with that?'

Her resumed consciousness sent the women into a flurry, and when several had left and come back again, Lucy was untied from the pole and brought out into the night. Though they'd been alerted into action by her waking, they took on the role of her relocation with a sluggish indifference. Two held her, one on each side. The other four walked ahead and behind in pairs. They were famished; drained mentally and physically by the sacrifices they endured during Amoritai. She was merely an obstacle, a disruption to the long-awaited end of their faithful observance. Lucy remembered being distracted from the anxiety of her hostage, by the rhythmical clinking of the bangles that hung loosely around the olive toned wrists of their free hands. They swung up and down, in effortless unison with each other, as though their stride had been synchronised over years of shared tasks like this one.

It was surprising how much of a chill was in the air. The day had been hot, and the night warm. She'd awoken sticky with sweat inside the tent. All Lucy could grasp of the campsite as she was led along, were several scattered pockets illuminated by the deep fire-torch glow along the path. But there was vegetation and thick undergrowth encroaching so forcefully across the camp that she couldn't yet appreciate the size of the settlement. The forest encroached into and onto their settlement, helpfully camouflaging tents and obscuring pathways. There was a small clearing where they took her. This was the assembly point below their leader.

Chupner, an enormous man, surrounded by small women on all sides, sat on a bamboo throne on the stone podium. His round brown head was quite easily more than triple the size of the other nearby men. His stomach ballooned out in front of him, but his body was taught with muscular strength. Slouched lazily in the throne it wasn't possible to truly appreciate his height, but he dwarfed by several feet the tallest of his followers. In each of the corners of the podium were baskets of colourful fruits, pink and lime green, banana yellow and brazen red, all buzzing with flies. They were long past being edible to anything else. On either side of the steps leading up to the platform were bulky men and women with weapons. Stoic senior members of the tribe, who would take it upon themselves to protect where necessary, to kill where necessary. But Lucy, quite clearly, wasn't much of a threat. They had been discussing her amongst themselves and fell silent as the women brought her along.

She was thrown into the dirt, in the space before the podium, and made to kneel. Several long and tense moments went by before anything happened. Chupner picked at his nails, chewed the edge of a large leaf, and took the image of her in. He was not a man to play cards with, that was apparent instantly. But nor was the Indawara tribe a group to hedge bets with. She realised when she turned her head, that they had Crumbs too. He was tied up within a small wooden cage off to the side, being guarded by a small child. 'Crumbs!' she cried out instinctively. The child wacked the cage threateningly and Crumbs whimpered. The back of her neck felt then the warm rough heel of a foot pushing downward instructively; *kneel*. There was muttering among the many spectators now gathering behind Lucy, having woken from their sleep to monitor this unfolding drama. They muttered words and sounds she could not understand.

In a murmur that thundered over the mild muttering Chupner cleared his throat, and an instant respectful hush fell over the crowd. He began speaking this same indistinct language of his people. But a wiry old interpreter provided some rough translation.

'It is not unknown, you is foreign. You is not belonging to this place. But why is the east back again?'

The deep-set hazel eyes stared her down impatiently, with contempt, waiting for her to confess to some crime she did not understand. Lucy trembled, confused, and looked carefully up at carved spikes on the wooden stakes before the podium. They looked to be made of bone, and would pierce her neck quite easily. But as she craned her head upward the rough heel pushed against her silken dark hair and forced her head back to the dirt, *kneel*.

Chupner made some grumbling noise that suggested his impatience was peaking. On the base of the bottom step, which she could see without lifting her head, Lucy saw the outline of a fluffy animal start to crystallize.

'Bear!' she called in a somewhat hushed tone, 'help me! What's going on, what do they want?'

The people remarked at the bear with wonder but seemed to not be afraid.

'Amoritai! Amoritai!' declared Chupner. The crowd agreed reverently.

'You have to tell them you're not from the east, he thinks you are either from Murder's Echo, or from Mazouri. Both armies have torn through here in recent years with this worsening east-west feud, and they've upset the Indawara on each occasion - interfering with the 'balance' of the forest way.' Bear addressed her very casually, but he spoke quickly, hoping the old translator would miss most of it.

Lucy's palms were still pressed against the soil, she craned her head up slightly but not so much that she could see. In a shaky voice, 'I'm not from east, I'm not from…'

Bear hushed her. 'Don't say you're from another world. Say you're from far across the sea.'

Lucy blinked, her head twitched with a frustrated anxiety.

'I'm from far far away, across the ocean,' she choked out. The old woman muttered something to her master.

Chupner looked her up and down and then waved his hand directing her to stand.

'Rise,' said the woman quietly.

Lucy stood, and was re-examined, and asked now to sit not kneel. Chupner spat away the inedible parts of the leaf he chewed, its juices were what he needed, and they ran down his chin in bright green stripes.

'It shows you very foreign,' translated the woman again. She was sitting on the second step, a bandana around her greyed auburn hair. She looked tired and only vaguely interested in the nights' events, 'but you not welcome, you disrupt Amoritai. What do you seek in my forest?'

'Nothing. I just want to be let past!' Lucy blurt out. Bear stirred, surprised by her sudden assertiveness.

Chupner took a stuttered breath, he shook his head, dismayed by the audacity of her spirit, 'you may not pass. Amoritai will be disturbed. I will protect Amoritai.'

His final statement was taken as an order, and the women swept her up into their clutches again, amid a crowd murmuring and grunting in satisfaction. A sheet was thrown over her in the same moment that she was pulled to her feet by her hair, the force of which also threw her backward, into warm and sweaty clutching arms.

They led her up a short incline. She was fastened this time to a shorter post on higher ground, above the assembly area, beneath a loosely fitted tarp that provided little shelter from the rain when it fell. The women pushed her into the ground with annoyance, yanking her arms up and around the base of the post. They were rough with her, but they were being kind. They could have made her stand.

'Please no, no.' She begged, as they steadied her torso by pushing down on her back with a foot. Naturally Lucy expected the immediate infliction of some sort of sanctimonious punishment. But once she was restrained, lying down on her side with her ankles bound and her hands behind the post, they left her again, yawning as they walked back down to join the rest of their camp.

It was hours she waited, body twisted uncomfortably, and mind on the brink of consciousness. The rain was heavy, intense, rain. The droplets, large and voluminous, saturated everything in sight within moments. In the dry patch in the centre beneath the tarpaulin, Lucy lay with her head on the soft earth, watching the foreground blur behind a stream of water. She looked up though, as much as her restraints would allow her to do, and appreciated how far reaching the forest was. Into the depths of the starry sky, which now seemed so far away, the slender trunks stretched, with fan palms and spider vines lurching off in every direction. In dizzying appreciation, she took note of them where the light fell, be it moonlight, or lamp light here by her feet.

Above again, she saw small mammals spring themselves between the treetops, seeking shelter. Their timing almost seemed to deliberately obey the rhythm of the tribal drums, which went on it seemed, throughout the night, despite the rain.

He hadn't mentioned killing her out loud. And no symbolism had been arranged around her to give her that impression. And yet - she had this sinking feeling that it was on the cards. He was grave when he muttered the last few words, relayed to her by the translator as meaning that some festival could not be interrupted.

It was unmistakable how much of an unwelcome intruder she was. Somehow her presence threatened to poison the purity of something they held in the highest esteem. To the Indawara people, Amoritai was integral to the continuation of their lives as they knew it.

But Chupner had a greater problem on his hands than impure blood on his territory. The observance of Amoritai was near its end. The people had faithfully abstained from all but the meekest morcels of food since the crescent moon rose above the treetops some twenty-four nights ago. No deer had been killed, no ground tortoloins hunted, no fish caught, since he declared Amoritai in force and they knelt together by the moon and kissed with thanks the earth that held their weight. Now his people eagerly awaited the end of the festival, where as well as their spirits being replenished from their sacrifice, they could finally refill their bodies with the sustenance they needed.

But this season was different. There were no deer in sight. He had sent seekers out to monitor the herds in anticipation of the festival's end, but each party had come back to report that the forest within their territory was quiet - still - as if a terrible spell had fallen over their land. The easy answer was to attribute this to the eastern girl they'd captured; an anomaly to find an eastern girl in their forest, and an anomaly for the forest around the camp to be devoid of game. Chupner feared though, that slaughtering the girl would not solve the problem, and this would terrify his people and polarise the camp. Outside of Amoritai observance, he would have sent larger parties further afield in search of answers, but Amoritai required them to be close to camp, and they would not venture further than a half mile in any direction. Amoritai would be over soon, but the hunters had not eaten anything substantial in over twenty days. The tribe was in recovery from fasting. No one would have the strength to venture out on overnight hunting parties, and it would be days on foraged food before that strength would return to them.

This dilemma shifted the way he saw Lucy's place in this moment in time. Over the course of the night he did not return to his catatonic state of sublimely conscious dreaming. Instead he stared at the girl on the hill under the tarp, watching her go blurry and then re-focus through the changing intensity of the rain. He watched her, and himself, in the glass cutting that propped up against the wall of his shack. He wondered as the image of her and the image of himself circled in his mind, whether it could be possible that enemy blood could be used to protect Amoritai - rather than destroy it.

Morning came with a welcome return to humidity and warmth. Curls of steam etched upward from the damp forest floor, as tubes of pale yellow light pierced the canopy. He had waited until most of the camp was settled into their morning routine before he had her woken and brought down to his tent. But the resulting attention was unavoidable, and the work of the camp was stilted and interrupted, heads turning, people creeping away from their stations, eager to be the first to watch the events unfold. The outcome the tribe expected, more or less, was a swift but meaningful execution. It was important to everyone that they be protected from any threat to Amoritai.

Standing before Chupner's tent, the hot mist of the forest morning dancing around her, she was coming to terms with this possibility. Her palms were sweaty, her tired muscles and weakened system incapable of even the mildest defence, and her mind racing for anything she could say to remove herself from this situation.

She was brought through. Chupner was holding a rusted blade in his right hand. He rapped it against the arm of the bamboo chair to the beat playing in his head. A provincial song he'd heard some Archmonders sing once when they were crossing through his territory. He'd enjoyed their singing, as he and his men watched them from the cover of the jewel ferns. But he'd had their throats slit nonetheless.

He looked up at her, the droopy shadows of sleeplessness across his face were missed by Lucy, who only focused on the knife. That and the intensity of his gaze.

'It is custom to kill the intruder,' he muttered his words almost silently. The interpreter's translation echoed coolly from the far right of the tent. She was almost invisible in the shadow covering the left side, but the vibrant outline of her red hair made it clear she was the same woman from yesterday.

'But there is something I need you to do,' he said as his eyes met hers, 'you do this - you return, you and dog are free to go. You cannot do this - or you don't return, we kill dog, we find you again.'

Chupner sent her out of his tent without direction, but with a clear mission of ascertaining why their camp surrounds were devoid of game. He could not let the tribe go hungry when Amoritai concluded. And he could not let anyone defy Amoritai by venturing far from camp to find the answers they needed. The game they had sustained themselves with for decades had very suddenly disappeared. Why?

Bear floated some distance above her, a dark mass encircled with silver light, as she was led out of the camp. The same bangle wearing women, who had originally tied her to a post in the tent the night before, were now releasing her, as if they assumed entire custody of her. There were no allowances given to assist. No dry clothes. No food to fend off the faintness swimming in her head. They had however, supplied a mesh bag and some rope, to somehow bring back any creatures she managed to catch. Which was of course as likely as her catching a falling star. This mission - much like the mission of shrouded prophecy that brought her into this alien world - was clearly futile.

Many herds of shepherd deer normally gathered in pockets to the north of the camp this far into the season, which her escorts communicated to her with both weariness and mild hostility. The ground tortoloins were usually plentiful around the banks of streams and ponds just beyond the river. The 'information' was largely conveyed through rather oblique markings in the sand and sound bites she half understood - but the overall picture seemed clear. Deer north, tortoloins north east over the river, but where now? So reluctantly, if only to try and have her dog and things returned to her, Lucy headed toward the river.

The lapping of water over rocks, the repetitive trickle it made teased her sense of direction; an audial illusion. She walked in silence toward it, but as she circled round and round toward its call, she was no closer.

'From where the sun sits, north appears to be, upward, mmm…, over the incline.' Amongst the tops of the fig branches, Bear was squinting with a craned neck toward the sky. 'Did you hear me?' he said when she failed to respond. Her clothes were still damp, plastered across her. She threw sticks angrily out of her path, exhaling in irritation.

'What am I doing?'she exclaimed, her hands pushed up against her hairline. She looked up at him, 'you knew about them, didn't you?'

Accusation was blatant in her tone as she repeated herself. 'You knew about the tribe?'

Looking away she walked straight ahead, against his suggestion.

'I knew *of* them. But I fail to see how that justifies your snappy tone.'

'You presented yourself as a guide - and yet led me straight into a trap.' She walked faster now, as if not caring for his reply.

Bear lowered himself amongst the canopy to her eye level, floating nearer til her eyes met his.

'I do not,' he said very slowly, alighting the tips of fingers with violet florets, 'control the weather, the seas, the forest, or the tribes in it for that fact. It's hardly my fault they decided to blame you for this game-less festival.'

Lucy marched faster despite realising that the trickle of the stream was growing fainter.

'You can hardly take issue with my guidance if you're not following it,' he muttered with subtle undertones of sass. Without acknowledgement Lucy stopped, changed direction, and headed up the incline. She was forced to cling to spiky branches and vines for support as her shoes sunk into the wet earth. But over the hill, there was the stream she'd been hearing, trailing into a shallow grey pond further upward still, encircled by a network of bulbous rocks all glimmering in the hot sun.

'Mercy,' she whispered to herself and scrambled deliriously toward it. The smooth shale was almost hot against her torso as she pressed herself into it; first on her side, and then collapsing over onto her back.

'Well I'm not much of a tracker, but I'd hazard a guess that you're not going to locate any deer on that rock.'

Perched on a spotted flaxen branch he continued spurting out commentary. The branch hung flimsily bending down to the pond, but his figure would momentarily disappear into the thick of the foliage as it swayed up and down. She heard his voice fade until she could hardly hear him over the guzzling of water down the incline. In all her life the sun had never felt so magnificent, thick splendid colour fell everywhere across the clearing, not that she could see it. Eyes closed, comfort enveloped her, as her clothes started to dry under its warmth. She felt the tranquil pull of sleep, but she wouldn't let herself go under. She couldn't let herself sleep here.

The previous night at Archmond Castle.

Ron rubbed the hair off his face. Soleman had interrupted him in the small hours after midnight. He believed he had received messages from Bear through a dream. Although, both leaders acknowledged that it is not in Bear's repertoire to communicate through dreams. Soleman sat on the very edge of Ron's elongated olive lounge which sat in the centre of Ron's dimly lit bed chamber, rehashing the details in the hazy way they came to him. *There were the sounds of drums and singing, no not singing, chanting. And I was strolling through the castle gardens but they turned into the forest, and then Bear was…he came in as a shadow, no it was more of a reflection, in the pond, but the pond was in the forest… and so were the gardens.*

Ron was not amused. He'd already had difficulty falling asleep the last few nights with factions of the nobility becoming more and more restless about trade issues they were having with Trimany and Que. He'd had almost no help from Soleman in these negotiations, because Soleman had *insisted,* that his time was better served with quiet worship to the powers that be. Tonight, he had only managed to eventually drift off after having a rather large dose of Lyadell Leaf in his tea.

But now, sufficiently roused, he propped himself up and bore the weight of his tilted head on his ring and middle finger. Soleman had been awake a good hour. He was fully dressed, sprightly, and holding a cup of hot lemon water.

'But….anyway…yes, that's what I was getting to. What the point was, the point was, that she's crossed paths with the Indawara tribe. That was clearly the point of the drumming and the chanting, and the painted symbols on trees…'

'The Indawara?' Ron's attention was caught now but his gaze was still skeptical, 'aren't they observing Amoritai at this time of year? That's why we reasoned it would be safe if she kept north. How on earth would she come into their territory if she took the northern route? Unless she's gone the wrong way.'

'Well that's exactly it!' exclaimed Soleman, 'the impression I got was that they came to her. They sought her out.'

'That's rather disturbing.'

'It is,' Soleman said, sipping his lemon tea, 'but then I felt like he was telling me that she is on the way through it. As though some kind of deal, some kind of challenge, is being offered for her freedom. But I didn't get all the details. No, oh dear, I can't remember...' Soleman pinched the bridge of his nose, and then put his tea down as though it was all too much for tea.

Ron sighed, and succumbing to the idea that he would have to rise, he got out of bed and went to the basin to wash his face.

'Well we all know how that will go down, don't we? Pretty typical of the Indawara, make their sacrifices dance first.'

'Well, well, well... I mean... I don't know that we can say for sure what the situation is. I don't know what it is they're asking her to do.'

'We know the Indawara. I don't think there's anything she can do that will be enough. Unless Bear has a trick up his sleeve?'

'He can't use his powers during Amoritai - and even if he could - there would be war.'

'Well, perhaps you should start praying again,' Ron uttered coldly, and went to open the curtains. They could see the first light of dawn starting to push away the darkness on the horizon.

Back in Chupner's Forest...

Lucy woke when the sun was no longer warm, and cool grey shadow and gentle breeze blistered her comfort until she stirred. Bear had brought food, it seemed. He was sitting by it rather proudly, waiting for her to acknowledge it, and him. Some form of fruit and three little fish, dead but raw, lay by her ankles.

Lucy wasn't inclined to trust. She was also not inclined to express her distrust because it created animosity, which could lead to confrontation, something she shied away from at all costs. And so there was certainly something about this metaphysical creature she did not trust, but it was only the generic blanket distrust that she cast over all strangers. Somehow his form and his unexplained origins didn't conjure any more reticence than usual, and so this small gesture was getting further with her than others had.

She poked at the fish, 'how do I cook it?' Her voice was still dreary, strands of ebony hair fell across her eyes.

'Fire?' Bear suggested, and began making sparks in the shrubbery beside the slate.

'What do you think the tribe would say if I brought them back a fish each instead?'

'I think they'd eat your dog,' he said casually, as he flicked away the bones she'd discarded.

She continued north and the sun continued east. There were well walked paths clear in the undergrowth, and she used them, assuming they were the paths used by the Indawara. The forest had its own disobedience to the seasons, it was hot while the sun perforated the canopy, but it was cold when the grey afternoon shadows came over everything. There were flowers blooming and fruit ripening with all the excitement of spring, and yet as she pushed through the wilderness, yellowing leaves drifted down around her. A small crescent leaf, with marmalade tones of decay, landed across the bridge of her nose as she looked up. She wiped it away and looked over to Bear. He floated along beside her, about a foot or so away, a few inches above. He had an almost nonchalant air about him. Staring blankly straight ahead he had a relaxed smile; as though they were old friends on an ordinary stroll through the local park, and he was content with this ordinary suburban existence they shared.

But he must have felt her gaze. 'What?' he said turning to her.

She shook her head to mean nothing, but then she caught another glimpse of his eyes. She had taken them in already, had regarded their obscurity, but before she was certain what she had seen was crossed stitches with a central button, sewn into a face. Now, these two blackish circles opened inward, peering into chasms of the cosmos; tiny iridescent galaxies were sparkling from within.

'Hasn't anyone told you it's rude to stare into someone's galaxy?' he said with a smirk. Her mute response told him he was correct, 'my eyes do that from time to time,' he eventually added, 'I don't know why.'

The sustenance from the food had stimulated her in more than one way, now her mind was wandering to many places. She was phrasing her thoughts into questions as she watched a bright green lizard, no bigger than her thumb, scurry across the path and disappear under the fallen leaf litter.

'Are you alive?' she asked. The bluntness of her own words startled her, but she wouldn't have put it differently.

He seemed affronted, the galaxies in his eyes closed up and the empty blank buttons returned, 'I'm here, I'm talking to you. What else could I be but alive?'

'A ghost, an illusion?' The suggestion gave her chills just as they moved into a thicker part of the forest. The trees were taller here, with bulbous roots that perforated the clay before them, and the pale afternoon sky all but disappeared above.

'And you? Are you a ghost - are you an illusion?'

Lucy scoffed, but he was serious.

'What is the difference between your question and mine?'

'I'm flesh and blood. You can see I'm alive,' she said.

'I can see you. You can see me. What does blood have to do with it?'

Lucy started to explain, but the word 'everything' caught in her throat. She was wrong about something, but she couldn't place it. The undergrowth scratched her as they pushed through it. A thin, inconsequential scratch, but small red bubbles formed in a paper-thin streak along her forearm.

'Well, were you always like this? As far as you recall were you always a floating, semi-transparent bear?'

He shook his head, but she was not watching.

'If that's what you mean, no, but that's a rather depressing story. Another time.'

The champagne glare of the afternoon sun had been hidden beyond the canopy's emerald ceiling, but now the wind began to tumble the treetops, and allow sharp rays to cut through shifting gaps.

Momentarily blinded, Lucy stumbled sideways. It was hardly an incident. The wind eased quickly, and the sharp rays withdrew from the shadowy forest. She'd barely gone a few feet from the track. But it steered her attention toward a bulbous tree with vivid orange fruit hanging off it like Christmas baubles. It was alien to its surrounding oak-type neighbours, which made it even more obscure. When she got closer, stepping over the undergrowth in her way, she realised the disfigurement was partly due to the strangulation of a wooded vine.

'It gives me the heebie-jeebies,' called Bear, keeping a good distance.

Lucy stood at its base for a moment, transfixed in the shadow of its lumpy form.

'Some of this fruit,' she said bending down and Bear lost sight of her behind the shrubbery, 'it's been eaten, recently.'

'Often what happens to fruit, eaten by the wildlife, circle of life and what not,' Bear replied glancing around.

'No. Not wildlife. It looks like someone has peeled it.' She presented the curled rind and his sarcastic expression fell into one of alarm.

'It's still wet, juices…'

'Lucy come back this way,' Bear ordered anxiously.

'No, look, come here,' she ignored his growing concern. Reluctantly he floated over to her. It was instantly clear what had caught her curiosity. Between the mushrooms and wildflowers, two distinct lines, approximately a metre apart disappeared off into the forest, crushing the forest floor beneath it.

'A cart,' said Bear.

'A cart,' Lucy agreed.

The day was quickly turning into evening and the chorus of the night birds was beginning to stir as they made their way back west, following the cart. They followed the tracks against Bear's better judgment, but on the faith of Lucy's good feeling. It was about a half a mile before they saw where it led. They found themselves at a man-made clearing, forty or fifty square metres of forest had been cleared and the dirt upturned as though ready for seedlings. But the clearing was quite visibly an enclosure, divided into four pens. Wooden posts and wire surrounded the edge, and thicker wooden gates were used to divide the enclosure into quarters. It appeared new and unstable; a quick job. In the furthest pen from where they stood, about fifty or more shepherd deer, with their speckled mustard coats and enormous hooves, were crammed uncomfortably together.

They had stopped just shy of where the canopy opened-up, smart enough not to wander into the open moonlight. Before either of them could say anything, they heard voices coming from the other side of the enclosure, and slipped back somewhat behind the trees.

'It's always like this though, ain't it? I end up doing all the grunt work and you're all there carrying the rope…making up work to do so you don't have to help. Oh, the wheel needs fixing, does it? Wheel's perfectly fine. You just couldn't be bothered helping carry the load!'

The accent was distinctly identifiable, they were Archmonders, albeit likely from the Rolling Hills district and not the city. Lucy and Bear crept lower, and watched. Her vision was partly obscured by a fern, but she could clearly make out two stumpy male figures, one of them wheeling a cart. The deer riled up at their approach, grunting loudly and rearing back on hind legs.

'Illegal hunting,' Bear recognised the set-up, 'hasn't happened for years - or so we thought. Archmonders can't hunt in the forest, the castle and the Indawara have an understanding.'

'Looks like they're doing more than hunting, there must be sixty deer in that pen alone.'

'How have they herded them in there?' Bear asked, but rhetorically, 'we need to get in closer,' he eyed her sternly, 'but be *quiet*'.

They crept around the perimeter toward the furthest pen holding the deer. The shadow of night hid them, but the breeze had died completely. It was as still as death, and painfully quiet between the periodic calls of the night birds. But the men were muttering, arguing, as they prepped equipment pulled off the cart, and it was enough to muffle the sounds of the forest squishing and crunching beneath her feet. She stopped as they went quiet. The older and larger man stepped back a bit while the slender of the two raised an arrow.

'If you couldn't do this bit, I would've gotten rid of you a long time ago, so get it right.'

It wasn't an ordinary bow, it had been crafted to shoot five arrows at once, two of which were connected to a joint trigger.

'I always do,' grumbled the young man defensively. He had just finished loading the fifth arrow into place and was raising it up toward the pen. It was unclear just how this was to be used on multiple herds crammed together in a tight space. The arrows though, were also aimed right at Lucy, standing in the trees beyond the clearing. Instinctively, she flinched back alongside the nearest tree, and rustled the branches and leaves around her.

'Whoa, whoa, wait, you hear that?' said the older one. The lad changed his position and shot one arrow into the darkness. It hit the tree before her, she could smell the friction burn across its slender shaft.

'There's definitely something out there, and it hasn't moved again. Let's go,' he continued, bloodthirsty. The sharp sound then of a blade leaving its sheath.

She rushed a hand to her mouth. From this view looking down at her, Bear could see she was either going to run, and be shot running away, or sit here frozen, waiting for their knife. He watched them come nearer and could see it in them, hunters, with no limits about what and who they kill.

'They sent you to find their deer. This is their deer. This is the Indawara's deer,' Bear whispered beseechingly, his words racing.

Lucy's panicked breathing was audible, and leading the boy with the arrow nearer.

Bear pressed an ethereal paw upon her hand, sending shivers through her body, 'do something brave, you have to,' he begged. The night was fresh but hardly cold - yet a cold sweat was forming across her trembling hands.

'They'll kill me,' she spat out, forgetting herself.

'The Indawara will kill you,' Bear seethed through gritted teeth, 'right after you watch them eat your dog.'

Her whole body trembled now, brushing against the coarse bark of the jek-wood tree, while an intense heat started to bubble from somewhere deep inside her. Bear could see it happening. She shot up to confront the young man - just as he and his arrows sidelined her tree.

The young man was dumbstruck at the sight of her. He said nothing but stood back, eyeing her up and down with immense suspicion as his compatriot caught up.

'Oh, what's this!' the older man chortled, 'a girl! A bleaking girl!'

'An eastern girl,' corrected the younger one. The old man blinked with disbelief, and a sense of dysphoria came over him. He looked around.

'What the heck is an Easterner doing out here?' The question was directed at his co-hunter, not at Lucy, as though she were inanimate, or incapable of communication. He glanced around and his body language stiffened, he was on guard. But he regarded her once more; she was a mess. Muddy clothes, matted hair, her eyes were hidden by the shadows, but they looked swollen and tired.

'She ain't here with anybody,' he sneered menacingly.

'The deer,' muttered Lucy, 'let them go.'

'Aye?' the older man was puzzled and the younger one laughed, they both looked at each other with amused disbelief, already they were imagining retelling the story to chums at the tavern.

'That what brought you out here, rescuing deer? You some sort of 'deer girl' are you? These your deer, are they? Your little friends?' the younger one asked, laughing as he spoke.

'They're not my deer, but they're not yours, they belong to the Indawara,' Lucy said. She was still shaking but they couldn't see it in the dark.

'Oh, is that right?' The older man came near and put the knife gently against her neck, 'you belong to them as well?'

Lucy froze, her arms trembled violently. Knife pressed into her larynx he turned back to his friend, 'hey Elin, ever had an Eastern girl before?'

'Oh shit!' Elin cried. Bear had just come forward out of the shadows, illuminated by a faint purple hue.

'What the heck is that?' the older one cried jumping back.

'Wait… wait… I know that thing! I know that thing! I 'seen it before, with the wizards.'

Their eager expressions had turned to fearful revulsion.

'Bear, do something!' Lucy begged.

'It's Amoritai, I have no power,' he whispered quietly into her ear.

'You made fire before,' she hissed.

'Hardly magic.'

But he understood her point, that it could in the circumstances, be enough. He clapped the flint between his hands, letting the sparks fall to the floor and alight the leaf litter.

'I represent both His Majestic Eminence and His Imperial Lord,' Bear said as he moved forward through the flames, 'I know both of your families. I know where you both live. And I know that the castle will not take kindly to a hunting scheme which seeks to destabilise the unity between the Indawara and Archmond. So, before I materialise into that castle and have the army march into the Hills, I suggest you go home, and you make yourselves disappear.'

It was not for the men to know that he could not leave Lucy at this time. It was also not for the men to know that he in fact had no power, because as his purple hue moved through the glow of the burning earth below, he looked nothing short of demonic.

'You said this was authorised,' Elin snapped to the older one. The older man though, was still dumbstruck.

'Screw it Simon, I'm out,' said Elin. He threw the arrow to the ground and ran. In several moments, Simon ran after him. They left their empty cart and their equipment behind, and you could hear their speed increasing as they went.

Lucy and Bear stood in silence for several bedazzled moments, watching the debris burn before them.

'What do we do with the deer?' Bear posed jovially.

'Let them go,' she declared and walked out toward the enclosure. The Indawara only wanted to be able to hunt deer, she saw no need to serve them up.

They took the makeshift enclosure apart, tossing the loose posts in a pile by the tree, wrapping up the wire in case it had some use later. It transpired that the men had already killed one herd of deer that day, as they made the grim discovery of two carts full of carcasses, not far off from the pen.

A while later Lucy turned to Bear and asked, 'do you think what he said was true? That it was authorised?'

'Authorised? Hmm, authorised by who is the question. Certainly not by Soleman, but it does make me wonder,' Bear said cautiously.

'Wonder what?'

'Why some Hills folk are so desperate that they'd risk war with the Indawara.'

Bear looked down at her as she stopped again to catch her breath. She had dragged one of the overfilled carts at a painfully slow rate through the forest. His glow meant he was often the only thing visible around her, but she could hear everything else, and occasionally caught glimpses of things slithering along just beneath her feet. As she looked up, his light illuminated her puffy face. She was physically exhausted, but mentally alert, and on edge.

They'd left the other cart behind, merely because they had no possible way of transporting it. Bear had declined her request to teleport the carcasses directly to the campsite, claiming it was beyond his abilities even outside Amoritai. 'Besides,' he'd said, 'this way you get all the credit.'

But it had started to seem that whatever the influence of this religious observance, he could use his powers, if he really had to.

'Can I at least ask that you be sure to lead us back the right way?' she sighed, desperate.

'That,' he said grinning, the glimmer in his eyes somewhat menacing, 'that I can do.'

It was beginning dawn when they arrived back at the camp. It was the last day of Amoritai. The sentries were asleep at their post. The fires had died over the preceding hours. A smoky haze filled the camp through to its centre. Beyond the forest the sun had begun to cast itself, but in the confines of the leafy fortress their world remained devoid of colour.

Lucy parked the cart outside Chupner's tent, catching the side of it as her legs began to buckle. She hadn't noticed him at first, in the shadows of sleuth bushes that reached up around the entrance, creating both a camouflage and a shifting mural. The bushes were common throughout Archmond and beyond. Technically they were a weed. They had a network of thick central branches, from which hung spindly tendrils budded with leaves and tiny dark flowers. They were nature's curtains, blowing about in the wind. But he watched her from under their murky veil. He had heard her coming; heard her footsteps well before she crossed his sleeping sentries out at the camp's northern border. It was his pipe she saw, or rather the curl of its charcoal smoke that slithered out and across the slither of orange light marking the tent's opening. When she saw him it seemed impossible that she hadn't noticed him before, he was so imposing in stature.

He stepped forward and peered straight past her to the cart. His face was unreadable. His examination was intent, as he pushed his purple beige lips around the pipe again, inhaling gustily. Smoking tetra dried leaves was common among the Indawara. They elevated its consummation to a 'quasi-spiritual' rite. Contrarily back in Archmond the use of tetra was considered purely psychotropic and had been made illegal. Chupner's eyes were glazed as he stepped forward with odd gait, beyond the platform of his tent. He was exhausted, not intoxicated.

He was without his interpreter, so did not speak. Yet he appeared to listen intently as though he understood, while Lucy attempted to explain simply and slowly, with gestures and key words, the altercation she'd had. She mentioned hunters and suggested they'd been depleting the forest's wildlife at an unnatural rate. But if he understood he didn't show it. His expression was neither pleased nor displeased. He somewhat accepted the communication as though its triviality bored him, but he did examine with some intrigue the cart of carcasses behind her. When she was silent for some time he began to smirk, but it was only because he recognised the frustrated desperation on her face. Evidently it brought him some joy to see her so tired, so desperate.

He laughed to himself, a deep ricochet across his exposed brown belly, and leaned inside the tent calling out instructions in native Indawara tongue.

Several moments of shuffling led to a trio of young men emerging sleepily out from the tent. They were sluggishly rubbing their eyes and looking to Chupner with bland doe-eyed obedience, but their temperament became invigorated at the sight of all the deer. One of them made a joke at the other, the third laughed. The insulted one grabbed the joker's face and held it close-up to his, almost piercing the man's eyes with his own. Then he shouted something upbeat and shoved the man back. They all ran to the cart and began to examine the deer. The chatter between them was full of laughter, they shouted things back to Chupner. Without understanding the words, they were clearly given a liberty not usually allowed. The expression on their faces was one of cheek. It seemed that this good news was granting a temporary relaxation of protocol.

As they left with the cart, Lucy was left staring at Chupner, and he was staring back at her. He seemed glad now, but glad at what, that was not clear. He took a few more puffs of his pipe before he muttered in her language, 'your dog, you can see him tonight.'

Lucy blinked as some bangle-clad women, in fact the same bangle women from before, emerged to take her into their custody.

'You said if I…you said I could go if…you promised to give him back!'

Chupner was already inside his tent though, his figure was starting to disappear into the shadowy firelight. 'Tonight,' he called back, but his pronunciation confused things.

Against the clutches of the women's arms Lucy spun around, looking for Bear. She was glassy eyed and angry, but too bewildered to express it. She eventually saw him, dressed over the knoll of a branch of a small tree. He shook his head as he saw her, looked away, chuckled and commented, 'tribal folk are *so* unpredictable.'

Lucy's day progressed rather rapidly through a series of micro-sleeps. In the original tent she'd been held hostage, she was instructed to lie down and rest. But the sense of this experience was markedly different; it was obvious she was no longer a prisoner. But she was too weary to care. She woke from one of many short sleeps to find Crumbs nuzzled against her in the bed. Wearily she embraced him, but her joy was subsumed by overpowering exhaustion, and she rapidly fell back into sleep.

'Nooshi.' Now late into the evening, the ever-impartial interpreter encouraged her to finish her drink in local tongue. Lucy obliged.

After the initial hostility, the flattery she felt to now be on the reverse side, could almost compel her to do anything. They were at the feast they had kept her here for. The closing of Amoritai. Rows upon rows of tables, constructed from unevenly split trunks of various trees, extended into the end of firelight's boundary and beyond into mild darkness. The sun hadn't set but the forest fell into its own shadow long before the rest of the world did. Lucy was still somewhat distracted by the patchwork of colours across the sky. It was almost disconcerting; a ludicrous canvas of bright yolk and orange was blotched with technicolour pink and violet. It seemed less of a sunset and more of a hallucination. The sensation of which increased as she stared, head craned uncomfortably to the sky, the incessant unrelenting rhythm of the drums pulsing through her, shaping her heartbeat.

Chupner was on her table, or she was on his rather. Each table had at least twenty, but Chupner's had nearly thirty. There was a status of being among the leadership that escaped her in her ignorance and bewilderment. He'd kept her close enough to make eye contact with her. He wanted to take in every moment of shock that crossed her face. He hated foreigners. The culture of hatred for the east and the west that permeated the tribe, trickled down from his own desire to unify them in solidarity against the outsiders. But despite this hatred he maintained a fascination with the outside, and he delighted in tricking and deceiving those he considered were inferior to his people, which was everyone.

He had waited anxiously as Lucy was brought out to the feast, enjoying the drop in her expression as she realised that she was not a prisoner but a guest. She was about to enjoy a privilege most will never know. That was his own perspective. But truly the feast that observed the end of this subservient spiritual festival was a unique experience most all outside the tribe would never know. Throughout the day he had deliberately encouraged her misunderstanding, to indulge her fear and worry, only to have it wiped away in this dramatic display of bountifulness. She had not been restrained in the tent, but two men outside ensured she was not to leave. She had been offered a shower and food but had been treated with hostility. But after the true nature of the situation dawned on her properly, she began to relax. As she relaxed more and more, and her pensive guard came down, Chupner found himself bored.

The feast was not its finest in history, but they had roasted and smoked the deer carcasses they'd obtained at her intervention, having dragged over the remainder from where the makeshift pen had been. The sweet smoky smell of the game, roasting for hours, hovered over the chattering crowd like a haze. The litany of torches, decorative only for the evening light, though thin, remained, and cast a mood that was both reverent and energetic at once. The amount of food was in excess of what the tribe could possibly consume tonight, but that was the point. From the meat to the grain, to the bowls of concoctions, to their various forms of moonshine; it was symbolic. Swings and roundabouts. The days of fasting had been burdensome, the days of indulgence would be overbearing.

'You remind her of a small baby kitsha,' said the interpreter for one of the bangle women who had muttered an indecipherable phrase at Lucy and was staring at her intently. It was a stare without malice, but with no offer of friendship.

'What is a *kitsha*?' Lucy asked.

'Tweet tweet,' the lady linked her thumbs together and made flapping wings of her palms. A type of bird.

'With your hair and your face - like a kitsha,' the interpreter added, grinning. As dusk drifted off rapidly, the warm light from the torches between the tables began to burn through the interpreter's auburn hair.

The bangle women were to the right of her, laughing and sneering and snatching things from each other's bowls. They grabbed at each other's wrists and made pig noises in mockery of themselves. They had a rough, brutish sort of comradeship with each other. They were young, perhaps early twenties. The prettiest one with long brown hair scattered with braids and tiny orange leaves, had been the one who made the remark about the kitsha - much to the amusement of the others. She had an even-brown complexion, high cheek bones and dark eyes, was taller and more slender than the other two, but just as muscular. Well rounded arms and thighs were symbols of feminine beauty in the Indawara, and the impression, largely, was that these young women were at the very least, examples of what was to be aspired to. Their relationship to Chupner was unclear; daughters, relatives, servants or lovers all seemed possible.

'Kitsha *tasty*,' the pretty one said now, while eyeing Lucy and licking her lips. Lucy froze uncomfortably and the girl beside the pretty one hit her head and they let out with raucous laughter.

'Nobody eats kitsha,' the interpreter said dryly, grinning at the girls, who were now squabbling over the last piece of bone meat before them.

Lucy looked down; Crumbs had fallen asleep on her lap. A tiny furry ball of warmth. Beautiful to look at, but causing her thighs to sweat, and making it difficult to move. But a tremendous relief was still pulsating through her at knowing he was safe again. If there was one creature she should protect in either world, it must be him.

While the bangle girls continued their indecipherable, but in any case exclusive, banter, Chupner incrementally began to question Lucy about where she was going and why. But as she explained or conveyed what little she knew, he grew skeptical of her responses and then ultimately uninterested. He considered her remarks were either lies she was telling, or lies told to her now repeated. He asked (through the interpreter) questions about Trimany, and Que and whether their armies were coming to help her. More specifically, he asked whether the armies would come through his forest. But she didn't know anything about these cities, which concerned him. He asked her about her preparations for the frozen world and again she had no real answer for him, again claiming she didn't know.

'Honu, honu!' The shorter of the bangle girls, with jet-black hair cut short around her face, called out as Chupner grew frustrated. *She has a map.*

The attractive girl grunted in irritation and clambered onto the table on her knees over to Lucy, leaning past and snatching the backpack.

'Hey!' Lucy cried out but Chupner held up a flat hand instructing her to remain at ease. Chupner pulled out the map from her backpack and spread it across the flatter part of the log table. He gave her an expression of paternal disappointment that simultaneously beckoned her over to him. She'd barely had an opportunity to look it over since she bought it from the blind man's shop. But it was obvious now she clearly should have. Chupner showed her what he called the frozen world, some distance beyond the forest where the trees thinned, and the Alexandria Plateau after that. He pointed to Trimany and Que, and then moved his finger haphazardly across the remainder to the far edges of it. Then he slumped back into his seat and stared up at her condescendingly. It was clear he had no intention of giving her a lesson in geography; the lesson was that she was stupidly unprepared and should have already learnt all this herself.

Lucy understood though. After his look wore thin, she took the map back to her seat. The interpreter was chatting with someone at a nearby table and Lucy waited a moment for her attention to return. The eyes of the girls and others remained upon her while Chupner returned to his food.

'Will you ask if I can retire now? And if I can go in the morning?'

The woman snappily repeated the question, eager to return to her other conversation. Chupner laughed, threw a hand in the air and made several remarks that had his half of the table erupting with laughter.

'He says of course, sleep, then go,' the interpreter replied eventually when she'd stopped laughing, but it was clear he'd said more than that.

Some men, two of them, led the trio (Crumbs, Lucy, and her mystical counterpart) to the edge of the forest border. She'd never seen them before, they were thin, old and lower ranked with patchy beards. They had roused her early, while the campsite was still asleep and the air was still thick with a slightly cool morning mist. The bangle women she would never see again. The interpreter was not with the men, and their communication was poor, so she could only assume why they had been sent, and follow along blindly.

They'd walked in silence the entire way, the forest floor crunching as they marched, and the long-tailed kitshas cutting through the stillness with their occasional shrill coo. It had been a couple of hours. The mist had lifted, and the sunlight was blinding in the pockets where it fell, warm even. The forest was already starting to thin. Chupner's Forest was not as large as myth held it to be. It was fairly narrow on its east-west front, but stretched extensively north-south; a green wall separating Archmond from the rest of existence.

'I don't know what the marker is they're looking for, but they'll leave us soon,' called Bear from high above. It was the first time he'd spoken. The frail shirtless men looked up momentarily in response, but carried on as they were without trying to understand.

'Why do you say that?' Lucy said after some delay.

'The forest is thinning, can't you see? We're nearly at its edge. But there's obviously something they're looking for.'

A half hour passed, and Lucy's fidgeting reached a climax before she stopped abruptly and retrieved the map from her backpack. The elder men, her guides effectively, stopped and watched her without expression as she studied the map. Lucy spoke but she was not addressing them, as they well knew.

'If we are almost at the forest edge, then the nearest town or city is what, at least two days walk from here - or from there, where the forest ends?'

'Ahhh, yes, about that,' Bear agreed, but he was lying. It was much, much further. Her cartography skills left much to be desired. Lucy rolled the map in her hands and nodded at the men; they continued on. Several minutes later they crossed a struggling stream. A trickle skipped across the debris and stones in the centre of the mud crevice where the river once ran, like a tap not fully turned off. The guides started mumbling in native tongue.

'Esta, esta!' they were talking to her now, demanding attention. They were pointing upwards. The forest was thinning, and Bear was right, it had been gradually thinning for some time, to the point where now it hardly seemed a forest but a parkland of dispersed wilderness. They pointed to a patch of small trees to the right, that fell into the light of the mid-morning sun. The halo of sunshine was not the only thing that illuminated this group of wiry lacklustre branches; a group of eagles, with bright golden feathers, hopped around squawking at each other. Lucy looked back to the guides who were standing still, observing the eagles with a certain reverence.

'Esta,' said one when he saw she was watching him, but then they began to shift themselves. They were preparing to leave her. This was the place.

'What's going on?' Lucy asked, futilely.

'I told you they were looking for a sign of the end,' said Bear. Lucy ignored him, went over to them, and tried to ask them questions with hand gestures. It only seemed to alarm them, and they were quick to brush her away. *Esta.*

'Wait,' she asked, and then to Bear, 'tell them to wait.'

Bear muttered something to them in less than a breath, and they stopped momentarily and became transfixed with him.

'The nearest town is days away, what am I supposed to do for food?'

Bear gave an expression like he understood the seriousness, but of course he could not genuinely empathise with the need for food.

'Some of the trees, they are winter bloomers, they have fruit even in the colder parts, there will be some fruit if you can…or I can help you find it.'

The Indawara guides were muttering amongst themselves, formulating a way back. Lucy's stare at Bear after the fruit comment was almost palpable, but it was a look of completely innocent desperation. She had nothing to fall back on, and the promises that were given to her continued to prove false. Crumbs perked up noisily with excitement. He was suddenly full of energy, and was chasing after a forest rodent that had disappeared into the leaf litter by some tree-roots to the right of them. She lost herself for several moments taking in his gaiety before she realised a spear had been placed at her feet. Lucy looked up wanting to ridicule the absurdity of this offer through some very clever comment, but the guides were already disappearing into the distance.

'Are you any good at hunting?' Bear half suggested jovially, 'surely you could kill something with that?'

'Wait!' she called but they didn't turn, and they didn't stop. She heard the crunching beneath their feet continue after their frail figures became obscured by branches and undergrowth. She looked down at the spear, its rusted tip. A kind, but useless gesture. She hadn't the skill, nor the nerve, to kill another living thing.

I'm going to die out here, she thought grimly, casting another suspicious glance at Bear.

'There's a village,' as if reading her thoughts he chimed in with this added bit of knowledge, 'I don't know exactly where in the frozen landscape but it's less than a day…'

In fact Bear had not heard of anyone visiting or coming across the village in decades - this primitive little snow town. But it was still true that he knew of its existence. Yerkey, it was called.

Lucy eyed him dubiously, but the relief was all over her posture which was instantly and dramatically less hostile, 'a village? Are they friendly?'

'Oh, yes. Yes, very friendly. Neutral to all conflict. They love foreign visitors. Don't get many, but I hear good things.'

Chapter 7

An icy reflection

The land inclined steadily at the forest's edge. Shortly after they passed the eagle tree where the guides left them, its traction began to change, and so did their landscape. The trees became sparse and the undergrowth of ferns and forest litter gave way to a carpet of pale teal grass. This pale grassy ground was stony, and the incline was scattered with jagged grey boulders. Initially the gradient was exhausting. For nearly the entire first hour she hadn't the breath to speak her spiralling worries. It hadn't truly dawned on her when she left Archmond Castle, it was an abstract parcel in her mind, how am I going to manage in this strange world? How will I know where I'm going? Where am I going to sleep? How will I eat, bathe, drink?

But the gravity of those practical concerns had been kept at bay by the likes of Pepper and the busy, somewhat bountiful world of Archmond, where even in the derelict and sick villages of the forgotten hillsides there seemed to be help at every turn. The hostility of the Indawara was one wake up call. But now she was completely alone, and the gravity of those basic human needs was starting to bear down on her heavily. The weather was changing too. There was a rapid flux of cold air rushing swiftly down the hillside to meet them, almost visible as this hazy change of composition in the air. Lucy adjusted the deer skin draped around her neck, with the uphill exertion it was too warm to properly wear it. It was heavy to carry but the map alone told her she should be grateful to have it. The guides had given it to her at the start of their journey, but like everything that came from the Indawara it was really a gesture from Chupner. He had mocked her ignorance for going into the icy wilderness, almost delighted in it, as it proved what he suspected, being that all foreigners were inferior. But the coat was a gesture of goodwill, a recognition that she had, in fact, come in peace, and had in fact been the answer to their ill-fated Amoritai.

'So where should I start looking for this princess?' Lucy asked, once the gradient levelled out long enough for her to catch her breath. The air was starting to form a film of mist between the speckled trees up ahead.

'Anywhere and everywhere?' Bear shrugged, and then added with a tone that mocked their entire expedition, 'have you looked behind that rock?'

Lucy didn't respond. Several possible remarks of frustration passed through her mind, but she said nothing. Bear watched her, waiting for the response, but said nothing else to appease her. He reacted seriously to nothing; it was his nature. But it was no indication of how he felt. He had a deep connection with this mission. The desire to see the child-queen dethroned and the 'proper' sister accede was something he felt very strongly about. Actually, it was the only thing, that kept his clocks going. But he'd also had a hand in Lucy being the person brought forward for it. The decision was never up to him, but he had good reason to be consulted. They'd shown him the signs and the markings, the formulas and pathways, that had led them right to the village of Lockerby and the girl in the old manor. He ignored the methodology, but he channeled her and studied her intently. He told them he saw things in her, hidden things, but powerful things. They thanked him for his input and discharged him. He was to find out the outcome when everyone else did. And so, he did. Now she was here. Suffering this wilderness and on the crest of even more daunt-ingly alien landscapes ahead. He accepted responsibility for that, but it was a brash acceptance that moved quickly away from the guilt her puppy-blue eyes stirred up, and back to the necessity of the mission.

It was surprising how suddenly the air chilled, and how power-ful this stream of cold air poured down on them like a waterfall from up ahead. But the exertion meant the heavy deer skin coat was still too warm to wear. The gradient had eased, but there was still a gradient. Lucy didn't fail to appreciate, although half-heartedly, the fading intensity of the landscape. The sky was overcast. The grasses, the bushes, the flimsy clover that traced up the grey stony outcrops speckled across these seemingly endless hillsides, they were all paled of colour. To a girl from Scotland it was familiar, but it was a world apart from the vibrancy of Chupner's Forest. It was further still from the almost daunting displays of colour and extravagance throughout Archmond's WFB.

Lucy brushed her tongue against her teeth. The taste in her mouth was starting to sour further. She'd been able to bathe, again as this world rather seemed to force upon her, under the supervision of other women, the night of the feast. But she hadn't been able to brush her teeth, even in a makeshift way, since before she left the castle. The meaty metallic flavours in her mouth were starting to become normal.

'So you have no serious advice to give me then, about this bizarre task I'm to accomplish?' she asked rather timidly when they had been silent for far too long. Internally Bear sighed, he looked at her, realising the cold air had brought its own onset of moisture. It was starting to condense as they escalated, and heavenly ethereal beads of condensation were settling along the length of her thick plait of blackish brown hair. They also rested majestically on her eyelashes, beneath which these big blue lakes beckoned at him. An image he almost couldn't bear. He had no sense of attraction to other entities. But he saw within creatures, what was not yet. And when Lucy's eyes examined him it chilled him to see what was not yet - about her. But of course, now he was compelled to answer.

'No one knows where she is,' he muttered eventually, turning away.

Lucy tried to decipher a direction ahead, they were not in a fog, but the air was thickening nearly to that point. In the distance the shapes of the pines were only just made out. That is if they were in fact pine trees; the precise identity of the shapes could not be certain, like figures in the dark.

'Or *if she is*, as I understand,' she said, 'what if she is dead? How do we know?'

'Well part of the parcel is to find out,' Bear answered.

'And then? If she is dead? This is all for nothing?' Lucy swept away the spindly grass in front of her with the spear, which she'd taken to use as a kind of walking aid. Ahead, Crumbs' cocoa figure bounded in and out of long blanched spires. Between the cold grey rocks jutting out from the earth, thin and whispery lime creepers connected some of the stones like cobwebs.

Bear watched Lucy's expression, he somehow had this pride as it changed from curiosity to interrogation. It was as if every shift in mood was something he could pin to a personal growth in her, wielded at his hand.

'No, no, no. Lucy, if Cherry is dead, then we find someone else.'

Lucy pondered on this for several moments. 'You mean *I find* someone else?'

'No,' he felt suddenly short-tempered with her ignorance though he knew it was not her fault at all, 'if it transpires that Cherry Winters no longer remains a suitable candidate then I'm sure the relevant councils will reconvene and decide on a... look I'm not sure. Probably a relative.'

'Soleman and Ronald?'

'No...' he sighed. 'Not Soleman and Ronald.'

Lucy's walking seemed to slow as she felt a new sensation of scepticism. It wasn't simply that the gravity of her situation hadn't quite dawned on her, it was starting to seem apparent that the complete picture of her situation had been deliberately withheld. Bear sensed her slowing down.

'You, being here, is through the tenets of their wizardry, for the fulfilment of this prophecy but…this issue of who rules that island goes further than Archmond and its trade wars. Meta Emery exists as a de-facto central governing power. No one would be able to usurp the current Queen without full support of the other powerful cities.'

'Other powerful cities?' Lucy furrowed as she swept the spear through the grasses.

'Ahhh…well, I mean there's no easy answer to that, the power shifts often so…' he looked at her unimpressed face and answered, 'okay, for starters, Que, Mazouri, Trimany, Gemini.'

Crumbs began to bark around them, chasing a large dragonfly shaped insect. Aside from his yapping, the world was grey, lifeless, still.

Silence. There wasn't even a breeze to toss about the yellow-green grass. It made their conversation seem outlandishly overt and on display. Suddenly the edges of their surroundings, the outcrops and smaller trees that blended into the mist, seemed like the boundaries of a stage.

'Do *you* think she is alive? This princess? When was the last time anyone heard from her?' With every step the grass crunched beneath her feet, small stones shifted and rolled behind her several paces.

Bear hesitated some, he didn't want to go against the common line but what was the point of being obscure? The girl was here. She wasn't going anywhere. It was easier for both of them, if he helped lift this mist of misinformation that she had been fed by the troubled, nay *corrupted*, politicians of the west.

'No, I don't. The last time anyone heard about her or anything from her was over a decade ago. More maybe.'

Lucy stopped. She sighed. The foreground seemed to go on forever in perpetuity. Yellow grass, grey stones, and these small flimsy paperbark trees and shadowy pines, all eventually disappearing into the thickening mist. She was about to throw down the spear in protest, but it was evident she understood she had to keep going in any event.

'One way, or another, things will all play out. You'll see. It just might not be as simple as they all think back on the Wooden Floor Borders.'

As they reached the point where the gradient levelled out completely, and they moved along flat frosty ground, Lucy felt that her sudden onset of scepticism had morphed into a general feeling of foreboding. But it was not general at all. It was something above and beyond this practical uncertainty of where they would sleep and how she would eat; there was a very real feeling that was creeping into her veins connected to this place they had now become immersed in.

'Where are we exactly?'

Bear was above, to her left, but almost obstructively high. The air started to shroud his figure and Lucy beckoned him lower. They brushed past a crop of lemony grass bushes. Bear was uncertain and nonchalant about it. 'Somewhere between Chupner's Forest and the Alexandria Plateau?'

'But the air…' Lucy said, gesturing, 'we must be close… This frozen area? That's before the plateau?'

'I don't know it well,' Bear admitted, 'I have to say there's a lot I don't know about it. Least of all where it starts and stops.'

As they went on, the foreboding feeling in Lucy's head started turning. Her mind was wandering, somewhat artificially, to thoughts of home. She glanced around imperceptibly trying to gauge what about this landscape had sent her mind suddenly back to Lockerby. There was nothing. But she wondered if that was it. Whether this blank canvass of nothingness, devoid of any distraction, was all her mind needed to go back. There were one or two thoughts that popped into her head: Scotland, her crooked fence. Then it snowballed, and she started remembering all the things she had left behind; the town, the school, the parks…her mother. A bombardment of things, trivial and significant, good and bad; the turnovers at Mrs. Bates' bakery, the rusted bike racks outside the school, the men playing football on Tuesdays at the park, the view of the winter sunset from the hill at the end of the park.

Then at a rapid rate her thoughts started to go beyond Lockerby itself, and into the past. She felt strands of a memory come back, piece by piece. Her mother; the smell of her perfume. Jasmine was it? Jasmine and vanilla. She could almost smell it now, as though it was wafting off the bowing teal branches of the pines. Then the ludicrous checkered grey and purple gloves her mother had worn in the winter for years, before she'd left them somewhere never to be found again. Why did she always wear those gloves? They didn't match anything else she ever wore. She would grab them from the side table in the hallway, throw her strawberry blonde hair in a bun, cover it with the woolly black hat, and call to Lucy to get the coats and the pram.

Pram? Thought Lucy, stifled for a moment.

'What's wrong?' asked Bear quizzically

'Nothing,' Lucy said, 'let's just keep going. I'm hungry.'

But these visions of home persisted. They didn't let up. In fact, as they continued through this grassy wilderness Lucy started to feel as though this memory took on a life of its own, as if it were seeking her out, haunting her. As the hour stretched on and she watched Crumbs, bounding ahead still, her mind was back in the hallway, and she couldn't understand why. It was an innocuous sequence of events. Getting ready to leave in the colder months. The keys, the coats, the gloves, boots from the vestibule. But it was a particular memory of this being replayed to her. Again and again. This same vision was repeating itself over and over, her mother with the stupid gloves and the awful hat, Lucy seeing herself turn away from the milky light beyond the front door, walking down the dank hallway to get the coats. Then nothing. Then repeat.

'What can we eat, Bear? I'm starting to feel faint,' she asked as she noticed the frost on the ground thickening. They weren't going any higher. They were on flat ground, but the wintery climate was intensifying. Bear calculated it had been nearly a half day since they had left their guides, or rather their guides had left them, on the fringes of Chupner's Forest. Now that she asked, he wondered how she had gone so long already. She'd had a small canister of water they'd either given her or she'd picked up from somewhere, but she'd drunken it already. They'd barely stopped since dawn.

'I'll start looking out for signs of water. There's a very good chance that there's a stream or a river somewhere nearby looking at all these 'kespies'.' Lucy reasoned that the 'kespies', were probably the transluscent, stick-like insects buzzing around above their heads. She felt too lazy to check whether water meant there would also be a source of food, and so just hoped that's what he'd meant.

As they went on, and Bear muttered as he steered their traction toward where he thought this water source might lie, she was back in the hallway again. It was starting to visibly irritate her, and she didn't want to share what was going on inside her head. But she had to resolve it. So she stopped dismissing the memory, and instead she closed her eyes and let herself fall into it. Why was this insignificant moment replaying itself?

There she was, turning away from the milky light beyond the front door, down the musty hallway to the coatroom behind the staircase. Her mother had three coats she wore intermittently, an elegant black coat, a grey coat that was in season a decade ago, and a puffy red one. It was snowing outside, the puffy one was the warmest. She grabbed her own coat; also puffy but green. She threw the coats over the pram parked beside the coatroom, (she couldn't understand now looking back at it, what the pram was for, she didn't have any siblings) and pushed it back toward the door…

'Ahhh. Yes, there. Sort of a bit of a track there, and it's getting damper. The air is wetter, I think. It seems wetter to me anyway. So it must be that way,' Bear's smoothly aristocratic voice broke the vision and yanked her violently back to the present. Her eyes fluttered open to see Crumbs staring up at her somewhat desperately. Their eyes lingered on each other for several moments before he broke away to lick at the frost.

'Did you, did you hear me? You feeling that dizzy, are you? Come on - this way and we'll be sorted.'

She didn't dare comment on it, but she noticed he was becoming less sarcastic. Maybe even growing concerned for her.

To the left of their path, Bear led them to a slender parting of grass and rocks between the trees. It sloped only ever so slightly downward. There was somehow less frost and the pines thickened as though they were entering a plantation. The soil covered ground beneath their feet, littered with pine needles, was a pale grey. It could be relativity, Lucy realised, but this new place was almost completely devoid of life and colour. Without trying this time, the memory came back and finished itself.

She threw the coats over the pram parked beside the coatroom, she turned it around and pushed it down the hallway, but as the front entrance came into view her mother was gone. Lucy pushed the pram and the coats into the vestibule, looking out onto the front yard, but mother wasn't there either. She left the coats on the pram and went back inside to find her mother in the dining room.

She had tears streaming down her face. She was taking off her gloves.

'What's…'

'We can't go to shops now we've left it too late. It's too late now. Go on and put the coats back away will you,' her mother said sternly but softly.

'I thought we had to pick up…'

'No. No. We can't go now. Just look at the time. Four thirty it is, nearly, and I've not done a thing, and your father will be home soon, and I've not done a thing. You just go put those coats away and we'll… I don't know, we'll have to make do.'

Lucy's memory of the moment was that she was just as confused about it then as she was now. But then something odd happened. Almost in the same instant as Bear's announcement, 'and there it is, water, source of life,' brought her back to him and this grey world, there was the sound of her mother's voice almost echoing through the trees, *and go get your sister out of the car will you*.

'Sister?' Lucy bawled confused. Just then a shadow, like that from an enormous prehistoric bird, caught her eye, disappearing between the middle of the trees ahead.

'Sister?' Bear repeated, staring at her intently.

Lucy looked at him. But her mother's voice, the shadow and the memory, was all a bit disorientating.

'Oh, I don't know. I'm hungry,' she said, and then saw the river just ahead.

Bear started the fire, and they used long sticks to hold the bulbous white fern roots above the tips of the yellow flames, waiting for them to soften and become edible. They grew in the aqueous soil along the banks of the stream, so if they followed it Bear said, they would find more. Lucy pulled her stick from the fire, prodding the white root with a rectangular stone.

'It's got a while to go yet,' Bear said as he watched her. He was causing two more to levitate, but only on the condition that she hold one in herself.

'It's as much work for me to do this as it is for you to hold them. More pertinently I wasn't made as some sort of spiritual servant. Don't be foolish enough to think I was sent on some mission to help you. It was suggested I come along but I'm here of my own accord. Not to be taken as some navigator turned chef,' he had said to her tangentially.

'My arm's sore,' she forged the stick into the ground at an angle trying to lean it into the flames, but it kept falling into the dirt and she eventually gave up. 'I'm getting some water.'

My telekinesis is sore, Bear thought irritably as she crept down the bank, but kept a neutral expression.

Lucy pushed her palm against the boulder, steadying her weight against the loose damp soil that crumbled away at her pressure. She was reluctant to get her shoes or feet wet, but there were a group of flat rocks to her right that jutted out over the river. She ascended them carefully, the water canister dangling from a rope on her wrist, and made her way to the edge. The river bent and turned away just after that point, disappearing behind the misty barrage of teal pines. It was thickest here, almost deep enough to swim in, and while the silvery water picked up a pace as it skipped around the bend, the patch beneath the rocks was as still as glass. With the overcast sky behind her the reflection created a cool metallic surface; a mirror. It was the first image of herself she'd seen in days.

It threw her, this almost unfamiliar image; a squinty-eyed girl with flushed features and ghostly skin. She felt she looked stranger than she ever had. As though her eyes and lips had a uniqueness that was unpalatably alien. It never occurred to her that this might be the result of contrast, given the people she'd been surrounding herself with were all of a makeup very different to her own. Nor did it register in that moment, that there hadn't been a time in her life since infancy, where she'd gone days without seeing her reflection. In any event the image disturbed her, and she drove the canister into the centre of it, letting it soak up the water and pulling it out again. She drank thirstily and refilled it. But this second time, as her image on the rippled surface of the water started to reform, it was animated. It wasn't her reflection. But it was her. Or it was her image, just as she was now, but it wasn't *her.* There she was sat up upon these rocks, leaning over the glassy water but not looking down into it, crying into her hands…*its hands?*

Lucy jumped back, the canister spilled open and water ran over the rock dripping back down into the stream. She put her hand on her chest and caught herself, caught her thoughts. She was tired. It had been an extremely taxing few days. She had been through extreme circumstances. Now this wilderness and these memories were upsetting her and distorting her reality…Taking in the sound of the distant rushing water she took three deep breaths. Carefully and slowly, she braced herself, leaning over again, so she could show herself it wasn't real. But horrifically this girl, this *her*, was still there. Sobbing uncontrollably into her hands. Lucy stared transfixed. If the canister wasn't attached to her wrist it would have fallen in and floated away. She could hear the girl crying. Or hear *herself crying*? Then the hands came away from the face, and she looked at Lucy, or Lucy looked at herself. Her sodden eyes were of a sadness she'd never seen before - a despair of disbelief, of a grief unwilling to be truly accepted.

'You didn't help her,' the reflection sobbed softly, with a tone of self-pity, 'help me.'

Lucy jumped back. 'Bear! Bear! Bear!' she shrieked, each one louder than the last. Crumbs came bounding over, and Bear appeared alongside her.

'What? What is it?' he couldn't see a thing wrong. She was leaning backwards, pressed up by her elbows, her eyes fixated on the edge of the rock. He glanced around.

'What? What? What?' he demanded. He floated over to the edge.

'My reflection, is it still there?' she said, her eyes not moving.

He didn't quite understand the question. 'Ahhhh, I can see my reflection, because I'm over the water.'

Crumbs had arrived on the scene, he licked Lucy's shoulder and then went over to the edge himself to investigate. 'And now Crumbs can see his reflection because he's above the water…' Bear remarked condescendingly.

'My reflection… it wasn't me.'

'You've probably just had a bit of a - '

'No. It was me, but it was moving on its own, crying. It spoke to me.'

Bear's attitude became more serious. 'What did it say?'

'She asked me to help her.'

Bear's eyes darted around. Along the other side of the silver water he could still see the riverbank, and several rows of trees, before they became somewhat shrouded. They were alone. For now. But he was starting to think the stories they told of this place in rural Archmond might be true.

'It was probably just the way the water rippled, probably made it look like you were crying, it's very odd water.'

'How odd, Bear? I saw my own image, with my hands covering my face, while I used my hands to lean against this rock - is it that kind of odd?'

'Let's get back to the fire and warm up. It's too cold by the stream. Look, you silly girl, you still didn't even get any water.'

After that, they sat in silence while Lucy and Crumbs ate the roasted roots. Morsels of flavourlessness, apart from the faint after-taste of onion. A breeze picked up, a merciful break to the silence, the soft sounds of rustling near and far. It tossed tiny fragments of dead litter into the flames, some of them highly flammable, they burst and crackled.

'I can smell vanilla,' Lucy said after a time, 'I keep smelling it. Is there something that grows around here…?'

Bear thought on it. He thought about the wispy white florets that grew near the water's edge, of the solitary purple flowers at the base of the pines, but he couldn't think of anything with a fragrance. Lucy looked toward the stream, waiting for the odd food to digest, aware they should probably get moving soon but reluctant to do so.

Then like an apparition, like a ghost, she saw her mother stroll out from between the trees. A mouthful of the half chewed roots fell out of her mouth in shock. Whether it was a hallucination or not she couldn't tell. But there she was, by the edge of the river, her autumnal dress being blown about by a non-existent gale. She was looking around, apprising the location. It was as though she'd either lost an earring, or was checking the earth for an appropriate spot to sit. This was made difficult as she struggled to keep her honey locks from her eyes, staggering delicately in this micro gust that surrounded only her. She pushed her hair back with a hand and held it atop her head. Then her clear smooth face was revealed, and her green eyes met Lucy's. She began waving ecstatically, beckoning her over. This was most certainly her mother, but from many years ago. She was fresher, trimmer, radiant. It came back to her then, that they often had picnics by the river. There was a park not too far away with a creek and a playground.

The world started to warm up, the air around her dried out. It was early in autumn. The leaves on the hazel trees hadn't started to turn, in fact everything was still beaming with the thick green fullness of summer. The water in the river was pretty and blue. The sky was plumped full of voluptuous cumulus clouds. The open grass area stretched out before the playground she was so eager to conquer. She was not too old for play equipment, but old enough to navigate it a bit too easily.

'Lucy, honey, do you want to get the plates out? Then we can have some lemon cake.'

Lucy crawled across the pink blanket to the bag with all the things for the picnic. The sight of the straw picnic bag itself delighted her. It meant cake, it meant juice, it meant they were going somewhere. How many plates? Three. But they didn't need one for daddy. He was at work. He never came to picnics. Lucy counted them out. One for mummy, one for her, one for...? But of course! The third plate was for *Amber*. Amber...She turned around then and even in this haze of a memory it hit her like a thump to the head. A strawberry blonde lump of a girl, not older than two, was just crawling into her mother's arms. Amber the noise maker. Amber the terror. Amber her adorably annoying little sister. And this picnic was for the three of them. Lucy felt her stomach churn, Amber had been swept out of her life, and then out of her thoughts, and then out of her memories… until now. Why?

'What's wrong Lucy?' her mother said with a laugh, her brow furrowing as she tried to control the child's ascent up her torso, prying the little hands from the earrings they tugged on. But Lucy's stare continued to be one of disbelief, and the concern on her mother's face grew more genuine. Then from behind her mother and sister a gust of powdery white snow, threw the scene into disarray. The force of the cold blast, its trajectory into her face…she shut her eyes and turned away.

When she opened them again she could see the crackling fire, the mouthful of chewed roots in the soil, and Crumbs licking himself beside her.

'Where have you been?' remarked Bear, casually. Across the river, Lucy saw another shadow rush through the trees. This one was long and thin but black as night. The tiny soft hairs on her arms stood up.

'What?'

'I saw a shadow, actually it's the second one, high up,' she said, and pointed toward the trees, 'what…what is…that?'

The shadow had receded as instantly as it appeared and Bear couldn't see anything, but his expression became grave.

'Have you been having any, umm, bad memories just now?'

'Bad memories? No.'

Bear looked around, he floated above the fire and cast a paw over it, turning it to smoky ashes, 'we should get going.'

'Why? What's wrong?'

'Are you sure you haven't had any bad memories, what was that all about you going stone cold for several moments just then? And what about by the river?'

'That wasn't a memory, it was an image of me now, and I thought you said I was probably seeing ripples?'

'And just now, a moment ago?'

'Well it was a memory, but not a bad one, just a picnic I had with my mother.'

'Pack up your things.'

Lucy did as instructed, and called to Crumbs and they hurried off away from the river's edge.

'But why, what's that…'

'Sometimes good memories can be bad if they're connected to something now lost. Bittersweet,' he muttered seemingly to himself

'Why are you asking about memories? Why am I suddenly having these memories? They've come from nowhere.'

Bear was turning around anxiously as they hurried along. One of the shadows flashed away in the periphery of his vision. He could tell Lucy did not see it, and he chose not to mention it.

'There are rumours about this place, I remember now. This wilderness separating the frozen world from the forest. They say it brings up bad memories but…' he hesitated to go on.

'I'm just having memories but they're stupid, confusing. Not… *bad*. What are the shadows?'

They came to where they had been before they segued down to the river. Bear indicated the direction they should go, to keep them as much in the open as possible.

'Apparently,' he felt unsure of what he was about to say, 'the shadows feed off bad memories. They search for them in you, they bring them out of you. It's some sort of vice for them.'

'But what are they?'

'I don't,' he began and then looked at her plainly, 'I honestly don't know. I've just heard of people seeing them, and the memories, and I've heard of people…you know what never mind.'

'Tell me,' she said. She was a bit breathless. They were walking at such a pace, the heavy fur kept slipping off her shoulders.

'Are you sure your memories weren't bad?' Bear insisted. To his left he'd seen another shadow. That made four now, including the two Lucy mentioned. Four was too many. From what he'd heard of these entities, they were drawn to the dark thoughts people had, they thrived off the torment they carried within. In theory the shadows were single objects, scattered across the wilderness. He'd heard stories about corrupted convicts on the run from their guilt seeing two or three over the day, running back the way they'd come. In several hours they'd exceeded that tally. And there was nothing positive about the electricity he felt stir in the icy air around them.

'Or are they connected to something that disturbs you?'

It was that last phrase that made the penny drop. There of course *was* a connection. That connection was the existence of her younger sister.

They hurried along the rugged earth as it started again to incline. They hurried without running, a sort of organised chaos, driven by unrealised fears. It was haphazard and inefficient. Their step became clumsy as Bear in a hidden panic kept changing the direction. The mist had thickened, and direction could not be determined by visual markers. It had to be based on trajectory alone. But with their past trajectory also shrouded, and the panic that now consumed their current pace, the hope of being guided by instinct was lost. More than once Lucy tripped herself, though not into complete tumble, on the webbed vines that clambered between the shard rocks.

Whether Bear's explanation of the shadows had been entirely complete, or accurate, Lucy's memories of home started to spiral, although the detail clouded. The wind began with a terrible influx of sleet, and as she tried to keep it from her eyes she saw her father break the empty bottle by cracking it against the side of the bench, not in anger, but in defiance. She saw her mother's forced reservation, refusing to react. They'd rehearsed this, almost, it was not the first time. There was a correct and an incorrect response. And then - jutting forward in time - her mother crying, but trying to hide it while leaving the room, the scathed wooden door swinging shut, and then open again, and her father's smug face on the armchair, sniggering, *proud*.

The sleet rushed against her face and she struggled to keep track of Crumbs. The wind howled like a run-away train. She felt her exhausted body trying to fight against its strength. She spotted Crumbs eventually, close to her feet; a chocolate ball of fur bounding through the icy chaos, oblivious to any difficulty it was causing.

Then another vision of her father; tall, staggering down the hall. Nothing happened, but it was his eyes. They were so unfamiliar, as if he couldn't recognise his own daughter. He saw something else; an enemy. Just as everyone was his enemy and he was theirs. He glared at her with this contempt but mercifully continued past.

In Verity Palace the Queen seeks her uncle's counsel.

Leaning against, or on-top of, the porcelain shelf, she fanned herself, looking around for the help. But she was only mildly irritated. A thin linen dress of vanilla cream, with apricot floral emblems, clung with sweat to her pale skin.

It was far too late in the summer for things to be this warm, yet it couldn't be complained about that the harvests were strong and the oceans were at least becoming calm.

And the thing that bothered her, and kept her awake, made the sultry climate seem irrelevant.

'Why would someone who's never even met me, have so much dislike as to want me dead?' Abigail pulled at the white petals of the marshmallow flowers that dangled over the juliet fountain. They had between their silences, the tranquil sound of rushing water, as the fountain purposely overflowed into a stream below that trailed around her uncle's gardens. This was the northern end of the colonnade in the Winters Quarter of Verity Palace.

Norton craned his neck upward and to the left, for a moment thinking only of the stencilling, where the domed ceiling of the colonnade met the marble columns. Norton Winters was the Chancellor of the Citizen Finance Division of the PeaceKeep, and first bench on the Dynasty Council. He was using a lot of strength to keep himself present in this conversation with his niece. The tawny skin on his neck creased together in parallel ripples and settled again as he centred his direction back. It wasn't that he had excessive skin, but he was by no means a young man. As the greys in his black beard would indicate, he was well past the age of fatherhood. Yet in the way he had oft found himself for many years he was playing father to the Queen. Of course, she was not as young as she looked, or behaved, and not as old as everyone knew she was supposed to be.

'Abigail, it's just as I said. It's just as I said before. No different to last time. It's Archmond that need to be correctly handled, not some over-hyped whimsical creature they've warped into this mess.' As he spoke the servants brought back the cold drinks. Abigail looked up. She let her irritation slip away and instead thanked them. Over the edge of the balustrade a series of purring, gurgling and faint squeaking, called from the gardens. On the other side of the stream below, blossoms of fuchsia and apricot grew on the banks and up against the woody firs. A family of perots (small, slinky creatures, with auburn colourings) were inhabiting the space. They were seen as pests down in the city, but it didn't bother the Queen, and she'd made orders they be left alone.

Norton went on, 'the kingdoms of Coby, Gemini, Mazouri…they will all continue to support you on this.' He spoke dryly though, in a way that did not reassure her, 'they support the capital, that is the most logical approach.'

Abigail nodded, she had some of the iced tea. She looked around; they were alone again. She could tell her uncle was irked by this sudden summons on his time and didn't share her concerns.

'But you want me to send Thomas away?'

Norton sighed, 'he is a young man to whom you have become very recently betrothed, you are not man and wife. You can't let yourself become attached yet. You have many options, Mazouri for instance.'

Abigail chose not to respond to this. She turned away, and for several moments watched the water rush down the limestone into the stream. Her body language was emanating bitterness.

'He will not be gone long.'

'It cannot be that in this kingdom there can be two different men assigned for the jobs of being my husband and being my assassin? It has to be one and the same?' she asked, raising her voice now.

Norton was growing visibly impatient. He set down his tea and let his cupped hands rest on the table, the flowing black sleeves falling back to reveal the silver bangles beneath. His beady eyes, deep set into his face, gave her a piercing stare.

'He is not your husband.'

'He will be.'

He sighed. 'You want everything. And you want to understand nothing.' Very few would get away with such insolence toward her Majesty, but she had come to him for advice, as she had done for as long as she could remember.

She had been leaning forward pecking at the marshmallow petals, but at this she threw herself backward on the straw chair dramatically, letting her arms and the sheer white shawl drape limply over the armrests.

'She is coming for me,' she muttered in childish melancholy.

Norton did not buy into the hysteria about the threat that this 'other-worldly' girl posed, but he had to navigate the fact that his niece, the Queen, did. In fact, it was her will and irrational fear that generated such hysteria amongst the Dynasty Council.

'In that case let us prepare by strengthening our alliances with the closest port. The port, from which she would have to request safe passport? The shipping channel with Coby, are we going to give them the priority they seek?'

Abigail murmured. It was about preferences. In this case a fast track entitled to no other kingdom but Coby. Though a small city in comparison, Coby was most well placed geographically to engage in this kind of arrangement. It was more complex than that though.

'Their own supposed allies do not approve, Trimany, Que…'

Norton waved a hand in the air, equally dismissing both her comments and the flies. 'Both will come around. Especially if we finalise this special approval to Coby. Their ships will be sought after, their business will thrive, Trimany and Que will be pushed to support Coby and therefore support you.'

'It doesn't change how I feel about Thomas…'

'That is a different issue. One that's already been put in motion. Abigail…he's due to leave at first light. It's done. Focus on what we can do more locally and strengthen the alliance with Coby. The Council will meet about it in three nights, please, for everyone's sake try and regain some focus before then.'

Above them dark clouds with faint neon overtones were thickening, in the distance the faint crackle of thunder. The summer storms were frequent but not long lasting.

She was about to tell him she agreed, and that she would turn her attention back to this region, when a servant announced himself with a bell, and declared that Mica had arrived to take her Majesty to see the new horses.

'Oh, yes!' She rose, finished the iced tea and patted the edges of her mouth with the napkin. She stood in front of him, 'they're wild breeds, from the mainland! Wolchester wants to try and tame them. Did you know about this?'

Norton shook his head but smiled politely as if allowing her to leave, secretly relieved. A short while ago she had burst in on the brink of tears demanding reassurances he couldn't provide. Now she was almost prancing off with her personal adviser to look at wild horses.

Lucy's breath steamed out in plumes ahead of her. Snow was falling lightly, and starting to coat the trees like frosting. The land had leant upward still, forcing their ascent. But the mist had lifted, and despite the snow they could see clearly ahead. They had outrun the shadows, on Bear's advice. Though the running had been difficult and long they had stopped seeing them, and Lucy's head had also emerged from the fog of the past. The onslaught of memories had ceased, and she had been able to focus on the present, to keep track of where they were going and keep herself adequately warm. But that had only lasted so long, the shadows were creeping back again, or at least the memories were, which meant the shadows must be close by. The one she had just shaken off was less hazy, the telling events of the night before she fell into this world, but she could feel the start of something obscure, stirring to the surface from the depths of her mind.

'You're very quiet, I was expecting a barrage of questions.'

Lucy glanced at him briefly and glanced away again, 'I'm fine.'

'I wasn't suggesting you weren't.'

The silence between them resumed for several moments, 'how long until we can rest somewhere for a while?'

'Do you spot anywhere cozy?' he gestured the wilderness. The open plain that stretched out into the horizon had only a speckling of trees. They had long left behind the rocky outcrops of the hillside, and even the grassy bushes were slowly becoming lost under the white powder.

'And still, best we get some more distance between us and those shadows. Lest you get sucked into your murky memories again.'

'They weren't bad memories.'

'I didn't say bad, I said *murky*. And they'd have to have some connection to pain or fear or sorrow, else those things wouldn't feed off them so greedily.'

'Or you just don't know as much about them as you think?'

'Or perhaps you don't know as much about your memories as you think?'

Lucy rolled her eyes letting that comment slide away. Crumbs was still bounding ahead, leaping playfully through patches of snow as if it had arrived purely for his amusement. They'd barely eaten a proper meal and had walked all day.

'Seemingly limitless energy. Magic…' Bear remarked, reading her mind.

Lucy smirked, but there wasn't enough for a smile.

Lucy could smell distinctly, the candy strawberry essence of her sister's hair, as the child climbed up onto her lap. The lolly-flavoured shampoo, just one of several ways to induce her into cooperation at bath time. Amber's hair had been deepening slowly over the years from a honey blonde, to a warm chestnut, but it was as wild and thick as Lucy's blackish-brown locks.

'Umm okay,' Lucy laughed awkwardly, dropping the pen as Amber inserted herself between Lucy and the desk. This clambering was not usual. They had a peculiarly distant relationship as sisters. This was partly because of the difference in age, but little sisters often chased after and idolised their older siblings. Amber only chased after mummy. Only held her arms out for mummy. Lucy was regarded as this obscure older figure in their lives. And father was thankfully hardly around, but she seemed not to lean towards him when he was. Amber was only now starting to warm to Lucy at this age, the age of climbing and nonsensical utterings. She referred to Lucy as, 'Lissi'.

Lucy should have felt heartened by this unusual display of affection. From the adjoining living room her mother's eyebrows raised a little as if to say '*well, would you look at that?*'

But Amber's hands were sticky from the jam toast, and she promptly began spreading the droplets of jam over Lucy's homework, pressing her tiny palms across the pages. Lucy grimaced.

'No! Stop that!' she said as she snatched the paperwork away. Amber started to cry. Mother rushed in looking perplexed. Lucy could only give a confounded look of, '*what else could I do?*'

'Come here, darling,' mother's voice echoed in hushed, melodic tones, lifting up the eager three-year-old from where she now teetered on the edge of Lucy's chair. Lucy watched them walk away, back into the lounge room, and returned to her homework both irritated and rejected.

Suddenly, the force of the icy blasts hit her like a thousand tiny shards. How long had she been walking in that daze?

'Where are we?' she called out over the sound of the gale, looking around.

'Where have you been?' he responded curtly, 'I've been calling at you. The shadows are back. And they look bigger than before.'

'I thought we lost them, back at the ridge?' she cried beseechingly, feeling herself having to shout through the wind.

'They've caught up. *Following you,* no doubt. You and your bad memories.'

She could barely see him now the snow was getting thicker and he was hanging in the air several feet away.

'I told you, I'm not having bad memories,' she insisted.

But she was starting to recognise this as a lie. To herself really. There was a definite undercurrent to the memories of Amber. They had been disturbing to experience, these seemingly innocuous memories. They were coming like waves drowning her now, and each time she was able to rise up from one, and catch her breath back in the present, another came and pushed her under again.

This one had her wandering through the grounds of St. Maurice De'Ceille. Hedges lined up high either side of the stone path. The sky was unusually clear, and the sunshine sparkled off her mother's pearl earrings. It was just the two of them, wandering along. Her mother commented on the roses by the statues, on the lilies in the water features, the lavender, and the jasmine. Nearly everything they passed received a compliment. They had wandered for some time, and it wasn't clear now in this replay why they were here in the grounds, or why they were walking around alone. They were here for an occasion of some kind - but that detail escaped the nature of this memory.

'You're a clever girl Lucy, much smarter than I was at your age,' her mother said as they came to an area where orange poppies filled the garden beds on either side of them.

'I'm not smart,' young Lucy said.

'You most certainly are. You are aware of things. You understand things that other people don't.'

Behind them on the hillside, yellowing poplars shifted in the breeze. The sudden drop in temperature had her mother tightening her shawl, but Lucy felt like the sound the wind made was a call for her attention.

'Lucy? Are you listening? We may have some trouble getting home tonight as I know you're probably aware. Because you're aware of these things, aren't you? Got to get you to be my best girl for me tonight, and take care of your sister while I take care of your father? You got it?'

Lucy's attention was still backwards, caught up in the scene of the hillside.

'Did you hear me, Lucy?' her mother said, and yanked at her arm lightly. Lucy looked up at her mother, and her mother recognised the despondence in her eyes.

'Come on, it'll all be over in the morning,' she said.

They followed the path back around to where they started, where her father sat visibly inebriated, trying to strike up a conversation with uninterested patrons of the estate. Their disinterest was triggering the aggressive unrest of his intoxication. The people they had come here to see had already left.

'You don…you don't *believe* me?' he slurred in the direction of the other table where the guests tried awkwardly to avert their gaze.

Her mother went to get the staff to call a taxi, and her father's wandering eyes met hers. The look he gave her came from a place within himself deep with shame, but it was expressed as malice, and it filled her with terror.

The snowy presence came back only long enough for her to recognise Bear's instructions to move quickly, and she adjusted the fur around her shoulders and picked up the pace. She could feel the cold invading her shoes and dampening her socks. The ground was not yet covered with snow, but the patches of it were increasing.

Though internally she pleaded for no more of them to come, and fought the vision as it started to emerge, she was too late or too weak, and in seconds was standing in the fragrant air of late spring in her front yard. Amber's wavy ochre locks were catching the morning light in that dewy heavenly way. The light beaming through was in fact what produced these ochre auburn hues through the flyaway strands. Indoors or in the darkness of winter, Amber's hair looked a kind of dull chestnut, too dark for blonde and too empty for brown. But now in this moment it had its own vibrance. She was by the mulberry tree, facing it, reaching up into it. She had a patterned play dress on; red and white, a nice dress. They were going somewhere later but the morning was theirs, Lucy felt herself recall. She was watching Amber while mum finished up a few things. Amber was old enough to be left to her own devices a bit now, but not outside. She turned around then, her face and fingers stained with the berries she'd been foraging and devouring, and her eyes met Lucy's with the most haunting hum of innocence. It was almost as if the memory had warped now. She could not imagine why her nearly four-year-old sister would beckon her so beseechingly. But it clicked then. The painful truth of these memories was suddenly poignant. The thing she had been trying not to appreciate, the very obvious thing, that she was refusing to acknowledge which underlay all these memories, was that Amber was dead, and her death had fundamentally changed Lucy forever.

The snowfall had become an all-out blizzard, and it was impossible to be lost in the memories and survive through it at the same time. But as she struggled to move forward, and keep herself wrapped in the fur over the course of the next few moments, she was bombarded with a string of horrific images of her father, each only a second or so long. Her father throwing bits of food at her mother, laughing while he did so, but certainly not in jest, rather with the smug belligerent grin that all psychotic alcoholics harbour; her father crushing a glass bottle by the grip of his hand, the shards splintering into his palm and the vacant expression as the blood trickled down his wrist; her father smacking Amber around the head so hard she stumbled into the cupboard, after she had spilt cereal across the floor.

'Lucy!' his voice was finally loud enough to break through the spell altogether. She looked over and now saw that amongst the gale, Bear's grainy black image was flickering in and out of focus like a poorly tuned signal.

'Lucy, something's wrong. I'm not going to be *here* much longer. I can't stay…' He was struggling to explain it, 'I won't be *able to*,' he shouted.

Despite the thickening snowfall obscuring even their ability to see each other, they could both recognise that the multitude of shadows now circling was dauntingly grave. The number of shadows had increased, but individually they also seemed larger, and seemed to wail separately to the wind.

'Don't leave me!' she cried, but in the same moment he was gone. Crumbs was scratching at her calves, now finally attuned to the frightfulness of the situation.

She picked him up into her arms, adjusted her coat and the backpack, and did what Bear had told her to do the first time; run.

Chapter 8

Yerkey and the invitation

Neiy Mong squinted through the snow, trying to decipher the image in the distance and shouted out, calling his pack back to heal. Behind him they were hungrily pursuing some rodent up a tree or down a burrow. Yes, they were desperate, but no good chasing hunt too small for even the pack to devour.

He could see something in the distance he hoped may be a fallen deer. But it was beyond the trees, in the pass where the snow was thickest. From this vantage it was merely a darkish lump, statuesque.

The pack came back hastily, eager for new instruction. He lowered his hand down behind his back with his index finger out..., a command for them to fall into position behind him. They crouched. Heads lowered. Waiting. Eager.

Though he was not apprehensive of most things, he was aware they were well past the boundary of Yerkey hunting ground, and therefore it was wise to be cautious. Even so, he was more willing than usual to take risks today. The hunt so far had been poor. One elderly wolf and a pup. A disgraceful yield.

Still, he did not come out for the yield, he consoled himself. He came out to get away from the torment of being at home. He would do anything to be away from his wife, even if it meant hunting in the tail end of a blizzard. She was relentless, always had been, but tonight they'd argued more furiously than normal. It all traced back (as far as Neiy Mong was concerned) to her thinking she was too good for him. She had always thought it, and he'd always known it. It was at the very forefront of all their problems, whenever he dwelled on them. She had never forgiven her father for forcing the marriage, she even refused to visit him on his deathbed - that was the coldness of the woman he married. The last few days she had criticised him at length about the extension to their umbo. It was never done properly, she argued. He had done a lazy job, she said. And now, the wood was bending, the rocks were shifting, and the cold was getting in. Maybe also, secretly, she was angry because she had wanted him to be successful in gaining a spot in the hunting party. But he was too old for that. She knew that. But still, when he said they had taken up numbers already, she joked that probably he didn't try very hard, because it would mean he'd have to pull his weight like the young runners. She complained he didn't care about her and the children. There was not enough of anything to go around, but there would never be enough for her. They needed the walls fixed, they needed more wood for the fires, they needed new coats, more space. She claimed she wanted to do the repairs herself, but she couldn't finish anything with their youngest being so fragile and Neiy Mong was always out.

'Yes, always out hunting for us,' he'd thought bitterly. Tonight though she had scolded him for doing the only thing he could to help their situation, by arranging their eldest daughter to marry his cousin's son. One less mouth to feed was a great blessing. Somehow Karrichore didn't see it that way.

As he steeped his anger in this twilight hunt through the snow, (a hunt he left for in haste, which his wife had been sure to tell him would be pointless) he had stewed on all of this. Pulling the fur hat as far down as he could over his ears, he had reminded himself about how it was his wife's difficulty in their first few years of marriage, that had disinterested him in other women. He had deluded himself into thinking he could work hard to please her, earn her love, before he sought other wives. But she became so quarrelsome the thought of other women started to nauseate him. When he got over that it seemed he was no longer suitable for younger mates. He always resented her for that. Now, her outrage about their daughter proved everything he'd ever suspected of her. In her own mind she was above him and all his world. She opposed their daughter being further married into his family so much because, the way she saw it, this was the same 'injustice' she saw as having been done to her. And she was determined to prevent the same happening to their daughter…or was it 'her' daughter? He clenched his fists as he recounted all this now, and crept closer to the dark blur in the snow, his well trained and much practiced pack creeping with heads low, a few paces behind.

'Neycha! Neycha!' Neiy Mong commanded his pack back behind him, but with difficulty, as they yapped and ripped at the body, which he had rolled onto the sleigh with the wolf carcasses. They were so eager to devour any living flesh that wasn't him, it was hard to work up the right volume to scare them into compliance.

It was no deer. It was a female, human. A foreign female, and clutching a frozen creature, but human nonetheless. From the complexion, Neiy Mong considered she was either barely alive, or not long dead. It didn't really matter either way. He needed to get her to the Elder Circle at once. The foreign kind of her was eastern, not Archmond, not tribal. Easterners in these parts were a concern for all the west, not just Yerkey. It may even signal invasion, or war. And now he would be the hero that would unravel this by presenting her to the circle. Destiny had struck him. He smirked, despite the freezing of his limbs. Karrichore would surely eat her poison words now. This *pointless* hunt may have earnt their family prized approval from the Elder Circle.

The snow and wind had all but ceased by the time Neiy Mong's sleigh began to glide through the fringes of Yerkey's settlement. Lucy stirred ever so slightly with life. The warmth of the wolf carcasses had abated against the hypothermia and kept her on the brinks of life. She was too weak to open her eyes. She registered the warmth of the damp fleshy fur either side of her. She registered that she was moving. Thereafter she fell back into a daze that was barely conscious.

When she did open her eyes, still too stiff and fragile to move, the tops of snow covered structures appeared above the curvature of blackish fur pressed against her face. The structures repeated themselves as they went along, becoming denser. They were illuminated mostly by the glow of fire-lit lanterns that fell upon her intermittently; sunrise and shadow, sunrise and shadow. Yerkey was not technologically advanced in the way other kingdoms and cities were. It was better classed as a settlement than a city, and not a well-known one at that.

But it was an ancient settlement. Dating back well before the first seeds were sown in the farmlands around Gemini and Que. The ancient nature of this establishment and way of life was obvious to anyone passing through. It was by no means a primitive town, and it couldn't at all be compared to the tribal colonies of the forest. Yet, they had their own unique ways of subsisting in this frozen landscape. Ways they had never, and would never, shift from. While the other cities and kingdoms grew and evolved with new ideas and new methods, which created new problems, Yerkey over the last several hundred years, had largely stayed the same.

'Goee non, goee non.' The gentle call, perhaps a greeting of sorts, drew Lucy from the brink of another daze.

'Gia nan, gia nan,' she heard her rescuer (or captor) reply with weary caution. But that was all she could take of the exchange before the frailty of her condition once again consumed her.

Yinsoo had ventured out from the warmth of her abode to the edge of the settlement, because she knew Neiy Mong was coming. More precisely she had come because he was bringing with him the girl, and this was a momentous occasion.

'The girl, I will take her now, I have been expecting her.' In native tongue, Yinsoo explained herself calmly to Neiy Mong, with a contented smile.

Neiy Mong was insulted. He was in no way wanting to be 'relieved' of the foreigner; she was his prize. A prize found only because of his fearless travels beyond the brink of the habitat zone and into the tundra, which he explained to Yinsoo.

Yinsoo clasped her hands together in front of her. She smiled peacefully, but with an underlying confidence that enraged Neiy Mong, and bowed ever so slightly in respect. She knew little of Neiy Mong, and knew nothing of his troubles or his desire to keep Lucy as some sort of token to be bargained for social status. But she knew she need not fear, Lucy was here to be with her. None of this was an accident or a coincidence, it was her doing after all, that brought Lucy here to begin with.

'This is providence,' Yinsoo explained, 'this is to be, this from the late Reichi. She is destined. She must come with me.'

Neiy Mong knew Yinsoo was a part of the spiritual order, but she held no authority over him. Although he knew he may be reprimanded for ignoring her. He threw down his speargun in frustration, grasping that either way now his plan was defunct.

'What is this quarrelling in the evening before people's homes?'

One of two approaching young watchmen asked. Watchmen were identifiable by their black fur hats, but Neiy Mong knew these men.

He appealed to the one who had spoken, Leon, a young second cousin of his wife's.

'Please, Yinsoo lays claim to the girl, but it was I who risked much in the blizzard to find her. I sensed something was wrong - that's why I went out at such a time! I felt the air around the village stir. Something lurking, something needed to be brought to the Elder Circle. And something there was! Now I should bring her to them, tell Yinsoo it is so.'

Leon stepped forward and examined the sleigh. He parted the wolf carcasses and rolled the girl onto her back. Behind him Neiy Mong and Yinsoo stepped closer. Carefully, Leon's thick glove swept away the iced blackish hair from her face. Her plait had mostly come undone. Her skin was pale, with the trademark pink hue from exposure. But her eyelids fluttered rapidly without opening.

'This girl is alive,' Leon announced, disturbed and in awe, 'she must go with Yinsoo, Neiy Mong. We have a duty to protect all life, and it is the Reichi who nurse the sick back to health.'

'Elder Circle must know of the eastern presence,' Neiy Mong said, as Yinsoo began moving Lucy toward her own cart, pre-lined with warmed wool blankets. Neiy Mong was suggesting he could notify the circle now, hoping to savour some recognition out of this.

But Leon waved a hand dismissively as he watched Yinsoo wheel her cart away, the foreigner and small creature inside.

'Go home to your wife Mong. The circle will be told by morning - if they don't already know.'

Lucy awoke to a loud cracking noise as the largest log in the fire split, and its charred ashy splinters were expelled into the air. A haze of smoke drifted around her eyes. Her face was cinder-stricken. She coughed, surprised at how hard it was to take in air, and at the same time rising up from the rug on the ground to peer over the flames.

Yinsoo was only a few feet away, intently examining the contents of the pot as she gently stirred, in her pokey kitchen raised up from the rest of the umbo. She spun swiftly at the sound of the coughing.

'Ahhhh!' she exclaimed, excited, putting the pot down and coming over.

Lucy stared at the woman with unease. Although she would later recognise that this must be exactly the hospitality Bear hoped for. Now, quite naturally, she was vulnerable and confused. At the same time, Yinsoo stared at Lucy with the gleeful curiosity a child examines their pet bug, albeit with a slightly more maternal mindset. Yinsoo was long past child rearing age, and never had children of her own, but that had little to do with her fascinated gaze. She had been expecting Lucy for a long time, or her father had. Her grandfather was a great Reichi. He had taught Yinsoo from a young age, that she must make herself ready to play her part; her part in history. Yinsoo too, was special.

Lucy shuffled about trying to find her backpack, she felt its coarse canvas beneath the blanket and relaxed some.

'Where's my dog?' Her throat itched. Her chest hurt to talk. She put a hand to her throat.

'Eh, eh,' Yinsoo said. She indicated the bowl in front of Lucy and pushed it closer to her, wanting her to drink from it. When Lucy examined it, Yinsoo put her hands before her mouth, mimicking a drinking movement.

'I know how to use it,' Lucy said dryly.

Yinsoo grabbed a paper book from a nearby table and some coloured sticks. At first Lucy thought the old woman might suggest she do some 'colouring in' to entertain herself, but it was Yinsoo who drew.

She drew a stick figure, a girl, with black hair. She coloured the cheeks green. She showed Lucy, and pointed to her.

'You,' she said, her strange accent more apparent when speaking common tongue. Then she pointed to the bowl of liquid, and drew another stick figure, much the same, but without the green cheeks. 'Ahh…' she went to speak but then tapped the brown stick against her cheek for several moments waiting for the word, then with a flash of light in her eyes it had come. She pointed to the soup again, and to the non-sickly stick figure girl, 'better', she said rather proudly.

Lucy obliged, given all the drama, and drank the liquid. It was fine, some form of hot, salty broth.

'Where's my dog?' she asked again.

Yinsoo was waddling back up to her kitchen, but she turned and pointed. Crumbs was on the opposite side of the fire, under his own layers of wool and fur. He was in a deeper state than sleep, maybe far worse than she had been, because the sound of her voice would have usually triggered him by now. But she watched his chest rise and fall for several precious moments, and was at least assured by that. Lucy wanted to run over to Crumbs, but Yinsoo was right, she was very sick. She may have only been in the blizzard for less than an hour, but that would have been enough. Instead she watched Yinsoo hobble around the old pokey kitchen. She was a thin woman. Thin and frail and grey, her hair cut short across her head. Her smile, as she knelt-down, had revealed she was missing many teeth. This may have been why she liked soup so much, Lucy thought.

Lucy hadn't gotten a look at the man who dragged her here on the sleigh, she had little memory of any of it, except the occasional sound of his voice as he shouted at the dogs. Yinsoo, and Yinsoo's humble but cosy umbo, was her first impression of Yerkey. The woman wore a large oversized jumper, that was more like a poncho the way it floated off her, a long narrow skirt that covered her ankles, and fat thick shoes that flopped around. The umbo (the Yerkey word for home) was quite typical. All Lucy could see of it was the large circular living area; cream stone-walls and rug covered floor, the fire at its centre, and the raised little kitchen just off the side. The shadowy archway beyond the fire indicated there were more pokey rooms, but it didn't seem as though anything extended much further. Adjacent the shadowy archway, a set of shelves overflowed with poorly kept books and bundles of papers that continued in a pile either side of the structure. She sat up straighter now, both examining and stretching her neck. She made to get up and walk over to the books, but she felt the weakness in her and thought twice. Maybe she should continue to rest.

Lucy's sense of time was distorted. She woke assuming the memory of feeling herself starting to collapse with delirium in the snow was several hours ago, but in reality, she had been asleep in the umbo for over sixteen. One of the elders from the circle had already come to observe her while she slept. He returned with Yinsoo to the umbo, after she had gone to them at sunrise and declared the foreign girl to be the subject of her grandfather's prophecy. Though the Elder Circle, like most of Yerkey, were followers of the prophecy of the great Reichi, they had been skeptical about whether Yinsoo was wise enough to identify the right girl. Or rather, whether the great Reichi's eccentric granddaughter was objective enough to recognise an Easterner over a long hoped for prophetic child. Yinsoo had knelt beside sleeping Lucy, and had carefully untucked the necklace from under Lucy's garments. They had recognised the dangling metal shape, now pendant, as the key made for the late princess Gloria of Meta Emery, known to be in the custody of Archmond's wizards. Ironic that an eastern made trinket, dangling from the chain of an eastern looking girl, was the only thing that could convince them she in fact came from the west.

Lucy stood, legs wobbly, and moved around the fire to the shelves, craning upward to see where the iron chimney escaped out of the dome ceiling. There were symbols on the spines of both older and newer looking books that were familiar, almost Celtic, but she couldn't think where she'd seen them before, or if she even had. Her brain was fuzzy, the room was dizzy; too warm, or was that the fever? But she was alert enough to recognise that the books and papers were in multiple languages. The text that was open to be observed, had different compositions. Some book titles she saw were even in English. A dusty red spine read, 'An Introduction to Modern Geometry', while a small pocketbook on the floor appeared to be a reproduction of Thomas Moore's Utopia. A larger and older looking leather jacket at eye level had the inscription, '*Que cherchez-vous?*'

Lucy heard a whimper behind her and turned from the shelves. Crumbs' tiny legs twitched with energy, but he didn't rouse. Returning to the fire she knelt beside him. Unconsciously his spirit stirred at her scent and he licked her fingers as she stroked his jaw. Yinsoo had been preparing the second round of stew and returned from the kitchen, pot and ladle in hand.

'Ooooh!' she cooed at Lucy with Crumbs, and joined her on the floor, patting him. Eventually she indicated the ladle, and Lucy smiled with the obliging politeness of a good guest, and returned to her prior seat so she could eat.

'Thank you. For this. For all of this.' She broke a silence that had been starting to stiffen, at the half-way mark of the thicker bowl, after her rudeness suddenly dawned on her. This was the hospitality she had prayed existed somewhere in the wilderness, back when the ground was starting to crunch with ice beneath her boots, and the extent of her vulnerability and isolation had started to crystalize. The second dish was different to the first, which had been more like a broth, this was a kind of stew, the contents blended or melted together.

Yinsoo smiled in reply, almost bowing her head graciously, and Lucy became more unsure of the woman's grasp of her language.

Lucy nodded toward Crumbs, 'will he get better?'

Yinsoo was closer to him, she stretched wearily and scratched the back of her head, placed a hand on Crumbs' belly and said, 'better', then nodded peremptorily. Yinsoo then got up and fetched a cup of water from the barrel and placed it beside Crumbs. Lucy could only hope that the woman had seen her fair share of creatures come under the effects of exposure, and that her limited concern was based on a certainty of life, not a certainty of worth.

Lucy wondered how long she would need to stay here to shelter from the snow.

'How long will the snow last?' she asked, pointing to the fast melting patches seeping in under the iron-clad door.

Yinsoo laughed. 'Always snow!' she exclaimed, taking messy gulps of broth from the smaller bowl she'd let go cold while fixing the stew for Lucy, 'always snow.'

The next morning saw no relief in the amount of snow falling over the ancient settlement. The rocky outcrops, on its northernmost periphery, were indistinguishable from the umbos in their white coatings. From high above, the town workers slowly pushing the snow aside, made a honeycomb pattern emerge around the structures; creamy paths criss-crossing the white canvas.

In the relative reprieve of Yinsoo's umbo, the light and the colour had not changed. There was a persistent moody, earthen, warmth. The fire burned almost eternally, but the changing intensity lifted the shadows up and down the walls, and sometimes darkened the room to a fading winter sunset.

Lucy was sifting through the books in Yinsoo's makeshift library.

Yinsoo had indicated to Lucy that she was going out for food. That was not entirely a lie. She was stopping to get herbs from the apothecary, but the nature of her excursion was to secure the only good translator she knew for tonight's ceremony. Yinsoo knew that unfortunately he would be off hunting soon, so she'd have to catch him before he left. That also meant though, that the explanation of the ceremony to Lucy, the reason for it, would have to wait until the ceremony itself. It was delicate, but Yinsoo didn't know enough of the common tongue to start telling Lucy about it without causing crazed misunderstandings and unnecessary concern. She would have to keep the girl in the dark a day later. More time to recover, she reasoned.

Lucy had been left alone for more than several hours. She had flipped through the books with the familiar patterns for a while, and not got any closer to remembering where she'd seen them. Then she re-read parts of Utopia, which only made her confused about whether she was homesick, or whether Moore's reasoning was always meant to encompass life in all worlds, and not just her own.

But it was the book about Yerkey itself that had piqued her interest the most. It was written in her language, by someone from the outside, it seemed. The inside of the front page said - *Mathew Mathers,*

Trimany. This, 'Mathers', had either written the book, or once owned it. It began by claiming that many signs pointed to Yerkey being the most ancient settlement in all the world (perhaps just their world) and connected its religion to the origins of most other stellar based belief systems across other kingdoms. *'Even the constellation worship of the Mazourians, or the old religions of Meta Emery, can be traced back in some way to Yerkey's origin.'*

Estimates on population changes through the centuries, based on conversations with elders and records kept by the Elder Circle, was that of an unbelievably stable populace, not growing or shrinking for hundreds of years. The author noted about four thousand people lived in the settlement at the time of writing. Flipping through the flimsy guide, as it seemed to be, the author went on to say in the chapter on culture, that the religious beliefs of the Yerkey kept the culture traditional. They saw themselves as guardians of peace throughout the world, that somehow, their faith could save all life. Not through intervention, but through their persistent practice of symbolic gestures to the sky. Although seemingly less advanced than most settlements in many ways, they believed they were above the trivial struggles of other kingdoms, and their subsistence based way of life, following the tenets of their faith, would see them ultimately outlast all other civilisations.

When Yinsoo returned, Lucy had the map sprawled out in front of her, with small pebbles she found around the umbo holding it down.

To one side she had, 'An Insight into Yerkey', as well as several other books she could understand, opened up to random pages, face down on the stone floor. She had been trying to cross reference information in the books to cities and kingdoms on the map. But to no avail. None of the other books in her language had the purpose of being generally informative about geography. The closest she could get, was one that discussed what birds you could spot in the autumn around the fringes of a place called Rumustica. Lucy had located this region on the map. All she gathered from the ornithological commentary was that the region, which was many miles away, was rocky, mountainous, and more or less uninhabited. None of the books helped her get any closer to the answers she sought; information about the next cities and kingdoms she would encounter, how long it might take to get there, what side of this supposed east-west feud they were on, what language they spoke and whether there were any other small towns or villages in-between. After all, Yerkey notably, was not on the map. And yet, here she was.

Most importantly, she wanted to know which city (or kingdom) would have the most insight to offer about this world, the wizards who had brought her here, and how in the heavens she could possibly get home.

Yinsoo looked quietly self-satisfied in the doorway. Her basket was now full. Lucy looked up, her face brightened eagerly. The thirst for knowledge was written all across her.

She went to speak, but stopped, remembering the language barrier. She went on more carefully, 'these places, where do I…Do any speak my language?'

Yinsoo smiled and came closer. She set the basket down and stood looking over the spread map, as though she understood Lucy's question. She did not.

'Where should I go? What is the best kingdom to go to next?' Lucy asked and made walking motions with her fingers along the map to try and elucidate herself.

'Ahhh.' Yinsoo smiled. She nodded rapidly, 'go…you go'. Her index finger tapped the island of Meta Emery in the far east. Lucy's eyelids fell, the brightness in her faded.

'Right,' she muttered quietly.

Yinsoo fetched some water from the barrel and drank thirstily. She offered some to Lucy, but Lucy shook her head.

Then she took the basket back into her hand, and summonsed Crumbs with her eyes to the door.

'What's happening?' Lucy asked.

'*Come,*' Yinsoo called with her hand. There was no time for maps. Everything was now arranged. She would show the girl what she needed to see.

They walked through the now darkened streets, the passageways between the umbos, Yinsoo leading the way. Their pathway was narrow at times, because of the snow, and often blocked. Lucy wasn't properly attired for this weather, though Yinsoo had lent her a proper coat; the animal fur she'd been carrying was warm but impractical.

Smoke plumed from iron pipes at the centre of every snow dome, while warm yolk light glowed from under shut doors. Yinsoo, frail and old though she was, insisted on lending an arm to Lucy as they crossed each pile of snow. She worried for the girl's balance, and lack of experience. Lucy caught a glimpse of the woman's necklace, and wondered about the religion she'd read about in the guidebook, earlier that day. There was something about a connection to the rock here, was it a kind of emery? Rich in magnetite. She remembered reading something about energy from the rocks, being the reason why the settlement was built here, and the reason the generations of people remained committed to stay. But it was second-hand information, and she wasn't sure how much of it she understood. Still, it was a haunting thought, to think she may have been in the birthplace of all spirituality, for this world at least.

A shrill cry made her jump, amusing Yinsoo. A feral cat, prowling across the dome rooftop of a nearby umbo, was marking its territory. The slender silhouette shape arched its back, as though it knew it had an audience. There were a great many feral cats surviving in the snowy town; they would see several more on their way to the temple, their slender shadows seemed to play up their own incidence in the moonlight. It was only a crescent moon, but it was wondrously bright, and it seemed to call them all into heat.

As they passed a market area, empty at this hour, they heard the raucous calls of barking dogs; the party was arriving back from the hunt in a staggered procession. The area closer to the temple was filled with many Reichi buildings. The temple hall was at the end of them, closest to the rocky outcrop holding the emery they worshipped. But many auxiliary structures surrounded the temple hall, making the passage to it as narrow as any other part of town, despite it having its own space. These consisted of housing for the elders and their relatives, as well as storage buildings for relics and scriptures and other sacred possessions. Although Yinsoo was a granddaughter of an ancient Reichi elder, she chose to live away from it. Her thought was that she wanted to not be influenced.

As they neared the temple hall, Lucy saw the familiar symbols from the books again, carved into the walls of longer, elongated buildings. She recognised their same Celtic style, but at first, they were as foreign as ever. But as they turned into another laneway the edge of the temple came into view. It was as ordinary as any other structure in Yerkey; snow covered, plain, and she would not have recognised it as a temple. But she recognised that particular symbol, and then the relevance of all of them hit her in a flash of recognition that charged down her spine and hit the earth like lightning.

These were the same symbols that were etched into the paper notes that lured her here, through the reserve and onto a windy path that was, in her mind, the start of her undoing. Lucy stopped still in her tracks. Yinsoo turned to call her on, pointing to the temple, its ruby red wind chimes dangling from the overhang.

'No,' Lucy whispered, drawing in rapid icy breaths, 'where is that - where is that from?' she said, pointing to the symbol on the wall.

Yinsoo was confused at first, and then she remembered. In native tongue she tried to respond. She came forward, in a bid to mellow Lucy back into compliance. But Lucy drew away, 'no,' she said, louder this time, 'tell me who you are.'

Yinsoo rambled on in her own language, desperately wanting to explain.

'I don't understand you!' Lucy shouted, backing away. Crumbs began to bark.

Inside the temple hall, leaning over some scriptures to pass the time, Corso heard the commotion from outside. In this part of town, at this hour, the moon being high, it was almost unheard of to hear people in the street, let alone a ruckus. But he knew he was expecting Yinsoo and the young girl. He rushed outside.

Yinsoo was still rambling, and he called for her to stop. He turned to Lucy, 'please, I explain. She wants you know she brought you here, for very purpose of explaining…everything.'

Lucy took in the young man, he wore a thick green coat and had a round plump face with flat black hair, currently being speckled with the finite falling ice. She panted, looking back and forth at them.

'Please,' he continued, looking to the left as he attempted to remember the form of words, 'come inside, we tell you.' He then indicated the temple.

There was stillness, as Yinsoo and Corso awaited her reply. In the distance another feral cat screeched. In the narrow street Lucy watched the red chimes on the edge of the temple, spiral clockwise and then anticlockwise, in the imperceptible currents of air. The rubies in them glistened against a flicker of firelight escaping from inside.

'Fine,' she responded, somewhat bitterly.

Once inside, Lucy could see the roof of the temple hall was also covered with these same symbols. They transfixed Lucy as soon as she entered the double doors. Apart from the fire in its centre, and the altar at the end, the temple hall was empty. Its stone floor dusty and without comfort. The roof was also made of large stones, very different to the wooden thatching of the umbos. Against its dark grey surface, the symbols were almost invisible. But as the flames flickered, the bright white light from the centre of the room danced. The shadows weaved in and out of the carvings in the stone, revealing the patterns as some sort of orchestrated performance.

'Sit,' Yinsoo instructed, one of the few words she knew.

'Sit,' Corso repeated.

There was some simple décor; red cloth hung from some of the decorative internal awnings. A wooden stool sat in the far corner near the altar. Several large rocks were also placed in each of the four corners. But its centre was a bare, hollow space. It smelt damp and uninhabited. It hadn't been used since the last festival, several months earlier.

They sat around the fire, Lucy reluctantly, on torn and faded cushions awaiting them. Yinsoo began to speak to Corso.

'From now,' Corso said to Lucy, 'she will speak through me.'

Lucy nodded.

Yinsoo mumbled.

'She says you still seem very tense.'

Lucy scoffed and looked around. 'Who are you people?'

Corso translated, but Yinsoo only responded with the same question.

'She wants to know why you are now so closed?'

Lucy considered this. 'I guess I feel deceived.'

Once translated, Yinsoo smiled at this. She shook her head a little as she grinned to herself amused, then said something back.

'She says it is you who is the deceiver.'

Lucy fixated on Yinsoo with a new sense of unease. Yinsoo was smiling peacefully, as though she had merely complimented Lucy's hair. She went on though.

'She says you have been lying for a long time, most lies to yourself.'

The yolk flames grew white, with shades of both violet and rose. Lucy jumped back a little. But Yinsoo began to chant, ever so softly, as if not to cause anyone any disturbance.

'She is calling to the ancestors,' Corso explained, 'she wants them to help you.'

The rocks in the corners of the temple began to glow. Crumbs rushed to Lucy's lap.

'Help me with what?' she said, raising her voice. They were being somewhat drowned out by a sudden snowstorm beginning to rage outside the hall. The wooden doors rattled in its wake.

'She says you must find yourself. It is key to prophecy - for it to work - you have to want it to work.'

Lucy made a face, what did that mean? In all this, what could that possibly mean?

'These symbols. They were on the notes I got when I was back home, why? How are they connected?'

'That was our call to you,' said Corso, as he continued to translate, 'she says that was our invitation. She is glad you accepted.'

Lucy looked at Yinsoo, having finished her chant she was still once again, and her grey eyes were peaceful. It was as though she could not fully understand either discomfort, or contention.

'Accepted? I didn't accept anything.'

There was a pause, now Yinsoo looked confused. She and Corso exchanged many words before he said, 'you are here, you are here because you accepted.'

'I'm here because the wizards in Archmond brought me here,' Lucy retorted, she watched the snow race wildly past the windows outside, 'because of some prophecy.'

Suddenly the storm outside seemed not to roar but to hum, an almost beautiful white noise that was containing all they said. Yinsoo was shaking her head.

'Archmond wizards found you, but you are *our prophecy*, the prophecy of the great Reichi - grandfather of Yinsoo.'

As Corso said his name the building began to shudder, and for the first time Yinsoo looked rattled. It was possible she was displeasing his spirit. All the adjacent buildings were empty. They were alone out here.

'She says her grandfather predicted you in prophecy, many time ago. The prophecy well known, but very few know where it came from.'

There was a silence while Lucy thought on this.

'So, the notes,' she whispered, thinking on it again.

'Yes, they were from us, your invitation,' Corso said.

'I didn't accept any invitation,' Lucy replied, coldly.

Yinsoo threw a papery lavender box into the fire. It started to crackle and then steam, the misty smoke rising through the room.

'Yinsoo says you did. That you are here because deep down, you knew.'

Lucy choked on the proposition as well as the essence filling her lungs, 'I was brought here, against my will.'

She coughed some more, 'are you saying the wizards lied? They said they brought me to fulfil their prophecy. Do you each think this was your doing? Every town in this world has its own story, its own dumb prophecy?' she rambled a little, though meekly.

'It is the same prophecy,' Corso said, then listening to Yinsoo a moment longer, 'the wizards do not know all, they think they act alone, but they did not know you needed our invitation - before the path could be crossed.'

'I didn't accept any invitation, your notes called me a liar.'

'Mmmm. Liar,' Yinsoo murmured.

'An invitation,' Lucy said as she went back to it, 'an invitation to what exactly?'

'To your destined path. If you accept it, you save yourself, and you save this world too.' Corso offered this up as though it were self-evident, his palms gesturing outward. He shifted positions then too, leaning forward onto his elbows and stretching out his body behind him. At this point Lucy felt her senses being overcome; the air around them was thick with the incense from the box. Its effect was calming but she felt desperate to reject it. The persistent battering from the wind seemed also to subdue her instincts, which wanted to reject this nonsensical information and move back into a sphere she understood. The wind chimes outside came in every few moments with their clinkering spells of eerie whimsy.

'Why am I a liar?' asked Lucy eventually, after long elongated silences.

'Hiding is lying,' Corso translated. Lucy rolled her eyes, denying the anxiety she felt. But that statement meant nothing.

But Yinsoo piped in, 'your sister.'

Lucy's nerves were triggered then. 'What did you say?'

Suddenly Corso's translations became much clearer. Lucy was unsure of what she was perceiving because there was a light-headedness that was following the incense, but it seemed as though now Yinsoo need not speak.

'How long have you been hiding the fact of your sister's death? Let alone how it actually happened?' Corso addressed her plainly, without any of the effort he exhibited in translation.

Lucy made to crawl backwards on the floor, 'I don't know what you mean,' she lied. Her eyes were welling, her stomach churned.

'Yes, you do.'

Yinsoo began to chant again, almost inaudibly. Lucy looked into the flames, they were purple, and pink, and *Amber*.

'Why did Amber die Lucy?' Corso asked.

'I don't remember.' Her gaze was focused inwards; she was searching. She realised that she had only recently remembered that Amber had existed. She realised this was significant. Part of her knew there were more memories in there, locked away.

'You do,' he insisted, 'you do.'

'Who killed her?' Yinsoo asked, almost without an accent. Lucy flashed an accusatory glare at the woman, but it was too late. By then it had all started bubbling to the surface. As the visions broke through in volcanic bursts, magma, she fought against them. Eventually she relinquished control and let the memory play out. Once she opened the gates it came back to her like a tidal surge.

Her father. His temper. Amber was being naughty. In her room she was throwing toys at the wall, making noise, he went in to scold her. Mother wasn't home. Lucy came out of her room when the yelling became more ferocious than normal - Amber was only little. She arrived just in time. Or did she? Just in time, to do nothing and be complicit. Amber was struck in the head, and the force caused her to fall back and hit the back of her head on the bedpost. She was instantly unconscious. Her father turned to see her. 'Don't say a damn thing,' he whispered, with a drunken malice that suggested she would be next. He carried Amber to the bed and tucked her in, properly.

'She's sleeping. Like she should be,' he muttered, storming out of the room. By the next morning, she would be dead. For some reason, aside from grief, nothing further ever came of it.

Lucy opened her eyes, the incense seemed to have dissipated, and Corso and Yinsoo were glancing around the room; almost nonchalant. If she were any more coherent their apathy may have enraged her.

'What does this mean?' she asked shakily, her hands were trembling, her face pale. She shuddered, 'what does that…have to do with any of this? Huh?'

Whether the storm was still raging or not, she couldn't hear anything. The warmth inside the hall had fogged the small box windows above the doors.

Suddenly Corso had to translate again.

'If now you know the truth, you can start to see how the fates are intertwined - our fate - your fate - it is one and the same.'

'I don't see that,' Lucy spat out bitterly. Whether justified or not, she now felt an utter contempt for both of them.

Meanwhile, in the eastern wing of Verity Palace, at the easternmost edge of the easternmost island, a game of Lions is being played by three members of Meta Emery's Dynasty Council.

'Ah! Got it!' Norton exclaimed looking smug. In a small study overlooking the orchards behind Verity Palace, he had just won the second round in a game of Lions with his wife Locotier and Bevant Obsiddian (Chancellor of the Construction, Maintenance, and Transport Division of the PeaceKeep, and second bench on the Dynasty Council).

Bevant lowered his eyes, unimpressed, and drew in the green and gold pieces, 'another round?'

Norton looked at Locotier, who shrugged. 'Go on then, why not, the sun hasn't quite set.'

He looked out to the balcony as he said this. The glow of the sunset swept in through the open doors along with the breeze, carrying the sickly-sweet bouquet of the unpicked fruits, rapidly turning sour.

Bevant counted them up, twelve pieces each, all of them face down, then put the remainders in the central pile. 'You have that meeting tomorrow, don't you? With the Citizen Finance generals?'

Norton grunted, agreeing.

'He's not looking forward to it,' Locotier said.

'Oh?' Bevant turned over his first piece, a clove symbol, 'but I thought you called the meeting?'

'I did,' said Norton, turning over his first piece, a heart, 'but I'm not anticipating them being very receptive to it. I am trying to tighten up spending on the offerings, it's getting out of hand.'

The game went on and Locotier's second piece was also a heart, meaning she had a double score. She grinned patting down her blonde bob, it was a good start for her.

Bevant scoffed a little, and looked around for the attendant, asking for more water, 'this from the biggest proponent of the offering system?'

'Well of course. It's a brilliant system. Why shouldn't our best soldiers be paired with the best wives? I just don't see why we have to make such a song and dance about it. Handing out coins for all these lavish ceremonies, it's too much. Money's better spent elsewhere.'

Locotier looked to the left, beyond the window, as she waited for Bevant to have his turn. Although it was still some time before the sun disappeared completely, it had passed behind the rock-face behind the mountain palace, and the orchard beyond the balcony was falling into shadow.

'Well it keeps the girls' families happy. Makes them feel like they're getting something out of this too,' Bevant mused, then growled softly as his fourth piece was a dagger. Lions was a very simple game of luck and chance. Your first twelve pieces determined your score, more than one piece of the same symbol could double the score, three pieces could triple it, while a bird halved your score. But after the first twelve pieces you could choose, depending on what your predictions were about the pieces in the central pile, to give up two pieces for one, in the hope of getting something better. The risk, being, you might lower your score.

A dagger was a low scoring piece, so was a clove. Bevant so far, was coming last.

'Please,' Norton said, and sniggered through another mouthful of heavy wine, '*keeps them happy*. As if they have a choice.'

Bevant eyed Norton condescendingly, 'yes, that's the spirit.' Very subtle sarcasm. Bevant agonised over the fact that someone so lacking in tact, could come from such an esteemed bloodline. In his mind, Norton was not suited to leadership. He had no grasp of how to manage people, he just had his sense of entitlement, and an expectation of obedience. Norton half rolled his eyes and gave a little shrug of his shoulders. Secretly though, he felt foolish for that remark. He twirled his beard as he turned over his next piece, a crown, the highest scoring in the set.

'Anyway, you expect they won't want to rein in costs in that area?'

'Well, they won't want to bear the brunt of it, it's one of few allowances we give. Their officers will have to be the ones voicing the bad news to the families who turn up to collect - that's why they won't like it.'

'Well, the Generals of Citizen Finance are in your chancellorship - to use your words, as if they have a choice?' Bevant had a lousy hand, the losing hand really, so he chanced two of his pieces for a centre piece. It was a crown. He hid his satisfaction. He was now at an equal score to Norton, with Locotier to play the remaining piece.

'Yes, to an extent, but those Generals operating in Killenny may go to Pykeros and get his input, get him to side with them in an audience they seek with the Queen. You know how soft he is.' Norton was referring to the two-tiered hierarchy that military in Meta Emery operated under. The line of reporting moved by operational portfolio (ie as treasurer, Citizen Finance fell under his chancellorship, and the Generals in that division reported to him) but also by region, meaning stations in different regions also had oversight from the Dynasty members who governed that region. Killenny was sub-ruled by Evaniegh, Norton's sister and Abigail's aunt, and her husband Pykeros. The Generals with Citizen Finance stations in Killenny could compel Pykeros (or Evaneigh, but no one seemed to bother with her) to speak to the Queen on their behalf. Norton pursed his lips and considered his hand. The two attendants in the room noted the increasingly long shadows stretching in from the corners. They set about lighting the lanterns as it had now gone dark. They began to close up the doors that led onto the marble balcony.

'No,' Norton said. He spun around as his back was to the window. He waved his hand at them, 'leave it open please, I'm enjoying the breeze, can nearly smell the ocean in it.'

'Well, we all know how that would go don't we? Surely if you whispered into her ear first, there wouldn't be a problem,' Bevant said dryly. They were still waiting for Norton to have his turn. He took it, also gambling two pieces, but came out no better. His sum remained tied with Bevant's. It took him a moment to register what had been said.

'Sorry? No, what do you mean?' Norton sat up stiffly, leaning back into the chair, his brow furrowed. Clearly, he understood quite well what Bevant was implying.

Locotier slowly took her last turn, another heart. Her score was tripled, she won.

'Well come on,' said Bevant who also leant back in his chair, arms folded across his large round physique, 'we all know she's under your thumb.'

Norton gave a look of wide-eyed disgust, 'she most certainly is not. The Queen makes her own decisions, guided by all our counsel.'

Bevant rolled his eyes looking away for a moment, 'so when she was eleven, and I mean actually eleven, not under her youth spell, the new economic system and militarisation of all sectors of the economy, that was her idea was it?'

Norton's expression was stoic, his arms also stiffly folded. 'It wasn't her idea, it was something she was advised on, and accepted.'

'By you?'

Norton maintained his look of defiance. Locotier sat silently, but threaded her pearl necklace through her fingers, watching the tension between the men rise.

'Which I'm sure she understood perfectly as well,' Bevant added, grinning.

Norton's facial muscles tightened further, 'we had a child Queen with no regent, of course she was not going to understand the complexity in the detail of all the decisions she had to make. But someone had to guide her. Things could not, and cannot, stand still.'

'Yes, we're all aware of how well you guide her,' said Bevant, 'but I'm sure such a momentous overhaul of the kingdom could have waited until she was old enough to understand those complexities.'

Norton let his eyes fall to the side, taking in his wife's winning hand, 'I disagree.'

'And the re-zoning of the palace to absorb two new wings into your area? That was also her idea?'

Norton laughed. 'I see, so this is about jealousy?'

Bevant sighed, 'forget I said anything. I'm feeling suddenly very drained, I think I might retire. Locotier, I see you had the winning hand this round, well done.'

Locotier nodded out of politeness. Bevant signalled to his personal guards, and left the couple in the lantern light by the table, to begin the long walk back to the Obsiddian wing.

That same evening, in the westernmost kingdom, a not-so-secret meeting occurs...

Soleman had his hands clasped in front of him as he glided along. Bear was following, floating a pace or so behind. The dry grass crunched underneath his bare feet but there would be a path soon. Ron was alongside him, and Ayerie and Aramor behind them. After Bear appeared in the throne room, it was Soleman's idea that they take an evening stroll through the gardens. It was his not-so-subtle way of having a private meeting that excluded other ministers. But it was clear to everyone in the castle what they were doing.

'Well I just can't say what will happen to Trimany. Obviously they will act in their own interests, but…surely they will side with goodness. If values are given up under threat, is there any point continuing to exist?' Soleman muttered. Trimany was a segue, but that news too had been important. The midland city had been invited by Meta Emery to join a proposed trading alliance, which would require Trimany to prohibit goods bound for Archmond moving through its territory. It stung because Trimany was at the intersection of the only rail network across the lands, albeit the Archmond line had been defunct for some time.

'Say that to the people Abigail's government will slaughter, if Trimany doesn't eventually yield,' said Aramor.

'Mmmmm,' several of them murmured in unison as they thought on this grimly.

Soleman waved his wand in an effort to light their way. He was relieved not to have announced his intentions beforehand, because he failed somewhat, instead lighting the stream that ran adjacent to them. The water glowed with aqua luminescence. It cast illuminated reflections across the bulbous trunks of jek-wood trees that crowded together between the stream and the curtain wall.

'Oh, how pretty,' Ayerie remarked.

'…eh-um, yes, yes,' he agreed, 'getting back to the other news though, Bear, I really wish you hadn't left Lucy - at this juncture. I don't want to throw words around, but it does seem negligent,' Soleman's criticism was genuine, but his tone was soft, inviting rather than deeming.

'You appointed me as her guide, let me use the discretion that necessarily entails. I could see these memories overwhelming her, and I could sense that we were near Yerkey. That's the only reason I left.'

Soleman sighed.

'This process is largely introspective, what use could he have been to that?' said Ron, picking off petite rubbery leaves from a flimsy branch he carried, and throwing them off to the side as they rounded a bend in the garden. Above them, yellow light from castle balconies beckoned out into the darkness. The small heads of servants peering over them disappeared as he looked up.

'Yes, I know, it's just -'

'You are too overprotective. Stop acting as though she's our charge,' Ron went on. Ayerie and Aramor exchanged glances.

'Well…I mean how do we know she even got to this *Yerkay* place?' Soleman looked to Bear for guidance on the pronunciation, 'I've never been. Can't say I know anyone who has.' He was dismissive of it.

'I've never heard of it,' Aramor concurred.

On the inside Bear ridiculed them for being so unworldly, given their position it was embarrassing. 'She's not dead, she's with the people of Yerkey. I can sense it. I can still feel her.'

'So, what do Yerkay know of these shadow chasers, the bad memories in the tundra?' Soleman asked. He stopped a moment by a lantern, marking the start of a small bridge over the stream. Underneath its light you could see the orange flowers in the dannis weed growing between and around the wooden planks of the bridge.

'They have the oldest religion in the world, the Reichi. If anyone is going to help her through some suppressed trauma, it's them,' Bear insisted.

'Do they?' Aramor doubted this. They had crossed the stream now and were following a path lined with pansies and sunflowers, all shut up and turned downward in the night, 'I've never heard that. On the contrary, I was always told our faith is the foundation of belief in the world.'

Bear chuckled. 'The Mazourians think that too, we can't all be right.'

'But truly, Bear,' Soleman said, 'what do you think will happen to Lucy now?'

There was a flock of birds clearing the curtain wall, but it was impossible in the dark to tell what kind.

'Well presumably, with the memories, she will come to terms with the truth of her past and…well…' Bear's words dried up.

There was a collective drawing in of breath, but in truth none of them knew the precise details of her past. It was simply clear it could be nothing pleasant.

'A trying time indeed,' said Soleman, linking arms with Ayerie, for his comfort not hers, but she smiled tenderly, 'let's just hope the truth does not break her.'

'Well, if we have chosen correctly, if the prophecy is correct, the breaking is only the beginning,' Ron said.

They had turned the final corner at that point and reached the front of the castle. A golden moon was sitting just above the northern tower of the curtain wall. For several silent moments, they stood and marvelled at it.

In Yerkey's temple hall, the fire was dwindling.

Lucy felt as though she had woken from a trance. How long had she been sitting here? The fire was almost out, and while Yinsoo was still talking, it was as though she had only just become fully conscious of her surroundings. She had been catatonic for some time. Now she was tired, but suddenly alert.

There were so many thoughts spinning through her mind, so many questions of herself, so much disbelief.

But Yinsoo was offering Lucy a sword, and although she felt as though she had not been present for some time, she understood what the gesture meant.

The sword was largely symbolic. Her acceptance of the sword, or rejection of it, represented a fork in the road. She had to make a choice about her life now, going forward.

Without words, Yinsoo told her the sword was truth. Did she want to accept truth? But the sword was also courage. Did she choose courage? Or fear?

Yinsoo said something indecipherable. Corso, Lucy realised, was asleep on the cushion beside them.

But Lucy understood. *Take the sword, and become a new person. It is time to stand up. You must use this for protection only. You must protect yourself. You must protect those you love.*

Inside her, a great nausea stirred. But she reached out, and her hand gripped tightly around its hilt.

'I will,' she whispered, 'I will.'